THE GIRL

AT THE

EDGE OF

TIME

The clock chimes. The world turns.

ALEXANDRA JORDAN

Copyright © 2021 Alexandra Jordan

Teddy's Den Publishing House

ISBN: 9798536783023

All rights reserved.

PROLOGUE

Charles Braxton

Christmas Eve, 1923
Bakewell, Derbyshire Dales

CHARLES Braxton taps the steering wheel of his brand new car. The moneyed scent of soft leather rises up to greet him, and his chest expands with pride.

The car salesman, a tall angular fellow with smooth dark hair, perches onto the running-board to caress the shiny purple bonnet.

'She's a lovely thing, isn't she, Mr Braxton, sir? And she has that new Neverleak hood, so you'll find her warm and cosy. Just what you need today, the weather being what it is, sir.'

'Yes. Thank you, Albert.' Stretching out his long legs, Charles eases his aching muscles.

'A thing of real beauty, the Ruston-Hornsby, sir. Lovely piece of engineering.'

'She is, Albert, she certainly is.' A shadow crosses the sky ahead of them and he frowns. 'Looks like snow, Albert. I did hear something about it. You need to get yourself inside.'

'And you'll be wanting to get yourself back to Hathersage, sir. That lovely wife o' yours will be anxious to admire your new purchase, I expect, sir.' He jumps back down. 'Let's be getting the hood up, then, and I'll start the crank.'

'Thank you, Albert.' Pressing a five pound note into Albert's hand, Charles pulls out his pocket-watch. He realises that Walter took the horse and carriage back to the hall two hours ago. It's actually taken him this long to get used to the feel of the thing. But oh, he can't wait to drive it home.

*

The cluckety-cluck of the car carries him along the country lanes like a dream, despite the occasional pothole and the negotiation required whenever a horse and cart approaches. But he'll get used to it; these things take time. Outside the small village of Froggatt, just off the Bakewell road, a carter calls out to him, doffing his cap in admiration. Charles nods, smiling with pleasure. What a Christmas present. What a good start to the New Year. 1924, and all his hopes and wishes coming true. A beautiful wife. A loving daughter. A wonderful home. His three-storied manor house, with stone battlements and a spiral staircase made of elm, is set beneath the millstone escarpment they call Stanage Edge. The view upon entering his bedroom is wondrous, inspirational, and he has to pinch himself at his luck.

As Charles enters the quaint village of Hathersage, he's become used to the excitement building inside him, the feel of the car, the way it responds immediately to his touch. Now he knows why Albert referred to it as a she. So very appropriate.

He waves to old Bob Chandrey outside the butchers on the corner there, his bicycle laden with goods. He'll have been busy today, what with the turkeys and geese needing to be delivered.

But suddenly the heavens open. Flakes of snow circle round and round, falling and settling, gathering pace as Charles turns right onto Jaggers Lane. Pulling in briefly, he pushes open the windscreen to deflect the snow and continues on his way. Luckily, the snow is wet enough to slide off the glass. Not long until he's home now, anyway.

Coggers Lane is steep and curved, treacherous in the winter months. So he takes it easy, before taking another right onto Birley Lane. The oak trees here, usually so dark and brooding, are already white and oh, so Christmassy.

He turns onto his driveway. Lined with juniper trees dipped in snow, the house is just visible in the distance. Doris has already lit the lamps and the windows glow with an orange light that beckons him on.

CHAPTER 1

Enid Mitchell

Sunday 2ⁿᵈ December - Present Day
Lincoln, the Lincolnshire Fens

IF we could see into the future, we would know. We would know about faith and magic and truth. We would know that what is meant to be is just that. It's meant to be. We'd see not only the future, but also the past.

And how do I know all this? I know all this because of Peggy.

I know Peggy Fleming like I know the back of my hand. I know the colour of her nail varnish, the name of her scent, and just where she bought that lovely sheepskin coat she's wearing. Red Hot Rio, Patchouli, and second-hand off eBay. In that order.

But I've only ever seen her in this state once before.

Her face is wolf-grey. She stares at her empty coffee cup, her fingers gripping the handle as if she's afraid to let go. Chocolate sprinkles sit enticingly along the edge, while the heavy gold ring she wears catches the light of the bulbs around us.

Groups of people stroll by, excited by the day's events. Chatting, laughing, they're oblivious to Peggy's presence, to the stain of purple that surrounds her.

Me?

I just wait.

Eventually, she looks up. 'You see, Enid. Something doesn't sit right.'

I smile gently. 'Are you saying what I think you're saying, Peggy?'

Rubbing at the chocolate sprinkles with her finger, she places it to her lips, nodding quietly.

'You think we need to investigate Indira's place, don't you?' I say.

She sighs heavily. 'I do, Enid. I most certainly do.'

It's the second day of December. We've had the first snow of the season, but Peggy's still insisted on driving us into Lincoln. A beautiful cathedral city it is, with over two thousand years of history.

She picked me up earlier, her silver hair fastened carelessly into the bun she wears, her huge carpet bag and the sheepskin coat from eBay slung carelessly onto the back seat.

We've planned on coming to the Christmas Market for weeks, me and Peggy. Lovely, it is. Pretty. The lightbulbs and the cooking gases light the place up with a kind of magic, encouraging people to eat and drink and have fun. I get a warm glow too, seeing folks sauntering along with their torches and lanterns. From a distance, it looks just like a silver snake winding its way through the city.

Suddenly, though, there's a kerfuffle behind us. We turn to find two youths pulling at each other beside the coffee stall. Shouting and screaming.

'You bastard,' the tall one shouts, his face blood-red, unforgiving.

'She's not yours, mate - she never was,' teases the chubby one, smiling.

The tall one pulls back his fist and - crunch - the chubby one is on the ground. A girl screams from somewhere in the background.

Furtively, Peggy stands up, pulls off her ring and throws it into the air with long, scarlet-tipped fingers. The bulbs, torches and lanterns go out, the flames cooking the food fade away, and we find ourselves in total darkness.

'Away with you,' she whispers. 'Darkness and evil, be away ...'

The ring falls, she catches it, and I smile. Quietly.

There's a flash of light, a crack of thunder.

Then nothing. Only silence.

'Let harmony descend. Let peace remain. Away,' calls Peggy, softly.

Light floods the air, the food carries on cooking, and people continue to chat and queue and eat, just as they had been doing.

As if nothing had happened.

The tall youth pulls the chubby one up, checks he's all right, and they continue on their way without a backward glance. The screaming girl is nowhere to be seen.

Sitting down, Peggy sighs loudly. 'Hah. Rascals.'

I pull a small brown bottle from my bag. 'Here. Let's have some of this.'

'Cheers, Enid, you're a treasure,' she says. 'I could do with something a bit stronger, though.'

'A drop of brandy, you mean?'

She smiles. 'You remember that time we were in old Judy Savoury's kitchen and she was pouring the tea, and then we realised she'd laced it with brandy, straight from the pot?'

'I do. Thank god I spotted the bottle. Half empty by that time, of course. I don't know what possessed her.'

'She was getting over her husband, poor thing. But she poured it straight into the pot, with not a thought for us having to get ourselves home.'

'She was a scream, though, wasn't she?'

'Poor thing never got over it. Didn't last long herself.'

'Here, we're getting maudlin, Peggy.'

Pulling two clean tissues from my bag, I sprinkle a few drops of oil onto each. I mix my own remedies, you know. Nothing like a little frankincense and sweet orange to lift the spirits.

Breathing in deeply, Peggy smiles. 'Now, where were we, Enid? Oh, yes. So even though Indira was born and bred in Britain, her mother's from Delhi, and she still has that innate fear of djinns, as she calls them. She thinks they're kicking her out, telling her to move. Scared silly, she is.'

'So you want us to investigate.'

She rubs at her shoulder, as if pushing something away. 'Something's definitely not right, Enid.'

There's a group of carol singers nearby, huddled around a tall patio heater. They're collecting for Centrepoint this year, the homeless charity. A worthwhile cause.

'Away in a Manger, no crib for a bed ...'

'This takes me back, Peggy,' I say, wistfully.

And suddenly I'm a child again. Gathering up snowballs to throw at Sam, my brother. My fingers and toes are freezing, but I carry on regardless. And just when they're really starting to hurt, Mum calls us inside. Our Romani caravan is warm, inviting, and I'm breathing in the heat of the Sunday roast and the scent of fresh marzipan from the cake on the side. *The* cake. It was always *the* cake, our Christmas cake. Cinnamon, sultanas, cherries, a little brandy, the edge of the baking paper caught by the heat and burnt. And Mum, always busy, always on the go, wipes her hands on her red cotton apron while Dad smokes his ciggie on the caravan steps, nodding to us as we traipse inside.

I look around, beyond Peggy and the carol singers. Alpine stalls line the medieval square, positioned perfectly between the Norman castle and the wonderful Gothic cathedral.

The stalls are lit by long strings of blazing lightbulbs, and the food smells delicious. There's curry, paella, pizza, hot dogs, and sweet pancakes. Then there's gin, about twenty different flavours, and hot mulled wine and bottled beer. And coffee and cake, of course. Anxious to be fed, people stand in line, stamping their feet to keep warm, unable to resist the aroma of fried onions and cooked meats.

But I'm not one of them. I'm only here to buy some presents. For my Carol and her family. Jonathan too, my son, although I won't be seeing him until January now he's back in Dubai. And for young Tori, the girl who helps with the B&B. And of course there's Peggy, and Harry, my husband. Yes, we got married last year, correctly predicted by Justine with her pack of cards. The Ten of Cups it was, if I remember correctly. She always was good with the cards.

So this evening, with the melted snow solidifying into pools of ice on the cobbled streets, and with the sound of carol-singing and laughter in the air, Peggy and I have found a nice little table to sit at with our coffee and carrot cake.

'So what exactly is the problem with Indira's shop?' I ask.

Peggy shifts gently in her chair, and the heady scent of patchouli makes its way across the table.

'It was little Rishi who told me,' she says. 'They're looking at moving away. You'd think the bloody taxman was chasing them, the way he was going on. So I had a quick chat with Indira last week, and the truth is she thinks there are djinns in the shop. That's what she's calling them, anyway, her mother being Indian an' all.'

Confused, I shake my head. 'Sorry?'

'Spirits, Enid. Evil spirits.'

'But she's been living there a while now. They can't just have suddenly appeared?'

'They haven't, not that we know for certain. But there *is* something about that shop, isn't there? Something not quite right. It's always changing hands, haven't you noticed? People don't stay for two minutes. And now Indira thinks there are evil spirits telling her to move. I find it all very strange.'

The carol singers and their patio heater have left their spot and are being replaced by a brass band from the Salvation Army. They begin to play *Good King Wenceslas*, so we leave our table to stand and watch.

'Gosh,' says Peggy. 'There was a Sally Army band on nearly every street corner when I was a kid.'

'Only at Christmas, though. I don't know what they did the rest of the year.'

She chuckles. 'Soup, soap and salvation, Enid.'

Peggy places a five pound note inside the collection box. Pulling out my purse, I do the same, and we continue our walk through the market. The stalls are so enticing that we forget about Peggy's worries for a while, but then I remember.

'So come on, Peggy, what do you want us to do about Indira's place?'

'We need to call round when the kids are at school, for a start. Don't want them worrying any more than necessary. And then we're going to check out that old kaleidoscope Rishi found.'

'Kaleidoscope?'

She nods sagely. 'Indira thinks it all started after Rishi found an old kaleidoscope. We just need to see if we can make sense of anything.'

The scent of onions is making my mouth water and I look around. There's a hot-dog stall not far away.

'Do you fancy something to eat?' I ask.

She grins. 'I knew we should've brought bloody sandwiches. I had some ham ten days old we could've used.'

I know she's only joking, so I smile. 'I'll resist, then. I suppose I have just eaten a huge piece of cake.'

'You need to take your mind off it. Come on, let's find something for your Carol.'

As if by magic, the most appropriate wooden chalet appears just ahead of us. Necklaces dangle from the rafters. Sparkling rings, silver bracelets, and huge chunks of pink and purple crystal glisten beneath the lights. We head towards it.

Leaning across the display, I pick out a bracelet, silver with small purple stones set into alternate links.

'Real amethyst,' says the woman behind the stall. 'From County Mayo. Good quality, it is.'

It could be purple plastic for all I know, so I look up at Peggy. 'What do you think?'

'How much is it?' she asks, taking it from me and weighing it in her hands.

The woman fingers the thick woollen scarf slung around her neck. 'Eighty-five pounds. But it is real amethyst – there's a certificate comes with it.' She passes it to me and I pull out my reading glasses. It looks genuine enough, and the bracelet *is* pretty.

'Amethyst,' says Peggy. 'For healing and peace.'

'For balancing the Chakras,' I say.

'If you pay me in cash, you can have it for seventy-five,' says the woman, knowing a sale when she sees one. 'It really is a lovely thing.'

So I buy it. My Carol will love it, and it's sturdy, should last her years.

As we walk away, I turn to Peggy. 'Are you buying something for Ian, then?'

Ian is Peggy's boss. She's worked for him most of her life and he's become more like a brother, really, looks out for her. Not that she needs it. Not Peggy.

'I'll get him a bottle of something at the supermarket. I don't do online, as you know. But he likes a nice tipple now and again.'

'Fair enough,' I say. 'Let's find something for my Jonathan, then, and young Tori.'

'I need to get for Tori as well. She's coming over for her next lesson on Saturday. She's becoming a good little empath.'

'It's not going to clash with her work, though, is it? I've got guests arriving next weekend.'

She winks at me. 'It'll be in the evening, Enid. The bewitching hours.'

'Of course it is,' I say, smiling.

We see the two youths from earlier, the tall one and the chubby one, standing at a stall, queuing for beer. They're happy as Larry, chatting away as if there's no tomorrow.

'Now if we hadn't intervened back there,' says Peggy, 'they'd have been queuing up at the police station instead, and adding a bad record to their name. Not a good start.'

'Let's hope the girl has found someone else by now and will leave them alone.'

'Eeh, the joys of youth, Enid.'

'We live and learn, Peggy. We live and learn.'

She looks around. 'Those onions are making me hungry. Now where did that hot dog stall get to?'

CHAPTER 2

Indira Lambert

Monday 3rd December
Folksbury, the Lincolnshire Fens

HARVEY left me for a career in Hollywood. Sounds like the plot of some dodgy film, doesn't it? But no. Unfortunately, it is not. He gave up his job, a good well-paid job, to see the world. And I know they talk about men having a mid-life crisis, but honestly?

He's a TV cameraman. Worked away on location most of the time, came home for weekends and holidays.

But hindsight really is a wonderful thing. Because now I look back I can see exactly where he was coming from. He was full of resentment. Accusing me of sitting with my feet up, a coffee in one hand and a biscuit in the other. Of having lunch with the girls, chatting and laughing, gossiping, while he was working hard at putting food on the table.

But he was so, so wrong. Me, put my feet up? Me, have lunch with the girls? Not a chance. No. I was taking care of our home and our children, while *he* lived it up on film sets, mixing with the rich and famous. The writers, the producers, the actors and actresses. While *I* was busy waking up the children, feeding them, dressing them, packing their bags, taking them to school, cleaning the house, washing and ironing, shopping for food, preparing tea. Then of course I'd have to down tools to pick the children up at three thirty, to drive them to piano or football or swimming lessons, or birthday parties and play dates.

But they wanted for nothing, our children.

The truth is that Harvey wanted me to go back to work after Rishi was born. I used to be a geriatric nurse, you see, a good one, but the hours were prohibitive. There's no way I could have continued to work and look after the children properly. But he never thought about that, how it would affect them if I'd gone back to work. It would have been after-school club every night, or every morning, depending on my shifts. Then there'd have been homework to do at night-time, when they were too tired to even think straight. And very few parties. And no music lessons or football. No fun. No fun at all.

No. He just thought of himself, how he missed the money I'd been earning, how I was a *lady of leisure* while he had to go out to work. And we weren't like other families, with mothers and sisters and aunties to collect the children from school, to take them places. No. Other than my father and my sister Diti, my family are all in Delhi. And Diti didn't live anywhere near us, anyway. Plus, she has her own career as an air hostess to see to. To be honest, Dad didn't live too far away from us, but looking after the children and everything would have just worn him out.

So why did I marry Harvey? Why did I marry that no-good scoundrel who just dropped us once he'd had a better offer? Because I loved him. As simple as that. With his scruffy, dark blonde hair and his big blue eyes, and that slight stubble that would scratch my skin deliciously when we made love.

But then he left. He just left. Without a thought for us. Without a backward glance at his wife and his son and his daughter.

A Friday afternoon in May, it was, the day it all went wrong. We were living in Sudbury at the time, in a modernish semi we bought when we first got married. Sudbury is where I was brought up, where Harvey and I first met. In a bar on Midsummer's Eve. Romantic or what?

It was an awesome day too, warm and sunny, so I decided to leave the car at home and walk to school to pick up the children. If there was nothing to rush home for, I'd usually take them to the park and sit on a bench in the sunshine while they played on the swings and slides and roundabouts. I'd while away the time with the other mums and catch up on what was happening in school. Then on the way home we'd call at the post office on Harrow Road for ice cream. Marion, the postmistress, always made a fuss of the children, pushing an extra flake into their ice creams, or decorating them prettily with a handful of jelly beans from the jar on the counter. Full of energy, she was, never stopped.

So there we were, walking home eating ice-cream, when Harvey drove past, honking his horn, the Land Rover throwing out diesel fumes as if there were no such thing as global warming. It was so old, that car, and cost a fortune in repairs, but he refused to part with it. Not until he decided to fly out to America, that is. Oh, and then he was happy to sell.

'Indira!' he called. 'Come on, I'll race you!'

So we ignored the ice cream dripping down our wrists and began to wave, excitedly, noisily, Anika and Rishi jumping up and down like the crazy monkeys they are.

'Come on, Mummy,' said Rishi, pulling at my hand. 'We need to go.'

Harvey was working in Manchester at the time on some detective series, and hadn't been home this early in ages. So we quickened our pace to catch up with him, to welcome him home, and arrived just as he was unlocking the front door.

I really wished we hadn't bothered.

It was only later, as we were eating tea, that he told us.

'I've been offered a job in Los Angeles. A top-notch film company. Universal Studios. They want me to start as soon as.'

Talk about shock.

He'd never said anything before about applying for a job abroad, never said anything about us going to live abroad.

'What?' I said. 'Really? Why didn't you say something?'

His grin was shy, awkward, and I knew.

'Don't congratulate me, then,' he said, 'because it's an amazing job, a brilliant opportunity.'

I smiled. 'Congratulations, then. But come on, Harvey, what's the plan? What are we to do? Will we be moving? Do I need to be looking at schools? Or will you be flying home every weekend? Just how will this work, exactly?'

And there it was. The clincher.

He confessed to having applied for the job weeks ago. He confessed to his desire to get away, to leave us. He confessed to wanting to *do* something with his life. After all, he *was* thirty-six, didn't have much time left in which to make his name.

Talk about shock. Anger. Disappointment.

Hurt.

I loved him. Still do, if I'm honest. And the children? They were distraught, didn't stop crying for weeks.

I pleaded with him, of course. I cried and cried myself to sleep nearly every night. But he wouldn't change his mind, just carried on making his plans. Harvey's like that. When he decides on something, that's it. No backtracking.

So we sold up and we moved out. Lock, stock and barrel. I didn't want to stay around, anyway. There were way too many memories.

But I needed to work to earn my keep. I couldn't rely on Harvey sending money over, although he does send something. And there wasn't much left from selling the house once we'd paid the estate agents and the money-grabbing solicitors. So I rented this place, this shop with its living quarters behind and above. It just appeared on the website one day when I was checking out houses to rent, and I realised if I rented a shop rather than a house I could earn my living there, so I'd still be around for the children. It's important they have stability, you see. Also, Folksbury's not too far away from Sudbury, from Dad, but it's far enough away for us to make a fresh start.

Harvey messaged me last week, you know. Just to say he'd put some money into my account and to buy Christmas presents for the children. Said he didn't know what they'd want, so wouldn't be sending any presents himself, but to give them his love.

Love? He doesn't know the meaning of the word. Love isn't just thinking of yourself and your own needs. Love isn't walking out on your children at an age when they really, really need you. Love isn't deserting your wife on the spur of the moment, with no real word of explanation, or even an apology.

Anyway, I've used the money to buy presents for Anika and Rishi. I'm having them delivered to the estate agents next door so they don't see them arrive, then I'll sneak them round and wrap them once they're at school.

I just love Christmas.

This shop was actually a deli before we moved in, so it's ideal for me to use as a café now. The living quarters behind and above are warm and comfortable, and it has a good strong kitchen that's already FSA approved. And I'd recently developed a strong interest in Ayurvedic healing foods, so thought maybe I could do something with that.

If I'm completely honest, though, this place is starting to freak me out. It's no longer warm and friendly and safe and secure.

We need to move away. We *have* to move away.

I know I'm on the superstitious side - my mother's fault - but this is not a good place. It's not right. There are spirits here, djinns as she would call them. Bad, nervous, unsettled spirits.

They terrify me.

It wasn't like this when we first moved in, though. I loved it, despite all the upset of Harvey moving away and having to manage on my own. Although Dad did stay with us for a few weeks, and he was amazing, helping us move in, doing the DIY, setting up the shop, painting it, ripping up the carpet and laying the reclaimed floorboards. I had to concentrate on the business side of things, you see, which I'd never, ever, had to do before. The advertising, the red tape (change of use, FSA check), finding the best wholesalers, looking at the competition, seeing what prices I should charge. And all the while trying to come up with a good name for the shop.

Folksbury itself is really nice, though. A small village of about a thousand people, it's not too far from Sleaford and Grantham, so it's easy to get supplies when I need to. The school has an OFSTED rating of Outstanding, so it's ideal for Anika and Rishi, and there are some amazing buildings here. Some of the houses and shops go back to the 1800s, Saffron Silk being one of them. And of course there are modern buildings, too. Then there's the village green and the hotel, and generally a really nice feel about the place, welcoming. The Fens, too, are awesome. The long, rolling fields, the wonderful architecture, the craft shops that seem to fill every village and town for miles around, and the history - old airfields and engineering companies and the stories surrounding them.

So I kind of thought we'd landed on our feet when we arrived here.

*

But the djinns. I could swear it began the night Rishi found that kaleidoscope. It's only a couple of weeks ago, yet it seems like ages. He'd been messing about inside the old Grandfather clock, the one in the sitting room. It's oak, I think, with brass numerals and hands, and a lovely old picture at the top. Nice-looking, actually, not something you'd find nowadays, unless you happen to come across one in a second-hand shop. And it needs winding up with a key every few weeks, which is a pain, but I do love the tick-tock sound it makes. Well, I used to. I found it kind of round and comforting, filling the sitting room as it does. When it's not full of the sound of CBBC and cartoons, obviously.

But if you use your fingernails you can ease open the lower part of the clock, the box bit that sits on the floor. It doesn't look as if you can open it, and I don't think clocks do have an opening there as a general rule, but the hinges are on the inside and so very small that it's not obvious. And the winding-up key is hung from a hook just inside the main door at the top, so I'd never had any need to delve further.

But Rishi did. Rishi did have the need to delve further. I remember it vividly. It was that Saturday I was going through the decorations in the loft. I wanted to sort through them before Christmas, so we could make new ones if necessary. But there were four boxes of decorations up there, plus the old tree, which is a dusty old thing Harvey's mum gave us years ago and definitely needs replacing. So I brought the boxes down to my bedroom and began sorting through them, pulling out baubles, trinkets, lights and so on, and deciding which needed to go and which should stay. There's that gorgeous sequin-covered angel Anika made in school, and her cotton-wool snowman, and the reindeer picture Rishi made using his handprints. They would definitely stay. But everything else reminded me of Sudbury, of the children growing up, of Harvey, so it was really difficult, the decision-making. But at the age of thirty-two I needed to start afresh. I needed to create new memories.

I began to make two piles.

Anika was helping me, of course. She'd already done her piano practice, so I'd allowed her to come upstairs and help. In between watching *Frozen* on the bedroom telly, of course, and practising each and every dance move and song. So she wasn't that much help, really, but it was fun, messing about up there. We'd left Rishi to his own devices downstairs, and I was so busy I didn't even think about what he was up to. I just kind of assumed he'd be playing with a toy or watching something on the telly. My god, the thing could have come crashing down on him.

Using his tiny little fingers, he'd managed to pull open the door at the bottom of the clock. How he knew it was there is anyone's guess. But it must have been fascinating for him, this little door, so beautifully smooth and shiny. No handle, just an edge you can pull on. And that's where he found it, the kaleidoscope, tucked just inside.

Rushing upstairs, he came to show us. 'Mummy, Anika, look what I found.'

'Where did you find that?' I asked.

'In the big clock,' he replied, flushed and excited. 'In the little door at the bottom. I was looking for hidden treasure.'

Puzzled, I took hold of his hand. 'Come on, darling, show me.'

So he took me to where he'd found it, where he'd found his hidden treasure. Although why it was there, I don't know. It's not our clock, you see. The previous tenant had left a few bits of furniture, and I was happy to keep them. The clock's not quite in keeping with the rest of the apartment, with its pine shelving and its white walls, but it keeps the time well and is an interesting feature. And I like it. Or I did. But the kaleidoscope - now that's *really* old. It's not like the kaleidoscopes you buy nowadays, made especially for children. No. It's made of wood with brass at either end, and a brass wheel at the top that you have to turn to make the coloured patterns. And it's pristine, looks like it's hardly ever been used. But it's been fascinating Rishi so much I've ordered him a new one from Amazon. I'll throw that old thing away once it's arrived.

But that night was the very first time I heard it, I swear. I'd just finished tidying downstairs and had put my sewing away, checked the doors, switched off the lights, and was climbing the stairs. I was tired and so ready for bed.

I'd just reached the top stair when it began. A soft moaning, wailing sound that seemed as if it was coming from the cupboard opposite Rishi's room. But when I stood beside it, it seemed to move. And then I wasn't sure if it was coming from the landing window or the stairs or the bathroom. Pulling on the cord to the bathroom light, I peeked inside, just to check. But there was nothing.

And after what must have been only five minutes, during which time I sat on my bed trying to figure out what it was, the noise stopped and I was able to check everywhere, to see if there was a reason for the sound. But I found nothing, no reason at all.

So I got ready for bed and tried to sleep. But the emotion that had built up inside me was actually palpable, and it took me ages to get to sleep. I just felt so very, very sad.

For no reason at all.

CHAPTER 3

Sophie Dubrowska

Tuesday 4th December
Wells-next-the-Sea, Norfolk

I know, I know. It does seem a little weird. But a girl needs a man, doesn't she? She needs to feel a man's warm arms around her, the touch of his skin. Soft whispers. Kisses on her ear. The scent of cologne.

So when my Ant decided he was no longer interested in that side of things, well. One has to look elsewhere, play the field, yes? The Cold Pole, I call him. Well, he *was* fifty-seven last May, so what can you expect?

My first was Jakub, the young man renting our tea and coffee shop in Grantham. He was taking it on for a year, he said, to check out the market, to see whether it was worth investing in property himself. And there was something about him. Maybe because he was so transient, but also because he was kind and sweet and thoughtful. He asked me to stay for tea one evening; he was eating alone and would enjoy the company, he said. I'd only called round for the first month's rent, but Ant was away golfing in Portugal, I had no-one to go home to, and I confess to feeling a little lonely. So I stayed. And one thing led to another.

So he was the first. We'd meet every month, whenever I called for the rent. We'd go up to the flat above the shop, make love or have sex, or whatever the term is when you have a man ravage you. Then we'd drink tea, and we'd talk.

And now I sit and think about it, that was just over five years ago. Have I been cheating on Ant for all that time?

And do I feel bad about it?

Well. Kind of. But as I've said, what is a girl to do? Ant's quite happy in his own world, wheeling and dealing, jetting off to Portugal or driving up to Scotland, to play golf whenever he likes. Then he's happy to fly home, peck me on the cheek, buy property, sell it, watch the market, make decisions, and build up his portfolio. And I'm quite happy to spend our money and have a good time.

I mean, I do love Ant. Of course I do. But a girl has her needs. And I know some people would be shocked by all this, but the only alternative would be either divorce or masturbation. Both of which abhor me, if I'm honest. So, to my mind, this is the better alternative.

And as long as Ant never finds out - which he won't - then everything is hunky dory and no harm done.

Now don't get me wrong. Don't ever think I don't pull my weight. Because I do. I travel the length and breadth of Lincolnshire and Norfolk to collect the rents. I also check on properties every now and then, to ensure they're not being used to grow cannabis, or to hold illegal immigrants, or to carry out some other nefarious bloody activity. Seriously, you wouldn't believe what goes on in some rental properties. Keys handed over to crooks, tenants leaving without a by-your-leave, plans made months in advance so no-one suspects a thing. And the first time the landlord knows anything about it is when the police call round.

On the whole, however, it's a fairly easy living, as long as you keep an eye out. I mean, some tenants prefer to pay by direct debit, and that's okay as long as they've been with us a while. But Ant watches out for the newbies; doesn't trust them until they've proven themselves. Which is fine by me. There's always some young man willing to put up with me for a cut in the rent. And Ant never notices. He just thinks I've spent it on something pretty. Bless.

So today I'm visiting a small shop in Wells-next-the-Sea. It's on the main road, nestled in between an Oxfam shop and a run-down newsagents. An elderly couple, Mel and Idris Hughes, run it. They've been here years, even though they don't seem to make much money, and are always jolly and smiling. But they prefer to pay the rent once a fortnight in cash rather than through the bank, which is okay by me. They run a second-hand business called Hughes Hand-me-Downs, selling records, books, lampshades, handbags, and clothing. Anything that's old, in fact. I once had a dig round myself. Bought a cream waistcoat that had been part of a man's dinner suit, with stitched holes either side for buttons to be threaded through. So I bought some pearl cufflinks and used them instead. It looks amazing with a shirt and skinny jeans.

So I park up on the main road and walk in. There's a bitterly cold wind that freezes my fingers in seconds, and I'm so ready for a cup of tea. But Mel reads my mind like a soothsayer. Locking the door, she puts up the Closed sign and scrambles through to the kitchen at the back.

The shop has a damp quality about it, as if a basket of wet laundry has been left in the corner. Dusty ornaments made of china, wood, or plastic, perch precariously on overcrowded shelves. An old cuckoo clock hangs nearby, ticking away, reverberating through the shop, becoming more and more muffled as it reaches the clothing section. Shirts, sweaters, coats, trousers, and shoes.

The shoes. Men's old leather shoes, brown and shiny like conkers. They would have been really expensive in their day, but I mean - who wants to wear second-hand shoes? God knows what germs they're harbouring. It's not as if you can wash them, is it?

But I glide through the shop as if it's an everyday occurrence, ignoring the smell and the dust and the old shoes.

'I've put the kettle on,' say Mel in her Welsh sing-song voice. Soft as swansdown.

'Thanks, sweetie. Just what I need.'

It's pretty grim here in the kitchen, too. We do rent out some hellholes sometimes. The pine worktop around the sink is black from years of standing water. The gas cooker has definitely seen better days. And the lino is ripped along the edge - so much so, it's a tripping hazard. I make a mental note.

A glass vase of purple lisianthus, red roses and gypsophila sits at the centre of the old pine table, brightening up the place. And it needs it.

I smile. 'Lisianthus. My favourites, sweetie.'

'They're a present from my Idris. It was my birthday on Sunday, so we went out for lunch and bought them on the way back. Gorgeous, aren't they?'

She smiles with a twinkle in her eye that makes my heart sink. Ant hasn't had a twinkle in his eye for years. I mean, I do my best, I look after myself, I dress nicely, I keep busy. But no.

'How long have you two been married?' I ask, sitting down. The corduroy seat cushion has something like coffee granules spilt onto it. I brush it away with my hand, but it's dried on, so I sit down anyway.

Mel busies herself making tea, the mugs clinking together as she places them onto the table.

'Gosh. Forty-one years, it is now. We met at primary school, you know.'

'Where was that, then?'

'Merthyr Tydfil. We were there when the Aberfan Disaster struck, you know. I knew some of the children. And their poor mothers.'

'God, that must have been awful.'

'Yes, shocking it was. I doubt any of us will ever forget it.'

I only know of the incident through history books and the news, and that only when there's an anniversary of some kind. But the tragedy always hits home.

'I can't imagine what it must have been like,' I say.

'They were never fined, you know, the Coal Board. All those children. A hundred and sixteen dead. Just like that.'

She's pouring boiling water into the teapot, but her hands are shaking with the effort.

I jump up. 'Here, I'll do that, sweetie. You sit yourself down.'

She does as she's told. 'Sorry, Mrs Dubrowska. I don't think about it that much, but when I do it feels like it was yesterday. All those bodies ...'

I make tea in the big brown teapot that reminds me of my own childhood, and cover it with the striped knitted tea-cosy.

'I know,' I say. 'I do understand. Look, let me make you something to eat. A slice of toast or something. Or a biscuit? Or I could nip to the shop?'

She smiles, her nut-brown eyes wrinkled and worn. 'It's very kind of you, but I'll be fine. Anyway, I'm making lunch soon. It's only egg and beans, but you're welcome to stay and eat.'

'No, but thanks, it's very kind of you. I need to be getting back soon. Where's Idris, then?'

'Just popped out to the chemists for his prescription. Won't be long.'

I feel guilty. 'So shouldn't you be looking after the shop instead of talking to me? I mean, it's really kind of you, but ...'

'It's okay, Mrs Dubrowska,' she insists. 'We always put up the closed sign for lunch, so people expect it. And there's not been much business today, anyway. Far too cold for people to be coming out shopping.'

I stir the pot, replace the lid, and pour the steaming brown liquid into two mugs.

'Milk?' I ask.

She nods. 'Please.'

Splashing the milk in, I pass one mug to her, pick up the other, and sit back down.

'So how are *les enfants*?' I ask.

Her face creases with smiles; her eyes are bright with sunshine. 'Not so much children now, are they? But oh, my Ewan, he's doing really well. Been promoted to Sergeant, he has, just last week. Julia's over the moon. And little Noah - oh, I could eat him up he's so cute.'

'How old is he now, then? It must be getting on for a year or so.'

'His birthday's in January, so not long now. And yes, one year old, he'll be. Unbelievable. He's just about walking now as well. Into everything, he is.'

I remember the week Noah was born. It must have been a Tuesday, because when I called for the rent Mel and Idris were closing up early to visit the hospital, and I spent the following morning in Grantham, buying ice-blue baby clothes. And they were so cute I was loath to hand them over, but I did, of course. So once I'd folded each item nicely and wrapped them in pale blue paper, I drove down to Wells and gave them to Mel. Such a lovely day, that was.

'And how about your other son - Rowan?' I ask. 'How's he doing?'

She rubs her hand to and fro along the table, nervously. 'It's kind of you to ask, but if I'm honest he hasn't been the same since Cathy left. He'll get over it, I'm sure, but such a shock it was.'

I sip my tea thoughtfully. 'These things take time, don't they? A broken heart is like china. You just need to find the right kind of glue.'

'She fell in love with someone else, you know. They'd been trying for a baby as well, or so our Rowan thought. Been trying for a year, and he was beginning to think it might never happen. Then he found out why.'

'Oh, sweetie, how awful. So, what - she was taking the pill and didn't tell him?'

She nods. 'He was doing so well, you know. She wanted for nothing. Beautiful home and everything.'

'So what does he do?'

'He's an actuary,' she says, proudly. 'Works for Lloyds Bank. Such a clever boy, he is.'

The back door opens then, and Idris walks in. He's a slim man, pale and gaunt. Nodding at me, he smiles.

'Mrs Dubrowska,' he says. 'So nice to see you again. How are you doing?'

'I'm very well, thank you. And you?'

Placing a hessian shopping bag onto the table, he removes his mackintosh to shake off the raindrops.

Mel looks up at him. 'I've only this morning mopped that floor, Idris.'

He just laughs, cheekily. 'It'll be all right, love. It's clean water, isn't it? Now is there any more tea in that there pot?'

'I can make some more,' I offer, jumping up.

'No, no, no,' he says, throwing down his coat and picking up the kettle. 'Can't have the landlady making tea for us, now can we? It's just not on.'

I watch as he turns the tap.

'Looks like you need some new flooring, Idris,' I say.

His eyes move directly to the tear. 'You might be right. Will you be paying for it, then?'

'I think so, *mon chéri*. It's a tripping hazard. You could hold us responsible if you break your neck.'

Mel laughs. 'He can do that just from watching the rugby. The way he leaps up and down - you should see it. Like a child, he is.'

'Hey, less of that,' he says. 'If I can't enjoy a good bit o' rugby - well then, life's not worth living.'

I smile. 'Well, we'll see what we can do about the floor.'

Half an hour later, I leave their house of fun and laughter and walk back to the car. Mel has given me the rent in £50 notes. I've peeled two off the pile and handed them back.

'Buy yourself something nice for your birthday, sweetie.'

CHAPTER 4

Enid Mitchell

🐈

Wednesday 5th December
Pepingham, Lincolnshire Fens

SO yes, Peggy and I go back a long way. Back to just after my ex, Peter, and I got married, when we first moved to Lincolnshire. We'd found a lovely old house in Pepingham, and Peter extended it so we could run it as a Bed and Breakfast. Earned a nice living from it as well. Brought up the children on the income, made lots of new friends, and had guests who came back year after year. Until Peter ran off with one of them. But that's another story.

So, happily married at the time, I was out shopping in Folksbury, the next village along on the main road to Grantham, and getting to know the area, as you do. And Peggy and I got to chatting outside Folksbury Fruits, the fruit and veg shop where she works. Well, when I say *the fruit and veg shop where she works*, I should actually be saying *the fruit and veg shop she runs*. Because all her boss Ian has to do is drive out to the markets each morning and deliver the produce to Peggy. She sorts the rest. Admittedly, he does have other shops to attend to, but he doesn't have a bad old life, does he?

But you can find Peggy working out there in all weathers, rearranging the produce on the old cart outside, or stacking the shelves inside. The doorway is just behind the cart and is always pushed back, so the shop's open to the elements, even when it's bitterly cold. But Peggy soldiers on, her fingers wrapped in thick woollen gloves, a hat on her head, and her throat kept warm inside numerous stripy scarves. She keeps warm, she says, by popping to the back of the shop now and again for a quick cuppa or a hot chocolate, and one of her ginger biscuits.

But working there lets her keep an eye out, keeps her in the know as to what's going on. And boy, does she see some things. But then, it means she can help people.

And that's where I come in. If she needs me to help too, she just asks.

We're white witches, you see. Wiccans. There's a white witch in every village and at least one in every town. And yes, we perform witchcraft, but it's good witchcraft. We believe strictly in the law of three. That anything we do or send out, good or bad, will return to us threefold. It's a kind of religion, close to the law of Karma. We use our energies to worship nature, then we meditate, bending that nature to suit our needs, raising and channelling the energy within us to harmonise with it. It only takes a little practice. But the main thing is that we help people. You could call us private detectives, me and Peggy, only we don't charge.

It was actually Peggy who introduced me to Wiccanry in the first place. It was on a cold November night many years ago. Peter was out at the pub, the kids were in bed, and I was catching up with the ironing. Peggy had called round for a natter and we got to talking about her ex-husband, how she'd discovered his sordid affair, and how she'd sensed it was going to happen even before it did.

'It's funny, though, isn't it,' I said, 'how you know something's about to happen? I get the same sometimes. A kind of sixth sense.'

'It's a real gift, Enid. Don't knock it,' she replied, sternly.

'I'm not. It just fascinates me.'

'It *is* fascinating.'

She looked up at me then, watching carefully as I stood there, the iron steaming in my right hand, my left holding down the edge of a white pillowcase.

'Do you believe in witchcraft, Enid?' she asked, suddenly.

Well, I just burst out laughing.

'What?' she said, obviously put out.

'No, Peggy. I don't believe in witchcraft.'

'Why not?'

'That kind of thing is all in people's heads.'

'What? Don't you ever say a prayer when something's going wrong, or when you want something really important to happen?'

I thought about it for a second before I replied. 'I suppose I do, yes.'

'And don't you think that's a kind of witchcraft?'

'Possibly. Possibly not.' Folding the ironed pillowcase, I placed it onto the chair beside me. 'Why are we discussing this, anyway?'

'Well, don't you think it would be good to be able to control things a bit more?'

I looked at her curiously. 'What exactly are you trying to say, Peggy?'

She smiled. 'What would you say if I said I was a witch?'

'Sorry, Peggy, you're not making sense. Do you mean a *proper* witch, or are you in a play or something, taking after your mum at last?'

But her face was deadly serious as she revealed all.

So that's how I became a Wiccan. I remember it like it was yesterday.

Now, however, I'm a newly-married lady for the second time and have moved around the corner to Harry's house. We're letting out my old place, Chimney Cottage, and are using a website called Airbnb, something Tori suggested. And it's all working out very well.

Harry had already done up the house beautifully. With a bright yellow kitchen and a big black stove, and neutral but expensive-looking wallpaper in the lounge and dining room. A friend of ours, Mattie, designed it, did all the decorating for him. Lovely, it is. Although I have insisted on making room for my herbs. We're using the conservatory at Chimney Cottage for now, but Harry's promised me a small one for this house next year. Something to look forward to.

Genevieve, my cat and long-time companion, is settling in nicely too, although I don't think she's too keen on the bright kitchen. She's choosy, like most cats. Likes her bowl in just the right place, under the kitchen table, so she can eat in private. So it took a bit of getting used to when the table moved to the dining room and her bowl stayed in the kitchen, in full view. But we manage. She cleans herself in private, though, behind the couch, her knowing green eyes searching for predators. Usually my Harry, or Carol's children when they visit. She does make me smile.

So I've known Peggy since forever, and I'm as sure of her friendship as I am of my own breath. Whenever I visit her, though, I have to catch the bus. I don't drive, you see. Never have. So off I trots, climbs onto the number 26, inevitably chat to old Miss Pennycuik about her aches and pains, throw a little stardust her way, and alight at the bus stop beside the village green.

Folksbury's an enchanting little village. There's the Church of England school at one end of the main street, and St Andrews' Parish church at the other. The village green sits beside the school, and the Folksbury Hotel sits behind that - such a lovely place to sit with half a shandy on a summer's day. And in between the school and the church are the most delightful shops and cafés. There's a bank and a post office, too, even though many have closed down around here. How the ones in Folksbury keep going, I've no idea. And Peggy positively denies having anything to do with it.

*

Indira rents the shop just across the road from Folksbury Fruits. There's Haringey's Estate Agents on one side, and Kitty Crafts on the other.

She's a lovely girl, Indira, with the most beautiful ivory skin and long dark hair. Indian, of course, on her mother's side, but her father is British, from somewhere down Suffolk way. She wears a gold crucifix around her neck, so I guess she has some kind of faith, and has a gold wedding band, although I understand she and her husband split up a while ago.

She's given the shop a lovely name, though. It's called *Saffron Silk,* after the spice, and she's painted the door golden-yellow, the same colour. To be honest, the woodwork's getting a bit flaky now, but it's so bright and welcoming it kind of makes up for it. And it's a lovely old shop. Built of stone, with Georgian windows and bulls-eye panes of glass. All the shops on that side of the street were built a long time ago, you know. 1838, it was, the year of Queen Victoria's coronation. It says so on the wall.

Indira ran the place as a café at first, selling Ayurvedic snacks and drinks. I ask you - in the middle of Lincolnshire. And it was a novelty to begin with, so she did some roaring trade. But then the thrill wore off and folks went back to the tried and tested. To the greasy spoon with its egg and bacon, to the bakery with its posh cakes and pastries, to the hotel with its fine food and fussy waiters.

So Saffron Silk is now both a café and a home interiors shop. You walk through the door and there's a display counter on the right, all set for you to buy food and drink, with three small tables and chairs for people to sit at. And there's a long couch against the wall, covered in beautiful silk throws, and a sewing machine on the table beside it. On the other side of the shop there's a couple of old dressers, placed at such an angle as to entice you in, to make you want to touch and admire and buy. They've been painted in a matt cream colour, and are there to show off Indira's own hand-made creations. Cushions and throws and pictures, and the scarves and small dresses she makes.

She's very talented, you know. You can see her as you walk by. When she's not preparing food and drink, she's sitting there on the couch sewing, her machine zig-zagging, her slim fingers guiding the fabric along. She uses the old saris her mother sends over from Delhi to make soft furnishings and clothing. Beautiful, they are. She makes framed pictures, too, from the same fabric. Burnt oranges, vermilion reds, sunshine yellows, emerald greens and all shades of blue, shaped into elephants or trucks or rainbows. How many of her pictures have ended up in kiddie's bedrooms around here, I'll never know. But she's in an ideal spot. Mothers calling in for an organic coffee on their way home from dropping the children off at school, or taking them in for a treat on the way back. Then of course they see Indira's other merchandise on display, and they buy. She's enterprising, I'll give her that.

The first time I visited the shop, I was with Peggy. We went in for a coffee and to see what it was all about, this Ayurvedic thing. It takes me all my time to say the word, if I'm honest. But as we drank our coffee, Indira measured us up good and proper. According to Ayurveda, each of us is a mix of three basic constitutional types known as doshas. These affect your physical traits, personality and health. Understanding your dosha, she says, helps you understand the diet and lifestyle you should follow in order to keep yourself in balance and healthy. There are three doshas - pitta, vata, and kapha.

Peggy, whose mother was a professional dancer in the West End, is tall and leggy, walks with a straight back and a confident manner. Taking hold of Peggy's wrist, her fingers on the pulse, Indira studied her carefully.

'You don't sleep well, do you, Mrs Fleming? Too much thinking. Much worrying.'

Peggy nodded guiltily. 'But please call me Peggy. Mrs Fleming makes me feel so old.'

Now I must confess - that did make me smile. Practically all the folks around here call Peggy *Old Mrs Fleming*. Well, serves her right for staying in the same place so long. You'd think she'd be used to feeling old by now.

'You're a definite vata, Peggy,' said Indira, smiling. 'Now then, Enid, let's see about you.'

She took hold of my hand and I felt quite nervous.

'Kapha,' she said, after checking my pulse and studying me. 'You're definitely kapha.'

Peggy ended up with a warm rice drink, which sounds awful, but which she said was soothing and tasty. It had cinnamon and ginger powder, with liquidised dates for sweetness. There was also a small plate of cooked apple and raisins, and a delicate little spoon. I had fresh ginger tea with raw honey, and my apple dish had cloves and cinnamon instead of raisins. It all tasted lovely, and everything was so nicely presented on old china plates and pretty cups and saucers that we couldn't help but be impressed.

But there may be something in what Peggy says about the shop always changing hands. I can remember it having been a sweet shop a number of times, then an arts and crafts, an antiques shop, a haberdashery (twice), then a barbers, a sweet shop again, and then a deli. And that's only while I've lived here. So when Peggy said Indira was giving it all up, I wasn't really that surprised. The lease ends in March, so she's packing it all in and moving back to Sudbury, bless her.

But her kids are so upset. They've settled in nicely, just love their school, and have made some really nice friends.

And that's how Peggy found out. Because Anika and Rishi were playing outside their mum's shop last Tuesday when their football landed in the cart outside the greengrocers. By rights, they shouldn't have been playing in the middle of the road at all, but I suppose it's better than staring at a screen all the time. So of course they come dashing across the road, lift up their ball, see the potatoes, turnips and swede, and dare each other to a game of catch. Which is when Peggy caught them. But, bless her heart, she didn't chastise them at all. Not one bit. Instead, she invited them to the rear of the shop for hot chocolate and ginger biscuits. So they stood around, eating and drinking and talking, and that's when she got the story of them moving back to Sudbury, of having to leave their school and their friends.

'So why is your mum moving? Have you told her you want to stay here?' asked Peggy.

It was Anika who replied. 'She's scared, Mrs Fleming. She says there are djinns in the shop. She says they're telling us to move.'

'And why does she think that?' asked Peggy.

'She hears this strange noise after we've gone to sleep. She says it makes her feel scared, like it wants us to go away.'

'And it wants you to move back with your grandad – is that it?'

'But we want to stay here. Grandad can come up and see us any time he wants, can't he? Mummy should just ignore the djinns, shouldn't she?'

Peggy didn't blink an eyelid. She just carried on as normal, chatting to the children, sending them home, and selling her apples and potatoes and grapes, and chatting away to folks, just as she has been for years.

But after work she walked over to Indira's place, rang the doorbell to the apartment, and was invited inside.

CHAPTER 5

Indira Lambert

☆

Thursday 6th December
Folksbury

IT may of course be pure coincidence that the moaning sound began the night Rishi discovered the kaleidoscope. There might be some other, much simpler, explanation. But I'd never heard it before. In fact, I was really happy with the shop and the apartment, and we were settling in nicely. And the children just love their school. Rishi was still in Reception when we moved here, and now he's in Year One he's just flying. Anika's the same. She's made lots of new friends and has already been given a part in the end of year show in July.

The shop's been doing really well, too. When I began selling Ayurvedic food and drink, I was unsure of how it would be received. But it did well and I was amazed, if I'm honest. Then after the novelty wore off and business began to slow down, I started making household nik-naks and little dresses from the old saris Mama had been sending me. A shame to throw out such beautiful material, she said. Make some dresses for Anika, she said, you're so clever with your hands. So I did. I am very good with a needle, the fault of my mother, so it was easy to make clothing for Anika. But then I thought about making cushions and throws and bags and selling them, and that led to making framed collages for children's bedrooms. It was actually a picture Mama sent to Anika last Christmas that gave me the idea. A beautiful hot air balloon made from small pieces of silk, and the colours are amazing. So I copied it.

And now I've made a name for myself, now that people know about me and my products, I have to move. I suppose I could always find somewhere nearby, but I've looked all over and there's nothing. Nothing that would be suitable, anyway, and still within my price range. We need decent-sized shop premises with living accommodation of at least three bedrooms, and with a good school. Not easy. And the children would still have to change schools, wouldn't they?

*

Old Mrs Fleming, as she's known around here, came over to see me last week, just after Dad had rung for a chat. Yes, he's fine. Work's keeping him busy and he's planning a holiday to Hawaii next year with his new *friend*. No, I'm not shocked at all. I'm happy for him. He needs someone in his life. And he might stop nagging at us to move back to Sudbury if there's someone else to keep him company.

But Peggy calling round did shock me. Even though she works in the greengrocers just over the road, she'd never been round before, except to call in for coffee a few times. She said she wanted to discuss us leaving Folksbury. Because, apparently, Anika and Rishi had been telling her all about it.

The children were upstairs playing with their friends, Billie and Leo, at the time. Which meant Peggy and I could talk freely. So I invited her in, made warming ginger tea, and we sat down in the sitting room. And she came straight to the point, which is kind of what you'd expect from Old Mrs Fleming.

'Anika's told me you're giving up the shop and moving away,' she began.

I grinned. 'Do you know, Mrs Fleming, you can't do anything around here, but that everyone knows about it.'

'And sometimes that's a good thing, Indira. Because it means we can help. But I've told you before – please call me Peggy.'

I caught the edge of her perfume. Patchouli. Reminds me of the *Bangles and Beads* shop in Sudbury, just up the road from our old house. Now there's an interesting shop.

'Sorry, Peggy. I forget.'

She smiled, her hazel eyes watery from being out in the cold all day. 'It's all right, Indira. It's not really a problem, is it? Just me and my old vanity. But tell me, why have you decided to leave? You seem to be doing so well here.'

Embarrassed, I sat back against the arm of the sofa. 'This may sound a little strange, if I'm honest. And it may be pure coincidence, but ever since Rishi found an old kaleidoscope in the Grandfather clock over there,' I gestured towards it, 'I've been hearing a strange sound.'

Following my gaze, she nodded sagely. 'Okay?'

'The thing is, I'd never heard it before, and it's scaring me. And you'll probably think I'm crazy, but I feel as if it's telling us to leave, to move away. Before something really bad happens.'

She stood up, nodding at the clock. 'Show me.'

It's a beautiful old clock, and I'm not surprised Rishi's fascinated by it. It stands in an alcove beside the chimney breast, redundant once the gas fire had been fitted. So as Peggy walked over to stand before it, I pulled open the little door at the bottom to show her where Rishi had found the kaleidoscope.

Bending slightly, she glanced at the empty space inside. 'So what kind of sound is it, exactly?'

Slightly embarrassed, I tried my best to describe it. 'It's like someone whispering or the wind moaning, but really creepy and kind of sad. It only lasts a few minutes, to be honest, but there's something about it. And it's only at night, last thing, when the children are asleep and I'm getting ready for bed.'

'What do they whisper?'

I shook my head. 'I don't know. I'm not sure. It's not really a whisper, I suppose – it – I can't really describe it.'

'So where's the kaleidoscope now?'

'In Rishi's room. He's fascinated, won't part with it. But I've ordered him a new one, so I'll get rid of that old one, send it to a charity shop or something.'

She straightened up. 'So you've decided to move because of this?'

I felt stupid suddenly, idiotic. What was I thinking, uprooting my children, destroying my business, my life, just because of a weird noise in the house?

'I know,' I said. 'Ridiculous, isn't it?'

'Come on, let's go and get comfy.'

So we headed back to the sofa and our tea. 'Would you like some cake?' I asked. 'I have some freshly-made banana cake. Sugar-free?'

'No, but thank you. I have a holiday coming up, so I need to look after my figure. And even bananas have calories.' Settling comfortably into the sofa, she fastened back the strands of hair that had escaped her bun. She has lovely thick, glossy hair, actually, that seems to suit her personality.

'Sounds awesome,' I said. 'Where are you planning on going?'

'It's just a small Greek island - Koufonisia. The beaches are nice and secluded, and I do like to sunbathe topless if I can. It's the freedom and the sea air that I go for. There's nothing like it.'

I quite like old Peggy, but she is a puzzle, with her scarlet red lips and fingernails, and her topless sunbathing. Not quite in keeping with that old sheepskin she wears, and the layers of scarves and hats and gloves she wraps around herself through the winter.

She looked at me then, her expression stern and profound. 'I really don't think you should move, Indira.'

Inexplicably, I began to panic. 'I can't stay, though, can I? That noise really is freaking me out. And I'm all on my own once the children are asleep. I don't think I can cope with it anymore.'

She looked around. 'Have you checked right through the apartment? There could be an old pipe come loose, or something that's moving around a bit, like a mouse. Something that might only start up last thing at night.'

'I know, and I've thought about that. I've thought about pipes and floorboards and doors. But honestly, I've checked everywhere, and there's nothing. And why does it start at the same time every night? And why does it make me feel so sad?'

She shook her head. 'I don't know, Indira, but it's such a shame. You've done so well with this shop, and the children obviously love being here.'

'I know that, and the school's really good too. It would be great to be able to stay on, but I can't think of any other way out. I'm sorry, but this whole thing is making me really nervous, really unhappy.'

Her keen eyes surveyed mine. 'You know, I've worked across the road for longer than I care to think about. And I have to confess, people don't tend to stay in this shop for very long. I've never really thought about it before, but now you've got me wondering about it, and about the shop's history. Do you happen to know anything about it, or about the people who've lived here before?'

A cold shiver ran through me, right down to my fingertips. 'So you think there might really be some djinns?'

*

This week has been so busy. As if word has got round about my leaving. But I've not said a word to anyone, honestly, not even Billie's mum Mandy, who helps with the school run and who sometimes pops into the shop for a chat. Unless Anika and Rishi have said something to someone. I suppose that's possible. They tell their friends at school, they go home and tell their mothers, and word gets around.

But it's helped the business no end. I've been sewing and gluing like crazy, and my stuff is selling really well. How I've found time for the café and to take the children to their various activities, I have no idea. But I have, even though I've been up 'til ten o'clock some nights. So the coffers are full and my cup overflows.

Not that everything's been perfect this week. Oh, no. There was this one incident that completely freaked me out. Tuesday evening, it was, about seven o'clock. I'd just finished the picture I was working on, and had gone upstairs to tidy the rooms while Anika and Rishi watched a DVD before bed. I remember - it was the *Paddington* film. For the third time.

So I'd already tidied Anika's room and changed the bedding, and was just starting on Rishi's. His is the smallest room and there's not enough room to swing a cat. But it looks out over the fields at the back, there's an old horse chestnut tree in the garden that attracts the birds, and he loves it. But then Rishi just loves birds. Although he does get a little too enthusiastic when we feed the ducks at the beck in Ruskington. Poor things.

So, as I was saying, I was making up Rishi's bed. Clean base sheet, clean pillowcase, clean duvet cover. Pale blue and covered in trucks and tractors.

Except it wasn't a clean duvet cover. As I opened it out onto the bed, there was blood on it. A pool of dried blood, around twenty-five centimetres across.

I screamed. I couldn't help it. I just stood there and screamed.

You see, I'd washed the thing myself, dried it in the tumble dryer, ironed it and folded it away into the cupboard on the landing. Clean and neat and tidy. As always. So there was no way it could have been stained with blood.

No way.

Anika and Rishi came running up to see what was wrong. So I rolled up the cover, threw it into the pile of dirty sheets from Anika's room, and said I'd screamed because I'd seen a spider. Rishi's a proper little boy, not scared of anything, and I knew he wouldn't be upset by a wayward spider. So of course he offered to look for it.

While Rishi searched, Anika took my hand and led me onto the landing.

'Come on out here, Mummy. I'll look after you.'

She's been such a mother to me since Harvey left, and I'm so grateful, even though I've had to hide my tears from her, crying only at night when I'm safely in bed. But I couldn't possibly stay on the landing with her - I needed to make sure Rishi didn't find that damned duvet cover.

'Just let me help Rishi, darling,' I said.

'But Mummy, you're scared of spiders,' she cried, pulling at my hand.

'I'll be fine, I promise.'

We found Rishi still searching beneath the bed, his feet sticking out, his socks worn through at the back.

'Come on, Rishi,' I said. 'How about we all go downstairs and leave that nasty spider alone?'

'It's all right, Mummy. I can find it.'

Terrified he might start searching further afield, inspiration hit me.

'Ice cream, anyone?' I called.

'Yippee!' Rishi screamed, scurrying out from beneath the bed and scampering downstairs.

'Ye-es!' said Anika, following him, the spider all forgotten.

Bribery and corruption. There really is no substitute.

So I waited until they were downstairs before picking up the cover, rolling it into a tight ball, taking it to my room, and pushing it to the back of the wardrobe. Only when it was properly hidden did I begin to tremble.

Calming myself, I put a fresh white cover and pillowcase onto Rishi's bed, placed a happy smile upon my face, and went downstairs to find both children eagerly waiting for me at the freezer door. Five minutes later, we were watching *Paddington* with bowls of black grapes and vanilla ice cream on our laps.

But all the while my mind was working overtime. What on earth had just happened? How on earth *could* it have happened? That's not something to do with a mouse, I thought. Or creaking pipes. It's something that's not right, something over which I have no control.

So what the hell is it?

Once the children were fast asleep, I pulled the soiled duvet cover from the back of my wardrobe and threw it into the bin outside. It wouldn't have cleaned properly, and frankly I never wanted to see it again.

I've ordered a new duvet set with tractors and trucks on. Hopefully, Amazon will be more prompt in sending that than the new kaleidoscope. I can do without awkward questions from Rishi.

But I've hardly slept a wink since then. Tuesday night and Wednesday, I tossed and turned, and tossed and turned, until I'm exhausted. I've googled the Ayurvedic way of getting to sleep now, so I'll try that tonight. A warm glass of milk with a pinch of nutmeg and some saffron strands. I'll try some deep breathing, too.

And I've decided that, whenever I hear that noise, I'll summon up the courage to walk around the house, to try and pinpoint exactly where it's coming from. I really do need to get to the bottom of this weird phenomenon before it completely ruins my life.

But even if I do find the cause of the noise, I can't think of any kind of explanation, any reason, for what happened to Rishi's bedding.

CHAPTER 6

Sophie Dubrowska

☼

Friday 7ᵗʰ December
Grantham, Lincolnshire

TODAY it's sunshiny and fifteen degrees, but for some reason the road along the A52 to Grantham seems cold, eerie, other-worldly. It's the mist over the fields, I decide. The white fog hangs so low it looks as if a hand with long, trailing fingers is holding it up. But it's beautiful, it makes me feel good, and I smile as I sing along to the radio.

Ant got up early this morning to drive down to Cheltenham. He does occasional work as a consultant for Longford Structural, a local engineering firm, and they want him there to discuss plans for a new bridge somewhere. Devon, I think, but don't quote me on that. But that's how we met, me and Ant, because he worked full-time for Longfords when he lived in Nottingham.

I also lived in Nottingham, you see. I was at uni there, studying Art and Design. But as soon as I'd done my three years, I locked the door of the flat, gave back the keys, and flew out to Paris. I'd bagged a prestigious post-graduate placement working for the *Galerie Laurent Godin*, a gallery near the Pompidou Centre, for two years. It was such a fabulous experience to have under my belt, and I really should have been set for an amazing career.

But instead of moving back to live with my parents in Barnet when I came home, I decided to return to Nottingham. To a bedsit and a job selling shoes. I'd decided I needed time to look for the right job before settling down, before buying a place of my own. So of course I happened to be out one night with some friends, one of whom was Caroline, an old uni lecturer, and it was she who introduced me to Ant, or Antoni, to give him his posh Polish name. She knew him of old, you see, and thought we might get along. Which we did. It was a match made in Heaven – he wasn't always the Cold Pole. Well, he proposed a year later.

So I never did get a proper job. Ant had already built up his rental portfolio and just needed to keep updating it. He'd inherited a substantial amount of money from his parents at the tender age of thirty-two, you see, after they died in a car accident, bless them. So after inheriting, he decided to spread his wings and fly out to England to work for Longford Structural. He used any spare time he had to work on his investments, initially high street business properties, then later, houses that needed some kind of development. Ant's very good with money, I'll say that. And then, of course, when Mum and Dad gave me a huge chunk on my wedding day I was able to add to the coffers. So we've built up a good little business between us.

We did try for a family, me and Ant, but it just never happened. I became pregnant twice, but both ended in miscarriage. Miscarriages that I feel I'll probably never get over. And I never was very good with doctors and needles, so after one unsuccessful attempt the IVF route didn't appeal at all. So now I'm forty-three, childless, and semi-married. It may seem like a sad state of affairs, but no.

I have fun.

So today I'm driving out to Manningby's, a well-established kitchen showroom in Grantham. We need new worktops and flooring. And while I'm at it, I might just see about a new cooker. For the shop in Wells-next-the-Sea, of course. Just because they don't complain doesn't mean we should let them live in a hellhole. Bless.

And if Ant says anything, I'll say he should check out the property owners' insurance policy. *All properties should be kept in a good state of repair, etc. etc.* That should do it.

It's ten o'clock as I pull up outside the showroom, and I'm ready for a coffee. So I call in at this little place I've spotted on Finkin Street. The scent of roasting coffee beans literally hits me as I push open the door. And it's warm inside, cosy, with the radio on in the background, a low murmur. I order an Americano, large, and pay with my card. The guy serving me is tall and handsome with a winning smile, so I drop a two pound coin into the tips jar.

The coffee is strong and hot and delicious, and I savour it as I stare out of the window. The sunshine has brought the crowds, but I guess the Christmas season approaching will have a lot to do with it, too. So I watch as people struggle with their bags, chat on their phones, or just walk along holding hands. Yes, even couples who look like they've been married for years walk along holding hands. It warms the cockles.

Suddenly, my phone rings. I hesitate at first as it's not a number I recognise, but then I answer.

'Hello? Sophie Dubrowska speaking.'

'Hello, Mrs Dubrowska. My name's Peggy Fleming. Are you free to talk?'

I nod at the phone. 'Yes ...?'

'Thank you. I'm actually calling on behalf of one of your tenants, an Indira Lambert. She rents a shop from you in Folksbury she calls Saffron Silk, and I run the greengrocers opposite.'

I recall the shop she's talking about. Delightfully old, set in a row of equally delightfully old shops. A nice tenant, as well. She runs it as a café of some kind. So what now, I think? Not more repairs?

'Oh - yes?' I say.

'I'm really sorry to trouble you, but I'm wondering if you could let me have some information regarding a Grandfather clock that's part of the living accommodation.'

What a strange request, I think. Is this some kind of joke? The woman sounds serious enough, but ...

'Okay. Yes. What is it you want to know?'

'We're just trying to trace its history, that's all. Was the clock included in the purchase of the building, or was it something you bought separately - can you remember?'

A chill runs through me. This doesn't feel right. Something doesn't feel right.

'I'm sorry,' I hear myself saying, 'but is it possible to speak to Indira herself? I - I just feel a bit awkward discussing her affairs with a complete stranger.'

'Sorry, Mrs Dubrowska, she's not here at the moment. Maybe we could arrange to meet at the shop some time? Would that be possible at all?'

'That should be fine. Let me call you back when I have my diary.'

*

I'm rather pleased with my choice. A freestanding gas cooker in matt grey. Classy and understated. Then while I was choosing a new worktop, I realised that if I replaced the cupboard doors as well, the worktop wouldn't have to be made of wood to match. Because wood doesn't work, not when there's water being splashed about. So I've chosen a pale grey granite for the worktop. Only it's not granite; it's actually a manmade copy. But it looks lovely and is so much more practical than wood. Then we - the girl and I - decided on cupboard doors and drawer-fronts made of the same material. Silver grey with royal blue knobs. Then I spent even more time choosing lino, in the end deciding on a royal blue and grey tile-effect. But it's good quality, shouldn't rip so easily. And all in all it's going to cost way less than a new kitchen.

So my art degree has come in for something useful after all. Kitchen design. Who'd have thought it?

Yet all the while my mind kept flying back to that phone call. Peggy, did she call herself? So what's wrong with the clock? And why has she become involved? There's something going on here that I need to be careful of. That I need to push away.

Just a feeling.

'When could you fit it?' I ask the girl, whose name I later discover is Alicia.

She checks their work schedule on the iPad she carries everywhere and looks up, pushing back her dark hair thoughtfully.

'Well, assuming we've got enough stock in, we have a free day on Monday. If that's okay with you?'

'Brilliant. I'll get back to you with the measurements. Thanks.'

So, after a quick lunch of avocado and bacon on rye, I drive out to Wells-next-the-Sea. Parking up outside Hughes Hand-me-Downs, I push open the door to be greeted by Mel, a shocked look on her face.

'Mrs Dubrowska. What are you doing here? It's Friday.'

She looks worried, as if I'm bringing bad news, so I smile and reassure her.

'It's okay, sweetie. I'm just here to take some measurements. If that's okay?'

'Yes. Yes, of course. What, is it the lino?'

Closing up the shop, she takes me through to the kitchen. There's a pile of ironed laundry on one side, and I notice the beautiful flowers on the table have drooped a little.

'I need to measure up for lino, worktop and cupboard doors. I thought we might have a new cooker as well.' I'm busy pulling a tape measure from my bag, and as I look up she smiles delightedly. 'I hope that's all right?'

'Of course. Thank you.'

I pull out the tape. 'I'll need some help with this, though. Is Idris around?'

She shakes her head. 'He's gone off with our Rowan. He's got the day off, so they've driven out to the nature reserve for a nice walk. They've taken sandwiches and a flask, so they might be a while. But a good bit of fresh air and a chat always helps.'

'It certainly does. Here then, can you help me with this, please?'

We take the measurements and I note them down on my phone.

'Would you like a cuppa while you're here?' she asks.

'Thanks, sweetie - that would be lovely. But I won't stay long.'

While she fills the kettle, I pop out to the car, call Alicia at Manningby's and give her the measurements. She's already checked their stock and can confirm the fitting date. I pay with my card and the deal is done.

Mel is pushing chocolate digestives onto a plate as I return.

'So when will it all arrive, then?' she asks.

'They'll be fitting it on Monday. I hope that's all right.'

She turns, surprised. 'That soon? Gosh. Just in time for Christmas, it'll be. And we've got family coming over as well.'

I smile. 'Oh, sweetie, that'll be so lovely for you.'

Sudden tears fill her eyes. 'Thank you, Mrs Dubrowska.'

I swallow hard to stop myself from crumbling. 'No. You deserve a nice place to live, and you've been our tenants for years. Anyway, as I said before, this flooring's a tripping hazard. It's actually dangerous.'

She wipes her eyes with the backs of her hands. 'Thank you, all the same. It's very kind of you.'

The back door is pushed open at that point and Idris walks in, followed by Rowan. Much taller than his father, his brown eyes sparkle with health, his face is pink from the cold air.

'Why is the shop shut?' asks Idris, dumping his rucksack onto the table. He looks from Mel to me, then back again. 'Are you all right, love?'

She smiles. 'I'm fine, Idris. Mrs Dubrowska is here to measure up, that's all. We're having some new stuff fitted into the kitchen. Will you be wanting a cup of tea, you two?'

Hanging his coat around the back of a chair, Idris nods.

'That'd be lovely - thanks, love.' He turns to me. 'So what is it, then - that new lino you promised?'

'New lino, new cooker, and new cupboard doors and worktop.' I'm just bristling with pleasure.

His face is a picture, delighted and astonished all at the same time. 'Oh now, we weren't expecting all that, were we, Mel?'

'No. But it's lovely, all the same. Thank you, Mrs Dubrowska.'

I asked Mel years ago to just call me Sophie, but she's never picked up on it. So now I don't say anything. But I do feel guilty. We really shouldn't have been allowing them to live in these conditions. It should have been dealt with years ago. But when we have long-term tenants, we just tend to let things slide. It's only when someone moves out that we update a property.

'It really needed doing, Mel,' I say. 'So please don't thank me.'

'All the same,' says Idris, 'it is very good of you.'

Mel fills the kettle. 'So where did you two get to, on your walk?'

'Just the beach,' says Idris.

Rowan smiles. 'They were out walking the alpacas again.'

'Lovely,' she says. 'Here, there's chocolate biscuits if you want one.'

'Can you bring mine through, love?' says Idris. 'I'll just open up.'

As Idris goes to tend the shop, Rowan smiles shyly and pulls back a chair to sit beside me.

'How are you doing?' he says.

His voice is warm and deep and soft. Like his eyes. I could literally melt into them.

But I don't. Sleeping with other men is one thing. Falling in love with them is quite another.

Instead, I smile. 'I'm fine, thank you. But how about you, sweetie - did you have a good walk?'

CHAPTER 7

Enid Mitchell

Saturday 8ᵗʰ December
Pepingham

HARRY proposed to me on Christmas Eve last year, you know. He'd planned it all so carefully, he said, wanted it to be so romantic.

He'd lived in London all his life, Harry, only moving up here after his brother Bill died. But Bill's house, the one we're living in now, is just around the corner from my old house, Chimney Cottage, and we only met because Harry was up here clearing it all out. Filling the car with boxes of hoarded rubbish, he was. Decontaminating the house with more bleach than I care to think about. But it needed it, if I'm honest. Bill was an alcoholic, you see, lived on his own, never cleaned, hardly ate a thing, and was a bit of a sad case, truth be told. So I'd pop in sometimes with bits of food to help out. Only a casserole or a lasagne, or even just a few groceries. But we all did it, the whole village. We made sure he ate properly, that he was warm and safe and looked after.

Sadly, though, Bill died of a heart attack a couple of years ago. Harry had paid the mortgage for him for years, so Bill left the house to him in his will. But he's a good man, Harry. Kind and thoughtful. Intelligent. A quiet man. Tall and slim with neat grey hair and lovely blue eyes.

Even so, it was difficult telling him about my witchcraft shenanigans. Although I couldn't tell him everything, obviously. No, that would not have done. But I had to say something, didn't I? I couldn't just accept his proposal of marriage without telling him what he was getting himself into, now could I? He already knew I meditated regularly, of course, but then lots of people do that nowadays.

He'd intended proposing on the morning of Christmas Day, he said. The ring was already there, under his tree, wrapped in pretty paper, although I didn't know it at the time. But then our Carol, as disorganised as ever, made a last-minute call to say they were coming over for a few days. Which of course scuppered Harry's plans good and proper. So he got me to open my present before they arrived. He brought it round the night before Christmas Eve, and it's the most beautiful ring I've ever seen. Made me cry, which isn't something I do easily.

And it *was* romantic in the end. Confused and a bit nervous, I opened my present, a glittering solitaire diamond set into yellow gold. Well, I just stared at it. So Harry took my hand, his eyes dewy with emotion, and popped the question.

'Enid, will you marry me? Please? I can't get down on my knees or anything - I'd never get back up - but please say you will.'

I laughed and cried all at the same time. Then I began to tremble. Because, despite what Justine had predicted with her cards, I never really saw it coming. The cards aren't always one hundred per cent, are they?

But I couldn't just accept his proposal there and then. He needed to know what he was getting into. So, taking the box and placing it onto the couch between us, I took hold of his hand.

'Harry, there's something I need to explain. You need to know what you're taking on here, but I don't want to scare you off – please don't think that. I do love you.'

Alarmed, he stared at me, his eyes wide with fear. 'What? What is it?'

'It's nothing bad, so don't go getting upset or anything. It's just - I know we've discussed my upbringing before - the fact that I'm a Romani, that my childhood was not the usual kind of childhood ...'

You see, as a Romani kid I spent my childhood travelling from one place to another. Up hill and down dale, Dad making up for lost time after his years in the war. It was a lovely life, though. Carefree. Apart from when Mum made us study. But even that was good in a way as it meant the other kids didn't look down on us for being *gippos*. We were clever, Sam and I. I could have been a teacher too, I suppose, but I wanted to help people. People who were sick, people who were sad, or who had just lost their way. So nursing was the most natural thing for me to do, which is what I did until I married Peter. My desire to help people is also what nudged me towards becoming a Wiccan.

But Harry just smiled softly. 'That's one of the things I love about you, Enid. You're different.'

I hesitated. Would this knowledge put him off? Would he wonder why I'd never told him before? Would he feel he could never trust me again?

I felt Genevieve's eyes on me. She was sitting before the fire, egging me on, telling me to do it, to be honest. So I bit the bullet. It was now or never, and he really had to know. Taking a deep breath, I calmed my racing heart.

'Harry, I'm not just a Romani. I'm also a Wiccan.'

'Right ...'

He hadn't flinched, not one bit.

'Do you know what that is?' I asked, just to be sure.

He nodded. 'A type of witch?'

I squeezed his hand, sending streams of love shooting through his veins. 'In layman's terms, I'm a white witch.'

He nodded awkwardly. 'Okay ...'

'My herbs, my oils, and Genevieve, my familiar - they're all here for a reason. I perform witchcraft, but only good witchcraft. And Peggy Fleming is my High Priestess.'

'Okay ...' he repeated.

'There's nothing bad about it, Harry, not one thing,' I continued, persuasively. 'We worship nature. Then we meditate, bending that nature to raise and channel our energy. And we use it to help people.'

He looked sad suddenly, and I knew why, of course.

'I - I've not told you before,' I said, 'because I didn't want to scare you off, and you've made me so happy since we met. I'm so sorry, Harry.'

'It's okay. I just - it does kind of explain everything, I suppose.'

I grinned. 'The odd goings-on? The burning of weird-smelling oils and herbs, and the kind of women I mix with? Yes, it's all to do with that.'

Letting go of my hands, he sat back. 'Wow. Well, at least you're not an evil witch. At least you're doing nice things.'

So he forgave me, and we were married last February at the registry office in Grantham, with photos taken in Bourne Woods and the reception at the Belton Woods Hotel. Such a beautiful day, it was. Both Carol and Jonathan were there, and I had Carol's two in attendance - Rosie as bridesmaid and Adam as pageboy. My brother Sam and his wife Jackie came over from

Snowdonia, and of course Peggy and Genevieve were there. So altogether, it was the most perfect day.

*

As the result of our trip to Lincoln on Sunday, Peggy and I have agreed to meet up at Indira's place, Saffron Silk. Peggy's already been round for a chat, but she wants me to take a look as well. She only finishes work at five, though, so I've hopped onto the four forty-five into Folksbury. Bernadette Coombes is sitting there at the front, on the way home from visiting her daughter in Bourne. And she's full of it. How well her Sarah is doing, how well the grandchildren are doing, how wonderful their house is, and how she wishes she could go and live with them. Makes me shiver, it does. Moving into your kid's house with them. It's all back to front, isn't it? It's lovely for a while, of course, but then everyone begins to get in each other's way. So you can't meditate in a morning, or have your nice sleep of an afternoon, or put your feet up whenever you like. No. It's not for me. Bernadette's welcome to her opinion all the same, so I just nod and agree and wish her the best. But as we reach her stop and she stands up, she clings to the rail unsteadily. Leaning towards her, I gently touch her back with my forefinger. Wishes for independence and good health. Straightening up, she turns to smile, and I feel I've done my deed for the day.

Peggy's just shutting up shop as I arrive. She's already pushed the old cart inside, so there's only the doors to lock and the shutter to pull across.

'Won't be a minute, Enid. Bloody spuds had minds of their own today, I'm sure of it. All over the place, they were.'

I stand and wait while she locks up. Dropping the keys into her old carpet bag, she pulls off her gloves and hat and drops them inside, too. Then, pulling out a small black cosmetics bag, she applies carmine-red lipstick. Pressing her lips together and checking herself in the small mirror, she smiles and shrugs her shoulders.

'Let's get on with it, then.'

Indira welcomes us in, taking us through the darkened shop with its weird cinnamon-coffee smell, through the kitchen, and into the lounge at the back. It's a lovely room, with French doors set into a bay window that I know, even though the curtains are drawn, looks out over the fields beyond. Indira's already made tea, so we sit around the small coffee table, me on an armchair and Peggy on the blue velvet couch, her long legs stretched out gracefully. An old piano on the far wall is littered with children's books, and the pine chest on the floor beside it is open, bursting with toy animals and Disney characters. Indira's hand-made cushions adorn the place and I make sure to admire them. But she fusses around, not really settling anywhere. One minute she's leaning against the curtains, the next she's picking up her cup and sipping tea as she walks around.

I'm surprised. Indira usually has a very welcoming aura, thoughtful, serene, making it easy to relax in her company. But today she's the complete opposite, setting the place on edge a little.

'Anika and Rishi have gone to a friend's house for their tea,' she says. 'I thought it would be best.'

'It's a good idea,' says Peggy. 'Don't want to scare the poor mites, do we?'

I nod in agreement. 'So from what Peggy's told me, my dear, Rishi found an old kaleidoscope in the base of your Grandfather clock, and ever since then you've been hearing a strange noise.'

'It's not just the noise now,' she says, tearfully. 'What if I told you I found blood on a clean duvet cover on Tuesday? Just suddenly? From out of nowhere?'

Determined to let us know how very upset she is and how much she needs to get away, she describes the incident, becoming more and more agitated by the minute.

'Okay,' says Peggy, thoughtfully. 'And you're sure no-one had been near it?'

She shakes her head emphatically. 'Absolutely sure. It was all folded up, just as it was when I ironed it and put it into the cupboard.'

'Come and sit down,' I say calmly, and she obeys. 'Now describe this noise to me.'

'Well, it's like the wind moaning, or someone whispering, but sad and creepy all at the same time.' She laughs nervously. 'Sounds ridiculous when you say it out loud, doesn't it?'

I shake my head. 'No. No, it doesn't. There *are* such things as spirits, if that's what we're looking at here. Some spirits are kind and some aren't. So I suppose we need to find out exactly what it is that's causing this particular noise.'

'And there's a weird smell when it happens,' adds Indira, 'so disgusting it turns my stomach. But the sound upsets me so much I don't take much notice of the smell.'

'Can you describe it?' says Peggy.

Thoughtfully, Indira stares at the littered piano. 'Kind of dirty. Like a dustbin. Like a back alleyway, where shops store their dustbins and they don't get emptied properly.'

'Okay,' says Peggy, nodding. 'Thanks, Indira. Now I plan on doing some research on the clock and I've rung the landlady, but she's not got back to me yet.'

'So we don't know anything about it?' I ask.

'We know a little bit, Enid. We know it was manufactured in 1850 and the manufacturer was Thomas Harrison of Yorkshire – it actually says that on the dial.'

I walk over to the clock, and Peggy follows.

The clock face is lovely, embellished with flowers. And there's a painting above it depicting a large white house overlooking a flowing river, with trees growing alongside. A beautiful rural setting it is, peaceful. Leaning over, I turn the small key, open the glass door, and peer inside. The heavy brass pendulum swings to and fro. There's the smell of ancient wood, of wax polish and cotton dusters. There was obviously a time when this clock was really looked after. Maybe by a servant. Or a wife who took great pride in her home.

Kneeling down beside me, Peggy uses her fingernails to pull open a small door at the very base of the clock, the box part that sits on the floor. There's a door here that's not obvious until you're guided towards it. With enough space inside to hide a small object.

'Is this where Rishi found the kaleidoscope?' I ask.

Indira nods awkwardly. 'It's where he says he found it. We were upstairs, sorting out the Christmas decorations, me and Anika. And Rishi came running up to show us what he'd found. But I know he'd never have gone outside - it was too dark - so he must have found it inside the house somewhere. And there's no reason for him to lie, is there? Even though it does seem odd. I mean, why would anyone put a kaleidoscope inside a clock?'

'Well, that's what we're here to find out,' says Peggy. 'But I have an idea.'

'What?'

'Would you mind if Enid and I stayed the night? You and the children can stay over at my place, if you like. It's warm and cosy and you'd be very welcome.'

'What, tonight?' Her face has turned grey.

'Yes.'

'Why?'

'I just think we should hear the sound for ourselves. In case it's something quite simple, like loose pipes or creaky wood or some such thing.'

It's only as Indira goes upstairs to pack that I realise Peggy is putting on an act. She's good at that, her mother being on the London stage for years, Peggy watching from the wings.

I screw up my eyes thoughtfully. Just what is it she's not telling us?

CHAPTER 8

Indira Lambert

☆

Sunday 9th December
Folksbury

IT'S Sunday morning, and I'm so tired I walk through the front door in a daze. But the children are really excited to be home again, and that gives me a good feeling. We did enjoy staying in Peggy's cottage, of course - it was like a mini-break - but it'll be good to sleep in my own bed tonight. The cottage is a two-up, two-down, with a small utility room at the back that looks like it used to be the outside loo. And the garden backs onto a stream, with Mallard ducks and Canada geese climbing up and down the embankment. But Rishi was so fascinated this morning that he kept creeping outside to go and look, and I had to keep pulling him back in because it was raining. In the end, though, wrapped in our coats, Anika and I joined him, throwing bread to the ducks and laughing and joking. Then we sat at the kitchen window and watched them as we ate our breakfast. Coco-pops and milk. Not quite what I'd have imagined Peggy eating for breakfast. Although, thinking about it, the box hadn't been opened. As if she kind of knew we'd be staying.

So even though Peggy's little cottage is nice and homely with its reclaimed pine, its striped calico sofas, and the huge sprigs of holly hanging in the porch, it's not home. And if it hadn't been for the DVDs I'd crammed into my bag at the last minute, and the ducks, the children would have been totally bored. Well, there's no Disney Channel at Peggy's, is there?

As I walk through the shop, I find Peggy busy in the kitchen, tidying up. There's a strange-looking bowl on the worktop that she scurries away into her huge carpet bag.

'Indira,' she gushes. 'How are you? Did you sleep well? Did Genevieve look after you?'

Funny she should ask that. Enid's husband brought their cat over last night, insisting she stay with us for some reason. And of course the children loved the idea. But weirdly, she - Genevieve - did appear to be in charge of the place. If she wasn't walking round with her head in the air, ears perked, she was sitting beneath the radiator watching our every move.

I smile. 'I think she did take care of us, yes. But there was no need - we were lovely and cosy. We've left her with a bowl of milk, so I hope that's all right.'

'She'll be fine, don't worry. We'll call and pick her up on the way to Enid's.'

'Rishi was really taken with her, though, and with the ducks. His favourite trip out at the moment is to visit the ducks at the beck in Ruskington – he's just besotted with them.'

'Well, you can come and visit my place any time you like.'

'Thanks, Peggy, it's very kind of you. But how did you two get on last night?'

She nods. 'We had a great night's sleep, thank you. After the noise stopped, anyway.'

Realising I'm holding my breath, I calm myself, walk through to the sitting room, and throw our overnight bags onto the floor.

'You heard it, then?' I ask, suddenly anxious.

Enid comes downstairs at that point, still in her dressing gown and slippers. She looks kind of right in my kitchen, kind of at home. Although Enid probably looks right anywhere. She's a Romani by birth, you know, has travelled all over the place. She looks a bit like your favourite grandma, really, apart from the fact that she wears big golden hoops in her ears, a finger-length of heavy gold bangles on her wrist, and dyes her hair a bright reddish-brown. Well, it's not what either of my grandmas would do, that's for sure. Picking up her half-empty mug of tea, she sits at the kitchen table beside my jug of pink lilies, and smiles.

'So how was your night at Peggy's, my dear? Did Genevieve take good care of you?'

Her voice, warm and kind with just that slight touch of Cockney, puts me at ease. I've noticed that about her before, though, her ability to calm, to pacify.

'Peggy's just asked me the very same thing. Yes, Genevieve did take care of us. She watched our every move, even when Rishi went up to the bathroom.' I shake my head in bewilderment. 'It was strange, now I think about it.'

'She's a good cat,' she says. 'Did you let her out at all?'

'Rishi did, although he didn't let her out of his sight, not for a second, just in case she chased the ducks. I think he's a little in love with her, to be honest, but she definitely has a mind of her own.'

I realise Rishi and Anika are playing some kind of game over by the piano. It's getting louder by the minute, so I shoo them upstairs.

'Go put your toys and things away, please, then I'll make you something to eat. And tidy your rooms for five minutes, both of you.'

'But Mu-um!' protests Anika, pushing back her long dark hair.

'And tie your hair back.'

I wait until they've run upstairs before I ask the million dollar question.

'So what happened here last night?'

Peggy sits down beside Enid, her face drawn and grey without her lipstick. Unlike Enid, she's fully dressed. Her jeans and jumper are denim blue, and she wears a white hooded cardigan that's thrown loosely around her shoulders. Looking round first to make sure the children are definitely upstairs, she replies. Her voice is quiet, uneasy, conscious of the impact her words will have. Like a dark night descending.

'From what you've told me, and from what we discovered last night, it is possible Rishi has released some kind of spirit. You were right, Indira. We think the clock is haunted.'

I feel faint. I cling to the edge of the table. 'What?'

She puts out a hand to comfort me. 'Don't be afraid. If they'd intended harm, they'd have done something by now. It's possible they're just afraid or upset, that's all. I don't think they mean to hurt you.'

My shoulders freeze and I can't move. 'What? But what about Rishi's duvet cover? The blood? What's all that about?'

'If something is haunting the clock, then it's obviously been around a long time. It will have embedded itself inside the clock, and probably the entire house, by the looks of it.'

'It's okay,' murmurs Enid, softly. 'We can sort this.'

'What? How?' I say.

Enid pulls at me to sit on the chair beside her. 'You need to sit down, my dear. Come on.'

Feeling slightly sick, I obey.

'There's something you have to know,' she says, 'and I don't want you to panic.'

As if.

'You need to know that Peggy and I are Wiccans. White witches. We're good people, we use our energy to worship nature, and we meditate so we can control that nature. But only so we can help people. People like you.'

I definitely feel sick now. I feel like I'm in one of Harvey's movies. Maybe I am. Maybe this is some awful dream and when I wake up I can write it all down and gross millions at the box office.

Breathing deeply, I try to calm my thoughts, which are trying their best to spin out of control. 'You don't have to help me. It's fine. We can just move out - it's okay.'

But Peggy shakes her head knowingly. 'So what happens to the next person who rents this place? And the next person? Do they all have to go through the same thing? A strange sound every night? Blood on the sheets?'

'You could help *them*,' I insist. 'We don't have to stay, do we?'

Enid takes my hand into hers. Her eyes, coal-black suddenly, burn into mine, insistent, demanding. 'You've built up a lovely little business here, Indira. The children are happy, they love their school, and they've made lots of new friends. Why would you move away from all that?'

Tears threaten, but I blink and take control, thinking again of all Anika and Rishi went through when Harvey walked out.

I nod. 'Yes. You're right.'

She smiles. 'We'll help. We're here to help. And don't worry, because we've had lots of experience in this kind of thing. We know exactly what we're doing.'

'Most of the time,' says Peggy, grinning.

Anika and Rishi come racing downstairs at that point.

'Mummy! It's toast and jam time!' shouts Rishi, running head-first into me.

His huge brown eyes bring me back to reality, my heart pounds with love, and I hug him close.

'Typical boy,' I say, grinning. 'All he thinks about is his stomach.'

Peggy and Enid, my new Wiccan friends, smile knowingly.

'Come on, then, darling. Let's see what we can find,' I say.

*

I do love this place. The kitchen with its long, sea-blue tiles and cupboards, and the rooms with their tall ceilings and wide windows. Admittedly, the work surfaces in the kitchen are stainless steel because of FSA regulations, but otherwise it's awesome, with its pine table and chairs and the warm copper pendant light that hangs above. The sitting room is nice, too, with French doors looking out over the garden and the fields beyond. And I've begun growing vegetables out there -

to use in the café, of course, but also for ourselves. I've been doing so well with them, and it would be such a pity if we do have to leave. Even my courgettes did well this year, and they make lovely roast veg, mixed with tomatoes, peppers, onions and aubergine. My children just love roast veg, the colours are so shiny and appealing.

Then, of course, there are the three bedrooms and the huge landing. That cupboard on the landing is so useful. I store our bed linen and towels in there, and stuff I no longer use but can't throw out. Baby clothes and books, toys, shoes, and curtains that might come in useful if we ever do move. I know. I'm really bad at getting rid of stuff. A hoarder, my mother says. You're a hoarder, someone who can't let go of the past.

She's right. I can't.

I can't let go. I need Harvey in my life. I need my children to be babies and toddling around the house again. I need my parents to be together, happy and living in Sudbury. Instead, Mama's in Delhi running her mobile beauty business, and Dad's living the life of a widower.

Poor Dad. He was devastated when Mama left. Even though they hadn't been getting on for years. But she was always out, into every society and club she could rustle up from the pages of the Sudbury Advertiser. Dancing, walking, boules, macramé, bridge, jumble sales, coffee mornings. Anything to get out of the house. She worked part-time, too, as a teaching assistant at the local secondary. No wonder their relationship fell apart. They never bloody well saw each other. I thought I'd learned from that, made sure Harvey and I spent quality time together, got my friend Kat to babysit so we could go out, even if it was just for a coffee along the road. Not that it did any good.

Obviously.

So once more my life is being turned upside down. I really shouldn't be dragging the kids away again, should I? Another house, another way of living, another school. It's just - I feel as if they're in danger. It sounds utterly, completely stupid, I know. But it is how I feel.

Peggy's adamant, though. She insists we stay here while she investigates further. Quite how she'll do that, I dread to think. She has said if I'm really scared I can ring her, and we can stay at her place again. So sweet of her. I just hope it never comes to that.

And then, of course, there's another reason for me to stay.

A guy.

Isn't there always a guy?

His name's Mark and he calls in for coffee every Tuesday morning. Sometimes he wants cake and sometimes just a drink. I give him one of my avocado fudge brownies, always freshly baked and now his favourite, he says.

But he's really nice, with dark eyes and round glasses, and a trendy stubble that's not too long and not too short. Intelligent-looking, I suppose. He's actually a salesman, selling pharmaceuticals to chemists. Every fourth Tuesday he drives from his home in Whittlesey to Scunthorpe, which takes him along the A15, the main road through Folksbury, and it's usually around eleven o'clock when he walks through the door.

'Hi, Indira,' he'll call nonchalantly, as if we've known each other for years.

I'm usually still baking at eleven on a Tuesday morning. So I wipe my hands on my apron and serve him. He sits at just the same table every time, unless it's occupied. The one nearest the window, near the chaise longue. So he can watch the people as they pass by.

From what I've gathered from our various conversations, he has been married (to Jenny), but is now single. He lives all on his own, no dogs or cats or anything, and so he likes to chat when he meets people.

But we just talk and have a laugh. And he does make me laugh. I really like him.

But he's not Harvey. There'll never be another Harvey. He was the first man ever to make love to me, on our wedding night. He is the one and only love of my life. And I miss him.

But Mark is kind and thoughtful. *He* would never abandon his wife and kids for a career in Hollywood.

So yes, I am kind of thinking I might hang around a while longer. It's just that dreaded noise. That moaning, throbbing sound that sends a chill of terror through me, telling me to pack my bags, grab my children, and go.

I wonder if the previous occupants ever heard it. That's obviously something we need to look into, and is what Peggy's trying to do, she says.

But we need to look into it before I completely and absolutely lose my mind.

CHAPTER 9

Sophie Dubrowska

☼

Monday 10th December
Spalding, Lincolnshire

THIS morning I drove out to Fakenham to call on Serena and Tom Keacher. Just to make sure everything is okay with the shop and the flat, and to renew their contract. We give tenants a six month tenancy to begin with, then renew every six months if there's satisfaction on both sides. To be honest, we only get them to sign the papers after the first six months, then just allow it to continue.

Serena and Tom are such an adorable young couple, though. But the shop's tiny with not much potential, really, so they run it as a clothing boutique called Bijou. They began their business from absolute scratch, importing linens from Italy, and I have to say their enthusiasm is infectious. I spent quite a long time chatting to them actually, so by the time I left I was starving. So I called into the local Deli and had a ciabatta with hot onion soup, followed by an Americano. All of which was delicious and very satisfying.

But it's now getting on for three thirty, and it's dark and raining. The roads are shiny where they reflect my headlights, and I'm struggling to see. Then the rain turns to sleet and comes at me in hypnotic stair-rods, one after another after another. My journey home has already taken me through King's Lynn on the A17, and as I reach Holbeach the map on the satnav shows me the junction for Spalding. Yawning loudly, I slow down a little and think about pulling off to call on Radley. Just for some respite and a cuppa, you understand. Ant wouldn't mind. I'd just say I pulled in for a while to let the sleet ease off.

Then my mood lifts suddenly as I make a decision. So I indicate left, change down, and turn off to take the road into Spalding town centre, a lovely old market town. Indicating right, I turn onto Moore Street. Radley Gibbs rents a house from us here, a two bed terrace. It's nice, modern, built in the eighties, but before building firms began cutting back on land so much. And it's just as we bought it almost five years ago, with a small back garden that Radley tends religiously, and a conservatory built onto the kitchen. Radley moved in straight after the young couple with the baby left. Sonia, I think her name was. I can't remember his name, the boyfriend, but I know he'd got into some kind of difficulty, so they had to leave and move in with her parents. They had no idea how to look after money, bless them, never mind a baby. But Radley's been here two years now, and he's happy enough, will probably stay a while. Which is fine by me.

The curtains are open and the living room light is on, so I pull in behind Radley's Skoda. I pull out my phone and message Ant to say I'll be later than expected and wait for his reply. But there isn't one, so I take that as acquiescence. Switching on the interior light, I pull down the mirror, apply some lipstick, rub a little into my cheeks, and check my hair in the mirror. The sleet is coming fast now, so I lock the car, hold my coat above my head, and run to the door, ringing the bell incessantly.

Radley works from home, some kind of engineering design. It's nearly four in the afternoon, but he opens the door in his pyjamas, his shoulder-length hair a mess and his face unshaven. Although that's kind of *de rigeur* these days.

The scent of sugared coffee hits me as I step quickly inside. Closing the door, Radley looks down at me.

'Hi, Mrs Dubrowska. Nice to see you, and I must say you're looking as lovely as ever.'

I grin at the compliment. 'Hi, Mr Miller, *mon chéri*. How are you?'

'I'm dandy. But you're not here for the rent again, are you? Because I'm paying it straight into the account now.'

I look up into those gorgeous blue eyes. He's thirty-one and a hunk. And way too young for the likes of me. But he doesn't seem to mind. And if he does, he's not saying. Placing my arms around him, I snuggle into his warm chest, and the curly bronze hair peeking from the V of his pyjama top rubs against my cheek. Aroused, I look up.

'I'm sheltering from the weather, sweetie. It's like shit out there. I hope you don't mind.'

Sighing, he removes my arms, hangs my wet coat onto the door handle, and pulls at my hand.

'We obviously need to talk about this, Mrs Dubrowska.'

Three minutes later, we're upstairs in bed. The room is dark, but the curtains are open, allowing soft light from the street lamp to fall into the room. The sleet catches the light before it melts against the window.

Radley nibbles my ear, his hands exploring gently, enticingly. I yield, my mouth searching for his, my heart racing with excitement.

He sits back suddenly. 'If I'm not doing this for a reduction in the rent, then exactly why am I doing it, Mrs Dubrowska?'

I laugh loudly. 'Because you like me? Because you can't resist ...'

He screws up his eyes thoughtfully. 'That may be the reason. I will consider it. But you do know I have work to do, don't you?' Placing his arms around me, he gently removes my bra.

'Are you really that busy, Mr Miller?'

He grins. 'It's okay. I've considered it. And I'm sure my work can wait, Mrs Dubrowska.'

His cold hand upon my breast sends a shiver rushing through me, and I sigh deeply. His bed smells of soap and sweat at the same time, and we surround ourselves with the soft white cotton of the quilt, keeping out the cold and the dark.

And Ant.

A tiny part of me does feel guilty. After all, I'm a married woman. I swore to love, honour and cherish. But as I've said, Ant's no longer interested. And a girl has her needs.

Which Radley fulfils quite beautifully.

An hour later, I awake to hot tea and toast, dripping in butter and marmite. Radley brings it in on a large plastic tray, and I sit up to eat and drink and talk.

*

Ant calls just as I'm driving past Bottesford on the A52, so I answer on the hands-free.

'Hi, sweetie.'

'Hi, Sophie. I'm just letting you know I'll be home late. I'm still in this bloody meeting - just popped out for two minutes. It shouldn't take much longer, but I won't get home until at least half eight. Sorry.'

'That's fine. No worries. Do you want anything special for supper?'

'Anything will do, thanks. And a nice bottle of wine to go with it. That bottle of Sangiovese, I think.'

'No probs. By the way, and while I remember - someone called me on Friday about the shop in Folksbury. You know, the café on the main street?'

'Oh, yes?'

'They want to know where we got that old Grandfather clock, and I can't think. Did it come with the shop, do you know?'

'I think we bought it from the antiques place we visited that time. We bought a few bits, if I remember. Investments. I'll take a look when I'm back home - there'll be something on the bill of sale, I'd imagine. But that's a strange request.'

'That's what I thought. But the woman sounded genuine, so I said I'd look into it. Anyway, I know you're busy, so I'll see you later. Ciao, sweetie.'

'Ciao, Sophie.'

The sleet has stopped, the roads are clearing, and it's an easy journey home. So I turn up the radio, and I daydream.

I get to thinking about Mel. Their kitchen should have been fitted by now. I hope it looks good. Although it really should have been done years ago. We need to up our game, me and Ant. I mean, it's not as if we're struggling, moneywise. And it all adds value to the property, if ever we do need to sell.

And then I get to thinking about their son, Rowan. Such a lovely young man. Actually, he's not that young – he must be only a few years younger than me. Late thirties, maybe? But so sweet. So thoughtful. I like a man who cares about his mother.

I'll never have that, a son who cares about his mother. Now don't get me wrong. I'm not broody or anything, but I do sometimes wish we'd managed to have children. Maybe Ant wouldn't have got so old so soon if we'd had a child. Someone to play football with, or cricket, someone to keep him young. And me? Yes, I'd have loved a daughter. Someone to go shopping with, who'd talk about makeup and hair and clothes. Someone to spoil. She would have been called Daisy. Daisy Dubrowska. And the boy? He would have been either Richard or Stefan – I still can't decide.

But it's never to be. So I dream, and I live my life vicariously through other people and their children. Which is wonderful in a way. I get all the good bits without the tantrums and the dirty nappies and the school run.

What I wouldn't have given, though, to be able to bring a child into the world, to nurture it, to fashion it into the loveliest person, kind and considerate and caring. A real person. A genuine human being. Oh, the joy, the satisfaction.

*

Ant's round face peeks through the doorway just as I'm pulling the lasagne from the oven. I catch some sauce on the oven gloves and have to throw them into the washing machine. But the sauce is cheesy and bubbling and smells delicious. And I've made a fresh green salad that already sits on the dining table alongside the bottle of Sangiovese, uncorked and allowed to breathe. Just as Ant likes it.

'*Ukochany,*' he says, undoing his tie. 'I'll be just a minute.'

'Okay, sweetie – it can wait.'

He runs upstairs to change and ambles down two minutes later in a black tee-shirt and joggers. I spoon lasagne onto our plates and carry them through to the dining table, lifting some salad onto Ant's plate for him.

Pouring wine into our glasses, he smiles. 'Thank you. You wouldn't believe how hungry I am. We had lunch at half one and I've had nothing since.'

I sit down opposite. 'How was it, the meeting? Did you manage to reach an agreement in the end?'

Pushing some lasagne into his mouth, he nods. 'Mm, thank god. I never thought it would bloody end, though. They've knocked a few thousand off the fee, of course, but it's okay - we can manage that. So how was your day?'

'Not too busy, actually. I called in on the Keachers to renew the Fakenham contract, so I had coffee with them and then spent a while chatting. So it was quite an easy day, really. Except for the weather. Did you get any sleet down in Cheltenham?'

Shaking his head, he shovels in more lasagne. 'I've hardly seen daylight, Sophie. We had lunch at the local pub, but apart from the short walk there and back I was inside all day. Did you get wet, then?'

'No, I was fine, really. I did have to stop driving for a while until it died down, though – couldn't see a thing. How's the lasagne?'

He gestures expansively at his nearly empty plate, his pale eyes smiling. 'Delicious, thank you. Well worth the wait. Is there any pudding?'

'I have some frozen raspberries. I can defrost them, if you like. With ice cream?'

So we eat dessert, then clear away together. The kitchen is easy to look after, fresh and clean, with a large island at its centre. So it literally takes us ten minutes to pile everything into the dishwasher and wipe round.

Topping up his wine, Ant carries it through to the living room and I follow suit. I'm tired and looking forward to just being able to sit down for an hour or two. Switching on the Christmas tree lights, newly bought from John Lewis, I throw myself onto the sofa and relax.

We're watching a film, a World War One film called *Journey's End*. It's powerful, moving, and I'm really enjoying it. But as I turn to Ant, I see he's fast asleep. Bless. Gently, I rub his arm to awaken him and encourage him up to bed. I watch the film for another half hour, then follow him up. After a nice warm shower, I curl up beside him. He's sleeping like a baby.

Suddenly, I realise something. We haven't looked into how we acquired that old Grandfather clock in Folksbury.

And we haven't discussed why the very mention of it makes me tremble.

CHAPTER 10

Enid Mitchell

🐈

Tuesday 11th December
Folksbury

WELL. Saturday night was an eye-opener, that's for sure. Indira must never know what happened, must never find out how dangerous it was. But I can honestly say that, even though Peggy was with me, I was absolutely terrified.

Before Indira and the children left to stay the night at Peggy's, we asked her to show us exactly where the noise she'd described was coming from.

'It's upstairs,' she said. 'Opposite Rishi's room, I think. But it kind of echoes right through the house, so it's difficult to tell, really. But honestly, just how do we go about this? If it is something to do with the clock, it was already here when we moved in, so I don't know anything about it.'

'The landlord?' I said.

Peggy swivelled round to look at the clock. 'It is a beautiful thing, so I'm hoping we can get to trace its history. But I've already rung the landlord, Enid, and she's said she'll get back to me. Really, we just need to find out if anything untoward has ever happened to it. There's usually a murder or something attached to such incidents.'

'Oh.' Indira had turned pale.

Peggy touched her arm and I caught stars of calming light shooting from her wrist.

'Sorry, Indira,' she said, softly. 'I didn't mean to frighten you. It's unlikely anything bad will happen now. It's usually an emotion or an incident that's happened in the past that has somehow attached itself, and needs to be set free. Look, how about you show us round?'

So we trundled up to the landing. There's a kiddie's rocking horse nestled against the wall up there, with a large brown bear sitting on top. There's also one of these mirrors that looks like a leaded window. And then there's a proper window that looks out over the fields. I peeked out. The sky was moody, heavy with rain.

'You'll need to be getting to Peggy's soon,' I said, 'or you'll get soaked.'

'It's okay,' said Indira. 'I'm driving round there. We've got sleeping bags and stuff to take.'

'Well, don't leave it too long, then.'

'Actually,' said Peggy, 'I need to pop home first to get sleeping bags for us. Won't take me long, though. But there's plenty of food and drink in the cupboards, so just help yourself to whatever you want.'

'There's some of my apple and sultana pies in the freezer if you want one, too,' I said. 'It just needs popping into the microwave. Fifteen minutes, that's all.'

'And there's tins of custard to go with it,' said Peggy. 'I can't be doing with that powdered stuff.'

Indira smiled. 'Thanks, it's really good of you - both of you. And the same goes for me - there's plenty of food in the kitchen, so just help yourselves. But come on, it's along here, the sound. I think this is where it starts, anyway. Just outside Rishi's room. Then it seems to travel through the house.'

Closing her eyes, Peggy tapped the wall with her long slender fingers. We watched as she breathed in and out, meditating, slowly and carefully. Then, pulling open the landing cupboard, she examined the hot water pipes that run down the back of it. Turning, she smiled.

'Nothing we can't sort out, I'm sure. Now come on, show us round this lovely apartment of yours again. We need to know all the little nooks and crannies.'

So we had the grand tour. It's a lovely old place, with high ceilings and strong, thick walls. But as I've said, it was built in 1838, so there could be a million and one reasons for the wailing, whispering sound. Faulty roof tiles, a pipe that's come loose - now that would explain the smell - or a wooden door that creaks at a certain temperature. Who knows?

But none of that would explain what happened on Saturday night.

*

The rain was just starting and hadn't yet gathered pace as Peggy and I waved, smiling, as Indira and two very excited children climbed into her old VW. But our smiles fell as soon as they drove away. We had work to do.

'Right, Enid,' said Peggy. 'Let's eat before we do anything else. We're going to be needing our strength, I think.'

We found a couple of organic pizzas at the back of the freezer, some spinach leaves, black grapes, and a bowlful of cherry tomatoes. Peggy rustled up some salad dressing from olive oil, cider vinegar and mustard, and we sat and ate in silence, the kitchen warm and snug, nestled nicely as it is between the lounge and the shop. Satiated, I began to feel sleepy, but Peggy looked as wide awake and alert as a new puppy.

'So what's the plan, Peggy?'

She put down her fork. 'I think I'd like to take another look at that there clock. There's also the kaleidoscope, which is upstairs on Rishi's bed. I spotted it and asked him to leave it behind. He is a good boy, you know.'

'But I thought we were checking out the landing first.'

'We need to eliminate the clock and that kaleidoscope first,' she insisted. 'Then we'll check out everything else.'

I yawned. 'Okay, then.'

'But first we need to set up our sleeping bags in the lounge. God knows what time we'll get to bed, so don't fall asleep just yet.'

'I won't, don't worry. But I'll wash up these things first, then it's done.'

As I busied myself, my thoughts turned to Harry. I'd rung him earlier, just to let him know I was staying over and to ask him to take Genevieve and a litter tray to Peggy's house. Just as extra protection for Indira. But he'd have been enjoying his umpteenth cup of Earl Grey by now. He loves his Earl Grey, does my Harry. But he was quite happy spending the evening on his own, said he'd be able to watch some cricket with no interruptions. I ask you.

So once Peggy had finished setting up the sleeping bags and pillows, we made more tea and left it to mash while we went upstairs to Rishi's room. The kaleidoscope lay on the bed, as still and as innocent as anything. Just a child's toy, although it's not. It's more for an adult, being made of wood and brass as it is. It's an interesting thing, though, and not something we see so much of nowadays.

Perching herself onto the bed, Peggy picked up the kaleidoscope and looked through it, pointing it to the light and turning the wheel.

'Such pretty patterns,' she said. 'I used to love these as a kid.'

'I wonder if it really does have any connection to that noise. It looks so harmless.'

She looked at me knowingly. 'Anything can have a connection to bad energy, Enid. You know that.'

I thought of all the times we'd seen bad energy, of the people we'd helped when they needed to get rid of it, and of the good energy we'd tried to create in its place. Like those two boys at the Christmas market.

'I know, Peggy. I do know.'

'I honestly can't see anything surrounding this, though. It looks just like a normal kaleidoscope to me.' Standing up, she carried it to the door. 'But come on, let's have a look at that there clock.'

So we wandered back downstairs. The place seemed soulless without the children laughing and giggling. The only sounds were the pit-pattering of rain on the French doors and the ticking of the Grandfather clock. Peggy went to stand before the clock while she pondered what to do next. Tired, I merely sat back onto the couch and watched.

'So the clock had a kaleidoscope hidden inside. A very old kaleidoscope,' she said, turning the item carefully in her hands. 'And when it's removed, the house emits a strange, haunting sound. If that's what it is. What happens, then, when we place it back inside?'

Opening the small door, she placed the kaleidoscope inside and closed it again.

'Come on. Let's give it ten minutes.'

She waved me away, towards the kitchen, where we sat and drank our tea, and waited.

'Exactly what are we waiting for?' I asked.

She shrugged. 'No idea, Enid. I'm just experimenting here.'

Yawning loudly, I felt just ready for a nice sit-down and a good film on the telly.

'Have you really got any idea what all this is about?' I asked. 'You did say you'd be able to sort it.'

'Stop getting niggly now, Enid. I know it's Saturday night and you're wanting to relax a bit, but we need to help Indira, don't we? That's why we're here. We need to do some digging.'

I sighed, thinking of my lovely home, of my gorgeous new husband watching cricket, and of Genevieve looking after Peggy's cottage. I was missing them.

'I hope Genevieve is looking after Indira,' I said.

'She doesn't need to, not really. I placed a Duk Rak just inside the front door.'

'Did you?' I was surprised.

Duk Rak is the Romani way of protecting the home, like a guardian spirit. Old Grandma Delaney would use it whenever she set up camp with the family. As a child, I'd follow her round, watching as she placed flat stones along the camp's boundaries, one in each corner and one at every door and gate. She'd use egg-white to paint the ancient occult symbol of the pentacle on the stones, forming a protective seal. It's invisible once it's dried, so they look just like old stones. But you can use your hand instead of egg-white if you prefer, which is what Peggy must have used. There are minor chakras in the palms, you see, and psychic energy can be either drawn or expelled from them. Like when healers lay on their hands to cure people, but you can direct this energy into protecting a place or a property, too. You have to be quite experienced in the art, but the hands can be powerful tools of perception and healing. White witches use Duk Rak too, of course, as a religious symbol, and to protect against evil.

Peggy shrugged her bony shoulders. 'Well, it was quick and easy, and I didn't have much time. I only popped round for a couple of sleeping bags and the pillows.'

'Well, at least they'll be okay.'

She grinned. 'I don't think they'll come to any harm, anyway. The only creaks and groans I hear in that house are my knees.'

I laughed. 'Well, there's only so much we can heal with magic. And arthritic knees isn't one of them, unfortunately.'

'Although I do use a little chakra healing now and again.'

'I swear by my aloe vera. I break a leaf off each and every morning and rub it into my knees. And ginger root too, of course.'

'We all have our own remedies, Enid, don't we? We use whatever works, and we're all different.' She stood up abruptly. 'But let's take a look at that there clock, shall we?'

I followed her into the lounge. Which was far too quiet for my liking. The rain had stopped its pit-pattering now, so other than the ticking of the clock you could have heard a pin drop.

Peggy stood before the clock, partially blocking my view. As she knelt down carefully and slowly, I heard her pull open the small door.

'Here we go,' she said, placing her hand inside.

Her scream echoed through the house. Pulling out her hand, she held it high, trying to shake off the pain.

Breathless, I rushed towards her. Her skin was red raw.

'Oh, Peggy,' I cried. 'What on earth?'

'Water, Enid. Get water. And my bag.'

Running to the kitchen, I pulled Indira's pink lilies from their jug on the table and filled it with fresh water. Then I grabbed Peggy's carpet bag and ran back, my pounding heart fearful and erratic.

'Here,' I said. 'I've got everything. What do I do?'

'Pour the water into the copper bowl that's inside my bag,' she whispered hoarsely, 'then take my ring and throw it in.'

I did as she asked, quickly and efficiently. Luckily, the ring sits on Peggy's left hand, so I was able to remove it easily and throw it into the bowl, as requested. The water turned lime green and began bubbling fiercely, as if it was boiling hot. But there was no steam.

Moaning in agony, her face pale, eyes tight with fear, Peggy pushed her hand into the water.

Terrified, I held my breath.

After a minute or so, the water stopped bubbling and became clear again. The large crescent moon etched into the bowl's exterior that before had been copper-coloured, the same colour as the bowl, was now a bright putrid green. I stared at it.

Peggy sighed loudly. 'Stop staring, Enid. I'll be fine.'

'Are you okay, Peggy? Is there anything else I can do?'

Pulling her hand from the bowl, she grinned. 'You can see if there's a glassful of brandy in that there kitchen, that's what you can do. And make it a decent one.'

CHAPTER 11

Indira Lambert

☆

Wednesday 12th December
Folksbury

I still can't believe Enid and Peggy are white witches. If that's the truth. And even if I did believe in that sort of thing, it would still take some getting used to. So yes, I suppose they do have something kind of distinctive about them, especially Peggy, and it does explain the cat, Genevieve, who really does have a mind of her own, and whom Rishi can't stop talking about.

But white witches? Really?

So Peggy's convinced me to carry on living here, to wait while they investigate further. She insists we'll be safe, that no harm will come to us, just as long as the kaleidoscope is left inside the clock. And even though I dread the children going up to bed at night, I do my best to stay calm, to live my life as normally as possible. So I switch on the telly or the radio while I'm sewing or baking, which really helps. And I make sure to be in bed myself before ten. Even if it means downing tools at nine thirty, so I can get showered, so I have time to massage Vitamin E oil into my face (something else that's the fault of my mother: *You only have one skin, Indira, so look after it*), and so I have time to read for ten minutes. And so far, thank god, nothing else untoward has happened. No sound, no smell, and no blood anywhere.

So the kaleidoscope has been placed safely back inside the clock, and there it will stay. And I've threatened Rishi with no playing-out time if he so much as touches it. But poor child – he doesn't get much playing-out time as it is, not with the evenings being so dark at the moment. And at least his new kaleidoscope has arrived now, but I've decided I want it to be a Christmas present. A lovely surprise.

But it's been really busy in the shop today, despite the rain. It's a hustle-bustle kind of busy, with people coming in quickly and going out quickly, like one of those weather houses with two doors, where the man comes in as the woman goes out. Which is great. I really enjoy it. Christmas is just under two weeks away and I'm getting really excited. We've bought two trees (one for the shop and one for the apartment), and everyone, including me, is going mad buying presents.

But I've been advertising in the parish magazine and on Facebook for a while now, encouraging everyone to buy local, and it does seem to be working. Well, let's face it - it's far better for the environment than ordering online. Nicer too, to be able to walk into a shop and touch and feel something before buying. So if I do stay on here, I think I might go into making products that are more personalised. Stitching names or messages onto cushions, or making collages with names on - that kind of thing.

No, it's good that I'm busy. It's bringing in the money, and that's what it needs if I'm ever to own my own place. That's the future, you see. That's what I'm looking forward to. So I work all day and all evening in the hope that it will get me somewhere. I realise, of course, that I could go back to nursing if necessary, once the children are old enough, but I do enjoy doing what I'm doing.

Mark called in again yesterday. Bang on the dot of eleven, as always. And I was busy in the kitchen, as always, making sweet potato and beetroot soup, intending to freeze some, but also wanting to eat some myself at lunchtime with a piece of my coconut-flour chapatti.

'Hi, Indira,' I heard him call.

Flustered, I wiped my hands on my apron, checked my hair in the mirror, and ran through to serve him. He was sitting at his usual table, the one near the window, his long legs stretched out comfortably, wiping his steamed-up glasses with a soft cloth. There were two other customers as well, a mother and her daughter, sitting nearby, with their lattes and dairy-free cheesecake. A slight oxymoron there, but they seemed to be enjoying themselves.

'Hi, Mark,' I said, grabbing my pad and pencil and going up to greet him. 'How are you?'

'Fine, thanks. Traffic's a bit hellish at the moment, though. How about you?'

I smiled. 'I'm great, thank you. It'll be everyone out Christmas shopping - the traffic, I mean. Not long to go now.'

'You're so right. I should be more understanding, shouldn't I? It's just when you have work to do and appointments to keep, and some idiot nabs your parking space just as you're about to pull in.' He smiles. 'What are you doing over Christmas, anyway? Are you visiting your dad?'

It wasn't something I'd had time to think about, to be honest, so I shook my head. 'I've not really decided anything yet. I suppose I could ask him to come and stay with us – it would be easier on the children.'

He grinned. 'What, they think Santa won't come if they're not in their own beds?'

I laughed. 'Probably, yes. Although I'm not sure Anika believes any more – she's been asking some rather thought-provoking questions. Rishi definitely does believe, though.'

'I should meet your children some time. They sound delightful. Jenny and I never got round to having any, unfortunately, although it would have been rather nice.'

'Having kids is great, yes, even though they can be really hard work. Well, I think so, anyway. Obviously. So Anika's the serious one, happy to sit there with her little sewing box or her paints, and Rishi's the adventurer, always searching for hidden treasure, always up to mischief of one kind or another.'

'Ha! That's boys for you. Hunter gatherers, always searching for something.'

A young couple, smart and confident, entered the shop and began looking through the items on the dressers.

'So is it your latte and avocado brownie, as usual?' I asked Mark.

'Just the coffee, please. I'm having lunch with a client, so I need to leave some room.' He patted his stomach. 'Even though your brownies are delicious and I'd highly recommend them to anyone who cares to listen.'

'Thank you, it's kind of you to say so. So, one latte coming up.'

I watched the young couple as they browsed. The woman, slim and delicate-looking, had picked out a cushion in crimson and was discussing it with her partner. Dashing to the counter, I made Mark's latte and placed a small chocolate cigarillo onto the saucer.

'So what will you be doing for Christmas?' I asked, placing it onto his table.

'I'm visiting my parents, as usual. My sister will be there as well, so it'll be really good to catch up with everyone.'

A happy house, full of family and fun and food. That's what I want for Christmas. I want happiness, laughter, freedom. Freedom from the worries that surround me. Freedom from worrying about what Harvey's up to, freedom from my money worries, and freedom from that awful clock that sits there so innocently, tick ticking away as if there was nothing at all going on. I do hope Peggy sorts it out, and soon.

'Well, I hope you have a wonderful time,' I said.

'Thank you. You too.' He looked shy, suddenly. 'But there's a couple of weeks to go yet, and I was thinking - it would be nice if we could eat out together some time. If you'd like? Get to know one another a little more? If you'd like to?'

I was shocked. I felt myself blush. 'Thank you. That would be really nice. But, er, I'd need to organise a babysitter, and if I'm honest I don't really know if I'll have time. I'm working most evenings with my crafts and so on, and I really need to keep up with stock levels just at the moment.'

He caught hold of my hand. 'Look, I know you're busy. I understand. But have a think about it. We could make it after Christmas if you like, but it would be more romantic beforehand, with the lights and the trees and everything ...'

So lovely, I thought. So kind. But am I quite ready for this? Another romance?

And what if we ended up in bed together? What would he think to my wrinkled, childbearing, stomach? Would it put him off? Could I actually cope with another rejection? I'm still reeling from Harvey's little exit.

But then, if we ended up being together, we'd surely want our own child. So I'd still have the same childbearing body I have now. And yes, I would quite like another baby. If we ended up being together.

I smiled. 'I know, and it would be nice. I'll have a think about it, shall I?'

He pushed his card into my hand. 'Call me. But I'll be here next Tuesday, as usual.'

Out of the corner of my eye, I saw the young couple heading my way, carrying two of my cushions, one in crimson and one in mustard. A good choice.

'Thanks, Sam. And I will think about it.'

*

It's the school's Christmas party today and the children are just so excited. Anika's wearing her new dress, a silk smock in a cool mint colour that really suits her. How long she'll put up with home-made dresses I have no idea, but I'm making the most of it while I can. As for Rishi, he's wearing black jeans and a tartan shirt in shades of blue. So cute. He's going to be very handsome.

I made small slices of my nut cake with chocolate drizzle yesterday, and took them along for the party. They're a favourite of Rishi's, so I was amazed they even reached the school gates, but I made sure they did. Set inside a tray, all wrapped in foil, with a great big warning sign in case of allergies.

So today I'm spending time cleaning while Anika and Rishi are at school enjoying themselves. They don't need picking up until five today, and Mandy has said she'll bring them home for me. If I'm honest, the bedrooms all need tidying again and the windows need a good clean, but they'll have to wait until the weekend because I've been much too busy keeping up with demand in the shop to do housework. So for now I'm dusting and polishing downstairs, then I'll just about manage to get the bathroom done before the children get home. The kitchen and shop are cleaned every day, of course, as per hygiene regulations. But I've closed up early to allow me to get on, seeing as school is finishing late and there'll be no mums popping by on their way home.

I make ginger tea before I start. Always a good way to start anything, warming and energy-infusing. So, sipping it as I work, I begin by kneeling onto the carpet. There's a tin of *Mylands* clear wax polish on the floor beside me, and I scoop it up with my duster before rubbing it into the oak coffee table Dad bought us as a wedding present. Rubbing violently, I make it shine so much I can practically see my reflection. I've switched the radio on as I always do when I'm alone, so I start to sing along. It's a song by Kacey Musgraves, about someone who thinks he's the bees' knees and needs taking down a peg or two. It makes me think of Harvey, actually. So I sing, and I polish even harder.

Satisfied with the shine I've achieved, I sip my tea before moving onto the Welsh dresser, also a relic from our house in Sudbury. We bought it to match the coffee table, Harvey and I, so excited at furnishing our first house together. There's a photo of the children displayed here, the frame made from a pale satinwood. It's of Anika when she was three, and Rishi, eighteen months he'd have been. Sitting back onto the sofa, she has one arm wrapped around him, and they both smile at me through the camera. I just love that photograph, which is obviously why I decided to frame it. It just catches the light in their eyes, as dark and as sweet as chocolate.

So as I dust, I move the photo onto the coffee table behind me, along with a few knick-knacks I've acquired over the years. Another photo, this time of Mama and Dad and my kid sister, Diti. Taken after the school's nativity play when she was the Angel Gabriel. A misnomer, if ever there was one. No, actually, I love my sister. But she's unmarried, promiscuous, and will always be a thorn in my mother's side.

I move the horseshoe onto the table, too. A genuine horseshoe but hand-painted in pastel colours, given to us as a wedding present and supposed to bring us luck.

And a couple of papier-mâché plates the children made in school last spring, plastered with poster paints of red, yellow and blue. Then, finally, there's a white china candlestick holding an expensive beeswax candle I've never actually used.

So I polish and I rub, gathering up the dust that's accumulated these last few weeks while I've been so busy. But there's no way I can afford to run out of stock, not at this time of year. I've made more money over these past few weeks than I've made in the last six months.

Finally, wiping my brow, the duster scrunched in my hand, I turn to pick up the ornaments I've placed upon the coffee table.

And my heart misses a beat.

That picture. The photograph of Anika and Rishi, the one with her arm around him. It's missing. No - the frame is still there. And the photo. But it's blank. A white piece of photographic paper. But the picture itself has disappeared.

'What the hell?' I whisper.

'What the hell?' I scream.

CHAPTER 12

Sophie Dubrowska

※

Thursday 13th December
Folksbury

PEGGY Fleming is a cool character, I must say. Tall and slim with grey hair tied back into a messy bun, she must be seventy if she's a day. Crimson red fingernails at the ends of exceptionally long fingers. A smile edged with vivid red lipstick that seems to take in everything about you, as if she can read your mind. Really. Incredibly.

We've agreed to meet up at the shop. I've spoken to Indira and she's happy for me to discuss things with Peggy. And I just love the name she's given it. Saffron Silk. How gorgeous is that? The village itself is adorable, too. I'd kind of forgotten we owned something here. So it must have been Ant who showed Indira round before she moved in.

The shop, however, is in total darkness as I pull up outside. I'm surprised. It's only four o'clock, so I'd have expected the place to be all lit up, especially at this time of year. I mean, the rest of the street is just festooned with coloured bulbs and Christmas trees, but there's nothing here, nothing at all. Strange. Locking up the car, I go to ring the doorbell, and then turn as I hear a shout. To find a woman crossing the road towards me.

'Sophie?' she calls.

Smiling, I nod. 'And you're Peggy, I take it?'

She grins, and a deep cloud of patchouli drifts by, reminding me of joss sticks and unremembered uni parties.

'Yes, I'm Peggy. For my sins. But come on, I'll just shut up shop, then we'll go inside. Won't be a minute.'

So I wait patiently as she wheels the old cart into the greengrocers' shop across the road, locks the doors, and pulls the shutter across.

Hurrying back, she unlocks the door to Saffron Silk and ushers me through. Once inside the shop, its scent a strange fusion of coffee and cinnamon, she switches on the lights and takes me through to the kitchen. Which feels cold and empty.

'Tea or coffee?' she asks.

'Tea, please – thank you.'

She fills the kettle. 'I'm ready for one, too. Bloody freezing out there.'

'Is that your shop over the road, then?' I ask, to make conversation.

She shakes her head regally, dramatically. 'Oh, no. No, it's owned by a friend of mine. I just run it.'

'It's a good investment, though, a fruit and veg shop. We all need to eat, don't we?'

She smiles and nods as she searches for mugs and teabags and milk. 'What do you do for a living, then? Do you work, or do you just rent out shops?'

I laugh at that. 'Both, actually. I work at renting out shops. And houses. It keeps me busy.'

'I'll bet.'

She turns to me, and I feel her reading my every thought. Blushing hotly, I change the subject.

'So what exactly is the problem here?' I say. 'I realise you need to know about the clock we bought, but I don't quite understand why.'

'Come on. Let's go through and get comfy.'

Waving me through to the living room at the back, she switches on those lights, too. This room is lovely and open, with French doors that look out onto the garden. Brightly-lit fairy lights decorate the hedge outside. There's a Christmas tree in the bay window, but no presents. And I can smell some kind of furniture polish, and everything is neat and tidy. It's obvious Indira has children as there's a pile of kiddie books on the piano, so I'd have expected the room to be a bit more messy. But the truth is - I'm totally confused.

Nodding for me to sit down, Peggy passes me a mug of tea. 'Here you go.'

'Thank you.'

As I've already said, Peggy's a cool character. But there's also something about her that warms the heart. Smiling, I relax into the blue velvet sofa, at the same time admiring the gorgeous silk cushions that adorn it.

'So where is the tenant? Where's Indira?' I say. 'Is she ill or something? Is that what this is all about? Something to do with the clock?'

Sitting back into the matching armchair, Peggy's face becomes serious, concerned.

'She's moved out. But only temporarily, we hope.'

'So where is she? We can't really be leaving the place standing empty like this – the insurers would need to know.'

'It's not empty, not really. Indira's still running the shop, but she and the children are living rent-free at a friend's house. So don't worry about the rent being paid – she'll be paying it, regular as clockwork. It's just that she doesn't feel right living here. I'm afraid there have been some strange goings-on.'

Sitting upright, my mind racing, I place my tea onto the small wooden table beside me.

'Something to do with the Grandfather clock?' I ask.

We turn to look at it. It stands there, innocuous, old and solid and sturdy, its heavy brass pendulum swinging gently, to and fro. As if butter wouldn't melt. But for some reason, the very look of the thing makes me shudder.

Sipping her tea, Peggy studies me carefully. 'Do you happen to know its history? Where it came from? Who owned it before?'

I shake my head. 'My husband Ant says he bought it from a place out Gainsborough way. One of these big antique stores, the kind with loads of stuff hanging around that they need to shift quickly. He bought a few bits, all at the same time. They weren't cheap, he says, but they were an investment, something he could sell on further down the line. He didn't want any of it in his house, though - it's too modern for that - so he used it to help furnish our rental places. Ant has looked for the receipt, but I think it must be with the accountants. I mean, I could get it for you.'

'No, no, it's okay. Really. All we need to know is where it came from originally. We need to unravel its history, discover its secrets.' She smiles to put me at my ease. 'Much like rubbing the dirt off one of my organic potatoes.'

'Sorry. I can't really help you with that, I'm afraid.' Then an idea strikes me. 'But the shop might have details? They must keep inventories, I'd have thought.'

She sits upright, a gleam in her eye. 'You could be right. You could just be right. Can you remember the name of the place?'

'We could look online, I suppose.'

'Actually, would you mind searching out the receipt, then? We could really do with the date it was bought as well, don't you think?'

*

I recall the antiques shop now. I remember me and Ant staying nearby that weekend. The sun was shining, we were young, free and happy, and we decided to book a hotel for the night. There's a cute village we wanted to visit, and the shop happened to be not too far away. But we were in the first throes of love and Ant wanted to splash his cash around, trying to impress. If I'm correct, he spent just over four thousand pounds that day. Investments, he said. Building for the future. On the assumption that he'd have a family, someone to leave it all to.

It was the year before we got married, now I think about it. Ant proposed not long afterwards. And I remember - there was a shop opposite the hotel that sold hand-made chocolate. Properly hand-made, at the back of the shop. But the scent was to die for. It literally forced you to suck in air as you pushed open the door. I can smell it now. Caramel. Cocoa. Burgundy. They sold the chocolate in boxes, or as huge slabs wrapped in cellophane and ribbon, or as just one succulent chocolate at a time. There were shaped pieces, too. Cars, trucks, shoes, wine bottles, wine glasses. So clever. I mean, how on earth do they do that?

This particular day, however, I left the place carrying a huge red velvet box, heart-shaped and full of chocolates. I still have it. I keep cards in there. Special ones.

On a whim, I fancy taking a look at them.

So I go upstairs, pull down my old suitcase from the top of the wardrobe, and am just pulling out the red velvet box when my phone rings.

It's Mum.

'Sophie, lovely, how are you? Sorry I've not rung. I've been so busy just lately I've not even had time to check on my own daughter. How bad is that?'

I smile. 'It's fine, Mum. Really. You don't have to worry about me all the time.'

'But I do. You know I do.'

'How are you and Dad doing, anyway?'

'Oh, I'm all right - busy, busy, busy - getting everything ready. Your dad's still at work, as usual. Although he's finishing next Friday for Christmas. Not much going on at the moment, so he's taking some time off, bless him. What a year he's had.'

Dad works for Rolls Royce in Derby. He's in Sales and yes, they've not had it easy this year. A long drawn-out series of redundancies has led to each one of them taking on more work. But he enjoys it, says it doesn't hurt to take on a bit more responsibility, especially when other people are losing their jobs. He should count himself lucky to still have one, he says. Mum, on the other hand, would like him home more often. She's nine years older than Dad – he was a mere youngster when they got together. So she's retired from her job at Marks and Spencer and now spends her time playing golf, painting pictures, selling them (impressively), and raising money from coffee mornings and park runs for various charities in the region.

'It'll do him good to take a couple of weeks off,' I say. 'So are we still coming to you for Christmas?'

She sighs loudly. 'Oh, I was so hoping you wouldn't have changed your mind. I'm really looking forward to it.'

I laugh. 'No way would I be changing my mind, Mum. What, sit there eating chocolates while Dad does all the cooking? I still can't decide what to get him, though. What do you think?'

'Men are so damned awkward to buy for, aren't they?'

'I was thinking of a new waterproof or something, for when he goes walking. Is that a good idea?'

I'm busily searching through the red velvet box as I speak. There's a bunch of congratulations cards from our engagement party, and some from our wedding day. And a few birthday cards and Christmas cards. All put there since our engagement. So we definitely visited the antiques place the year before we got married.

'A good idea,' Mum was saying. 'That old thing he wears looks so bloody shabby.'

I grin. 'That's what gave me the idea, of course.'

'Nothing too dark, though. He's showing his age, bless him. But what about you, darling? What shall we get for you and Ant?'

'Oh, just some Clarins or something for me. I'm not fussy. Or get me a surprise. I like surprises. And Ant would be happy with a jumper or something. Or socks. Anything really, Mum.'

We chat a little more, then I ring off, tidy away and go down to make tea. I'm making steak in red wine sauce tonight. But I have my laptop open on the worktop so I can check my emails. Work never really stops in our line of business. So, as I sauté the shallots, I find an email from our letting agents, Walters and Sons. They've sent a list of potential tenants for a house we've only just advertised. It's a three-storey terrace in Southwell we bought at auction years ago and updated. It's a nice house, but the most recent tenants only stayed for six months before moving on. So we've had to get the decorators in, clean the carpets, hire a skip, and sort it all out again. It's much better and cheaper if people stay a while, really. So I scroll down, check the list, make sure they all work for a living, flag the ones I like the look of, and reply to the others. It's just a quick apology, thanking them for their interest, but saying they've been unsuccessful on this occasion. One has to sort the wheat from the chaff, as Mum would say.

There's an Anyes Brochet who looks interesting. She's a teacher and has just moved into a hotel after leaving her husband. That's okay, I think, but what happens once they've sold the house and split the equity? She'll then be in a position to buy her own place, I should think, and we'll be left with an empty property again. So no, she's crossed off the list.

But then I get to thinking. I mean, just what type of person does rent a house? Young couples and singletons that don't yet have a deposit to buy their own home. Or the unemployed, who claim their rent from the local council, and for whom we can't get insurance anyway. But let's face it - the majority of working people would much rather buy their own homes than pay rent. It's dead money. So if we insist on tenants who are working, they're highly likely to rent only until they're in a position to buy. If that's the case, maybe we shouldn't be so fussy about short-term lets. Such as the schoolteacher.

I decide to call Anyes Brochet in the morning.

At least we haven't left an old Grandfather clock causing weird and wonderful issues in the living room, I think.

CHAPTER 13

Enid Mitchell

Friday 14ᵗʰ December
Pepingham

EVERY day I begin with some morning stretches, just like Genevieve, and then I do my meditation. My Harry's got used to it by now, knows not to interrupt when I take myself into the spare room. So this morning, with Genevieve stretched out on the floor beside me, I pull in my stomach to support my back, stretch my arms to the ceiling, then down to the floor, and stretch up again, side to side, and backwards. Once I've done that a dozen times, I sit back into the pink basket chair and relax. Closing my eyes, I take a few slow, deep breaths and begin to meditate. Sometimes I begin with a speck of sunlight expanding from my chest, but this morning I'm trying to envisage a quiet beach, with the waves rolling in and out, in time with my breath. And it works. I'm there. The breeze blows my hair, the gulls soar above me, and I watch as the waves curl in and out. And I breathe.

The whole thing takes about ten minutes, but it relaxes me and centres my mind. It helps to keep me calm, I suppose.

And today I really need that moment of calm. I'm going to be busy, sorting out my pies for the school's Christmas Fayre tomorrow. My apple and sultana pies are well-known around these parts, you know. I use mixed spice for flavour, and add a few drops of lemon balm tincture, too. It helps calm the nervous system, lowers blood pressure and soothes the digestion. I actually make the pies to help raise funds for the school, something I do every year. And Peggy helps out by storing some in her freezer, and there are some in the freezer at Chimney Cottage, so between us we're just about managing to get it all done. But today I'm defrosting them and placing them inside brown paper bags. I usually charge £3.99 each, so hopefully they'll do okay. We sell slices of pie, too, warmed up with cream or custard, so all in all it makes a pretty penny by the time we've finished.

Now you'd expect me to be able to wave my hand through the air, the pies defrost themselves, fly into their bags, then the prices attach themselves, and it's done. You'd also think I could wave my wand, the house becomes all clean and tidy, the drawers are filled with perfectly ironed clothes, the cupboard doors close by themselves, and the floor is swept clean. Well, we've all seen *Nanny McPhee* and *Mary Poppins*, and of course countless other films about witches.

But the fact is I still have to do the defrosting, the cleaning up, the tidying away, the washing and the ironing. Harry does his bit, of course he does. But men aren't really any good at that sort of thing - not to my mind, anyway. And he does still go away on business sometimes, so I really should be doing the housework, anyway.

Thankfully, however, my old place, Chimney Cottage, isn't my responsibility any more. We have a girl, Tori, who comes round to clean after each let. She's very good, very thorough, and I know I can just leave her to it. She has her own key, so she lets herself in and locks up again when she leaves. She'll also call round and cook breakfast for people if they need it. But she's at university now, so we tend to just leave the eggs and bacon and suchlike in the fridge for them to help themselves. I think most people are capable of cooking a full English these days.

Tori's studying French and Politics at Lincoln University, and being so close to home like that means she doesn't have to pay for accommodation. So the extra money from the B&B goes to help with bus fares and suchlike. Well, let's face it, her mum definitely can't afford it. She's a clever girl, though, Tori, although when I first met her she wasn't destined for such great things.

No, she was more the flighty type, sleeping around, getting drunk, not bothering with schoolwork, staying out all hours. The only ambition she had was to grow up and marry her boyfriend, Raff Slater. Who is now, I may add, living in a squat in London. Yes, the rumours are flying. Such a good start he had as well, what with all the money his parents have. But we need more than money to help us on our way. We need love.

I have been sending good thoughts his way, though. Wishes for love, for peace and happiness. And they're sincerely meant. So let's hope they filter through the haze that must be his brain at the moment. I hate to see youngsters lose their way like that.

No, Tori's doing all right, thank you very much. She sees Peggy regularly for her lessons and is destined to be the next legally ordained Wiccan High Priestess, from what Peggy's been saying. But only if that's what she wants. And even if she doesn't want to, Peggy's anxious that Tori knows all there is to know. Things that even I don't know, although I've been a Wiccan for more years than I care to remember.

*

So I've been busy all afternoon, it's now five o'clock, and I decide to take one of my pies round to Indira, as a thank you for defrosting the pies stored at Chimney Cottage.

'I'm just off to see Indira,' I say, pecking Harry on the cheek. 'Won't be long.'

'Okay, love,' he says. 'See you later, then.'

He's busy in the kitchen making fish pie. He's not a bad cook, I'll give him that. Well, I suppose he did live on his own for a while after his first wife left him. He uses parsley, of course, but also a slight touch of Worcestershire sauce to add piquancy. Nice, it is.

Indira will be home from school with the children now. They're living at Chimney Cottage, you see. Moved in yesterday, bless them.

The reason she moved out, finally - the thing that really frightened her - was when a photograph of the children suddenly disappeared from a picture frame she was cleaning on Wednesday afternoon. But that wasn't the only thing to happen that day. Because as Indira was wondering what to do about the photograph, about whether or not to run over to get Peggy, the tumble dryer finished and she decided to remove the towels and take them upstairs. Then wished she hadn't.

The thing is, when the dryer bleeped to say it had finished, she automatically pulled the towels out, folded them up, and carried them towards the stairs, intending to take them upstairs to the landing cupboard. But because the pile of towels was obscuring her vision, she looked down to check the bottom step before placing her foot onto it.

But it had gone. Disappeared. The step had just disappeared.

That's exactly how she described it to us, to me and Peggy. The step had just disappeared. There was nothing but a dark, gaping hole.

Screaming, she pulled back her foot, lost her balance, and fell against the wall. As the towels tumbled to the floor, she just sat there, shaking and sobbing.

Poor girl.

Terrified, she was. So, picking herself up, she ran over to Peggy's and asked to move out, and straightaway. She'd had enough, she said, and I can't say I blame her. She was only doing a bit of housework, like you do.

Calming her down with a cup of tea, Peggy got her to recreate the moment. Then, locking up Folksbury Fruits, she encouraged Indira back into Saffron Silk and the apartment.

The bottom step was there, of course. As solid and as permanent as any step could possibly be. So Peggy picked up the towels, folded them neatly, and helped Indira take them upstairs. But it was while they were upstairs that another dreadful thing happened.

And now that I think about it, the whole thing seems ridiculous, crazy. But Peggy was witness to it this time, so we know it wasn't just Indira's imagination. To be honest, going on what's been happening, I wouldn't have thought it was her imagination for a second, but you never know, do you.

*

Peggy told me all about it yesterday, once we'd helped move Indira and the children into Chimney Cottage. We were sitting in our dining room with a coffee and one of my mince pies. Genevieve was watching from her usual spot at this time of year, her head poking out from beneath the radiator, and Harry was watching TV in the lounge.

'That third incident was just about the last straw, Enid. You know that mirror on the landing, the one that looks like a window?'

I nodded. 'I know the one. Lovely, it is.'

'It was black, Enid, black. All the lights were on, so there should have been a reflection of some kind. But there wasn't. There was nothing. That mirror was pitch black. No light and no reflection. Nothing.'

I'm turning cold just thinking about it.

'Oh god, Peggy.'

'I don't think God had much to do with it,' she said, her intelligent eyes still and cold. 'Anyway, I put the towels away quickly and rushed Indira back downstairs. But she'd already seen it. Well, you can't exactly miss it, can you? Shaking like a leaf, she was.'

'No wonder she's bloody well moved out. Bless her.'

'That kaleidoscope has been all through the house, Enid. It's left its trail of destruction everywhere.'

So Indira and the children went to stay at Peggy's for the night. Then when Peggy rang me yesterday, Harry and I agreed they could go and stay at Chimney Cottage. I expect they'll be there for the foreseeable. Well, we don't make much money over the Christmas period, anyway - folks generally like to be at home with their families over Christmas.

So, holding my pie in one hand, I knock on the door of Chimney Cottage. There's a rush of shouts as the children dash towards it. Then the door opens and I see a warm glow of toys, coats, hats, and boots, lying in a heap at the bottom of the stairs. Homely, it is.

Indira appears suddenly. 'Enid. Come on in. Shall I put the kettle on?'

I smile. 'You've just read my mind, Indira.'

There's a small Christmas tree in the corner of the hallway that Harry put there in case we had tenants. I breathe in its piney aroma, which is so welcoming, and which I always take to.

'It's lovely, isn't it?' says Indira. 'I think putting the heating on has made it smell even stronger.'

'I'm sorry it's only a small tree. If we'd known ...'

She shakes her head. 'No, it's lovely, it's fine. I'm just so grateful you're letting us stay.'

'Well, you couldn't have stayed in that house, could you now? Not when it's like it is.'

Widening her eyes in warning, she nods towards the children. 'Come on through.'

So I follow her into the kitchen.

'Sorry,' she murmurs. 'The children think you've invited us here for Christmas as a kind of holiday.'

'I know. It's fine, don't worry.' I pass her the pie I've brought. 'Here, apple and sultana. For your tea.'

'Ooh, lovely, thank you. That one we had at Peggy's was delicious. Even Rishi enjoyed it.'

'Thank you. It's kind of you to say so.' Sitting at the table, I make myself comfortable in my own kitchen, the table laden with defrosting pies.

'Tori popped round earlier,' she said. 'Mentioned something about you asking her to tidy up, make the beds and so on.'

I laugh. 'Did she? That's not quite true, but I'll forgive her. I did ask her to pop round to make sure you were okay, and to see if there's anything you need.'

She chuckled. 'Oh, she did that all right. Practically cleaned the place from top to bottom.'

'Well, that was kind of her. I'll make sure to thank her.'

'She's a nice girl. Studying French and Politics, I understand?'

'She is.' She passes me a mug of tea, which I sip gratefully. Tea tastes so much better when someone else has made it.

'So why is she still living in Pepingham if she's at uni?' asks Indira.

'Money. Isn't it always the reason? But she'll be fine, I'm sure. She lives with her mother and grandmother and they love her to bits. She's made some nice friends at uni, of course, but I think she's that determined to do well she rarely has time for socialising, anyway.'

'Would you like a mince pie?' she says. 'They're shop-bought, I'm afraid. I did intend making my own, but I've really not had a minute.'

I take one from the plate. 'Thanks, Indira. I'm actually quite partial to a mince pie.'

'Well, once I have some home-made, I'll bring them round. You live just round the corner, don't you?'

'That's right – Fulbeck Street.' Studying her for a moment, I realise the children have run upstairs to play. 'So are you okay still going to work at the shop? I realise you have to make a living, but ...'

Sitting down, she smiles ruefully. 'You've hit the nail on the head, Enid. If I'm really honest, I'm terrified, and then sometimes I just think it's me going mad. The thing is, I'd much prefer not to have to go into the place, but I need to keep the shop going, don't I? I can't just give it all up, not now.'

Leaning forward, I place my hand onto her arm comfortingly. 'Peggy will sort it, don't you worry. And there *is* something strange going on, so don't go thinking it's your imagination. We just need to get to the bottom of it, that's all.'

CHAPTER 14

Indira Lambert

☆

Saturday 15th December
Pepingham

I'VE shut up shop for the morning. Well, the children and I have volunteered to help sell Enid's pies at the school's Christmas Fayre. I'm confident people will call round this afternoon if they really want to buy something, so I shouldn't lose too much money. But Santa's going to be at the fayre, and it's going to be all Christmassy and exciting, so we can't not go, can we? But it kicks off at nine thirty, not long, so I'm rushing round like an idiot, trying to get Rishi fully dressed and making sure he eats his breakfast, and everything seems to take twice as long when you're not in your own home. Not that I'm complaining. Chimney Cottage is awesome, a lovely old place, not too small, and cosy and warm with its stone fireplace and the huge Chinese rug they have in the sitting room. Which is just beautiful, a faded pink with green dragons and flowers and coins. And yes, okay, the wooden floors do creak a bit upstairs, but we're kind of getting used to that.

I'm just grateful we don't have to stay at Saffron Silk. Although I realise the children might be missing out a bit. Anika would usually be practising her piano on a Saturday morning, for instance, but Enid doesn't have one. Well, there isn't really the room. But I'm sure Anika will catch up once we're back home. If we ever get back home.

Enid's young friend, Tori, popped round again last night, just to see if we needed anything. She reminds me a bit of Enid, actually, with her calm, soothing presence. And Anika just adores her. Well, she makes a fuss of both the children, which is sweet. She's outside at the moment helping Enid load up their car with the pies I've defrosted, and she's so patient, so still, as if she knows there's no point in rushing, as if she knows she only has to wait and whatever she wants will come to her. If that makes sense.

'Come on, Anika, you need your coat,' I call, holding out Rishi's coat for him to push his arms into. They seem to go on forever. He's going to be tall, like his father.

'I'm coming, Mummy,' she calls, 'but I can't decide which one to wear.'

She only has two coats that fit, to be honest. The pink furry one, a size too big, that Mama sent over last winter, and the navy blue one she wears for school.

'Just wear the navy one,' I say. 'It's only the Christmas Fayre.'

Her brown eyes stare at me in confusion. 'But it's the *school* Christmas Fayre, Mummy. There'll be people that I know. From Folksbury.'

Patting Rishi's shoulders as his coat folds around him, I smile. 'Wear the pink one if you want, then. But hurry.'

The school's not far away, just along the main road and off to the right, behind the United Reformed Church. It's a small building with a playing field to one side, and a car park that takes about ten cars and is already full. So I park up beside the church and we walk to the school entrance. There's a strong icy wind that first moves one way and then the other, blowing our unbuttoned coats open with a gust. But the children are so excited they don't even notice. They just race on ahead.

Pushing through the queue of people, I reach the entrance to find Anika waiting for me. She takes hold of my hand.

'Come on, Mummy, I've just seen Enid. She's in the hall over there - look,' and she points.

The dining hall is empty, apart from the stallholders who are setting up shop. The stalls are all set into a large rectangle, and there's an opening in the wall that allows tea and coffee to be passed through from the kitchen. The scent of coffee is making my mouth water, but I resist for now. I have work to do. Letting go of my hand, Anika runs towards Enid and I follow.

'Hi, Enid,' I call.

She looks up from her task of arranging the table. 'Hi, Indira. Thanks for coming, my dear.'

I smile. 'I said we would, didn't I? So what can I do to help?'

She grins. 'You can get me some of that coffee for a start. Stallholders get one free, you know, so get one for yourself, too.'

It's as if she's read my mind. 'Good idea. Thanks, Enid. So two coffees, coming right up.'

It's only as Anika and I head towards the kitchen that I realise Rishi isn't with us. I look around.

'Where's Rishi, Anika?'

Stopping in her tracks, she looks quickly round, surveying the room. 'I don't know, Mummy. He was over there.' She points towards a stall selling soft toy animals, but I can't see him anywhere.

Panicking, I dash forward to the stallholder. 'Have you seen a little boy, small with dark curly hair and a navy blue coat?'

The woman is elderly, sprightly, with alert blue eyes. 'No. Sorry, love. Do you need some help looking?'

I nod frantically. 'Please ...'

We search. We search the dining room, the kitchen, the two classrooms, the pokey staff room and the toilets with their tiny loos and sinks. Nothing. Nowhere. After all I've been through in the past few weeks all I can think of is that awful kaleidoscope. I begin to cry.

Enid comes rushing up suddenly, placing her arm around me.

'Come on,' she says. 'He won't be far, I promise. If he's not in the building, he must be outside somewhere.'

Taking my hand, she pulls me towards the entrance. But I'm unsure. I don't want to leave.

'He won't - he won't have gone outside ...'

But she continues to pull, and I follow meekly, pulling my coat around me as we head into the biting wind.

The school gates are unlocked and wide open. People queue patiently, their warm colourful hats bobbing up and down, their children running around impatiently. My heart races. Any one of them could have taken Rishi. Any one of them could have carried him away.

But Enid continues to pull at me as we turn into the car park.

'Come on, the car's just around here.'

We turn the corner to find Harry standing beside his car, chatting to Tori. Rishi is there, as large as life, holding onto Tori's hand.

I burst into what I can only describe as laughter tears. But I'm angry, too.

And so relieved.

*

The Christmas Fayre was a huge success. Santa spent two whole hours entertaining the children while Enid and I sold pies at the princely sum of £3.99 each. Tori was busy in the kitchen, selling drinks and mince pies, and warming up chunks of Enid's pies to sell with custard and cream. And Rishi and Anika were very well-behaved, once we'd got over that little incident. If they weren't queuing for Santa or for beakers of orange juice, they were sitting behind Enid's stall, playing or looking at books. I was so proud of them.

We left just before lunchtime to drive to the shop and open up, but first I took Rishi and Anika across to Peggy's. She'd agreed to look after them for me, even if it was only while they played at the back of her shop. But she'd popped to the local bakery, bless her, and bought sandwiches and cake for them. Such a kind lady.

So, back at work, I unroll the blinds, switch on the lights, and quickly eat my own lunch, a warmed-up chickpea burger with salad and pumpkin seeds. Then I fill the espresso machine with water, grind some coffee beans, prepare my kitchen, and settle down to some sewing - cushion covers in red silk with a small sunburst embroidered in orange thread. But I don't sit for long. There are only two Saturdays left until Christmas, everyone is out and about, and they all want feeding. My food promotes healthy living and not everybody wants it, but even so I sell out within the hour. And of course when they see my hand-made items, they snap them up. So all in all, I have a busy afternoon and am highly pleased with the day's takings. Then at four o'clock I lock up briefly to pop over to Peggy's. Anika and Rishi are sitting in deckchairs at the rear of the shop playing eye-spy and drinking hot chocolate. They hardly even notice I'm there.

'I'll finish at five,' I say, 'then we can all go home. But thank you so much for taking care of them, Peggy.'

She smiles, and there's a whiff of patchouli that I could swear materialises into a soft wisp of cloud above her head.

'They've been good as gold,' she says. 'So you can leave them as long as you like.'

'Well, the shop's empty and trade will be tailing off soon, so it'll be fine, thank you.'

I open up again, sell a couple of my pictures and a bag of organic coffee beans, then close up. Emptying the till, I place the money inside the old cotton shopping bag I use. Then, switching off the shop lights, I carry the bag through to the kitchen, empty it onto the worktop, switch on the radio as company, and begin to count.

I sort the notes into denominations. Fives, tens and twenties. The coins take longer, but eventually I have piles of them, adding up to £46.20. I keep this and a few of the notes as a float for Monday, then count the remaining notes, adding it up on my phone and scribbling it into the ledger. I've made a total of £681.20. Plus around a hundred in card payments. In just one afternoon. Which is kind of amazing. Awesome.

So, wrapping a rubber band around the notes, I squirrel them away inside my handbag and place the float inside a jar in the kitchen cupboard. And it's as I pull open the cupboard door that I hear it.

'Rishi ...'

It's only a whisper, a faint whisper, and I turn around, expecting to see someone. But there's no-one there. The doors are all locked, the shop is dark, and so is the sitting room. The only source of light is the copper pendant kitchen light above me. So I dash through to the shop, switch on the lights and check the door. It's definitely locked. The sitting room, too - the same thing - the French doors are locked and there's no-one there.

Then I hear it again.

'Rishi ...'

It's coming from the radio in the kitchen.

I'm sure of it.

I feel sick. My legs turn to jelly and I fall against the sofa.

I can't think straight. All I know, at the back of my mind, is that I need to get to Peggy.

And, after what I think is only a minute, she's there, banging on the shop door.

'Indira! Indira! Are you all right?'

Forcing myself upright, I make my way through the kitchen to the shop. Unlocking the door, I pull it back.

'Are you all right?' she says. 'I saw the lights go off and on, but then you didn't come out.'

*

We're spending the evening at Enid and Harry's place. There's me, Anika, Rishi, Peggy, and of course Enid and Harry. Genevieve sits beneath the radiator in the dining room, well out of the way. But she's keeping an eye out, I'm sure.

Enid has made spaghetti with veggie meatballs and salad, followed by ice cream sundae with cherries and hot fudge sauce. So we're having a nice evening fussing over the children, eating, and generally getting to know one another.

But we all know why we're here.

Enid's food is delicious, but if I'm honest I'm having to force it down. Because, if I don't eat it, there'll be questions from Anika, and there's no way I can tell her what happened. She and Rishi must never, ever know what happened.

So it's only after I've taken the children upstairs to bed, read them their story and kissed them goodnight, that we adults begin to talk properly. By this time, I've had a rather large glass of red and am beginning to feel slightly less freaked out.

'Duk Raks,' says Enid, seriously.

'Duk Raks?' I repeat.

'They're a form of protection,' explains Peggy, sipping her own wine. 'The Romani use them all the time.'

'And they work,' says Enid.

But Harry, who is sweet and I'm sure wouldn't say boo to a goose, rubs his hands together nervously. 'I don't know about this, Enid. What if there's something dangerous out there?'

Enid takes his hand. 'Don't worry, darling. Me and Peggy know what we're doing.'

Peggy nods. 'So Duk Raks it is, then. All around the shop, right round the back and into the garden.'

'And Chimney Cottage,' says Enid, 'just to be safe.'

I smile, but if I'm honest I'm feeling just as scared as Harry. With the best will in the world, Enid and Peggy are lovely, but they're just two very sweet old ladies.

So I have my doubts. And I'm scared. Terrified. Whatever is out there has a much greater power than they're acknowledging. And this - this thing - is not something we can play games with.

CHAPTER 15

Sophie Dubrowska

☼

Sunday 16th December
Callythorpe, Lincolnshire

ANT and I are heading out to Grantham today, even though the traffic, I know, will be nose to tail. We're going Christmas shopping, and I'm so looking forward to it you just can't imagine. But it's very early and freezing cold, minus two or something, and they've forecast snow, so I'm wearing my huge faux fur. I don't wear it that often as it has to be pretty cold before I dig it out. But I love it. It's pure black, and admittedly *was* a bit on the pricey side when we bought it, but Ant likes me to have the best. I mean, not that I'm complaining. Particularly as, when we rush out to the car, my phone rings and I have to stand in the cold to fish it from my bag.

But it's a number that's not recognised and immediately I'm suspicious.

'Hello? Sophie Dubrowska speaking.'

'Morning, Sophie. It's Peggy - Peggy Fleming.'

I recognise the number now. 'Oh - hi, Peggy. Nice to hear from you.'

'Now I know it's a Sunday an' all, and you probably have a lot planned, but I'm just wondering if we could meet up later.'

I second-guess what she's trying to say. 'At the shop, do you mean?'

'The antiques shop, Burton Antiques. If that's okay? I realise it's coming up to Christmas and you must be busy and all that, but ...'

Ant's just climbing into the driver's seat. 'Look, let me have a chat with my husband and I'll get back to you. What time is best?'

'Two o'clock? Would that be okay, do you think?'

'Shall we make it two-thirty, and then we can have some lunch? We're just about to do our Christmas shopping.'

'Oh. I'm sorry, then. I knew you'd be busy.'

'No, it's fine, Peggy, really. I'll just see what Ant says, then I'll ring you back.'

'Thank you, Sophie. It's just that this problem isn't going to go away. In fact, it's getting worse. So we could really do with some information as soon as possible.'

'No, it's fine, sweetie. Really. Don't worry.'

It takes us forty minutes to reach the Downtown store in Grantham. It's usually only a twenty-five minute journey, but as predicted the traffic is something else today. So on the way, I try to explain Peggy's call to Ant. He's still confused by the whole thing, bless, even though he did agree to search out the receipt for us.

'So this Grandfather clock is doing something to the shop, is it? Is it something I need to be worried about?'

Ever the entrepreneur is Ant. I shake my head.

'I don't think so. I mean, I'm not sure, but I think it's more to do with the tenant being haunted. And that might be something to do with a kaleidoscope her little boy found hidden inside the clock. Which is weird enough in itself.'

'Just a bit.'

'I'm not quite sure of what the problem is, if I'm honest, but it's obviously worrying Peggy. She's the lady who works just across the road from Saffron Silk, at the greengrocers.'

He watches the road ahead. 'Just what is it she wants us to do about it?'

'She wants to find out where the clock came from, its history. Not that that's going to be easy. I mean, it's just a Grandfather clock, isn't it?'

Changing gear and slowing down to turn right, he smiles. 'The Poles love a ghostly legend, you know. My father would have done anything to hear of me buying a haunted clock. He just loved stuff like that. And Nikolai.'

I'm surprised. My husband is always the sensible one, the analytical one, logical, rational.

'In fact,' he continues, 'didn't I buy it on Nikolai's birthday? I remember, because he rang me and we talked for ages. He and Patryk were celebrating with vodka – don't you remember?'

I turn to him. 'So you can remember the date, then?'

'Of course. I even remember what we did afterwards.'

He chuckles to himself, and again I'm surprised. So the old Ant is still in there somewhere.

'So you bought the clock on your brother's birthday?'

He nods. 'July twenty-first.'

'That's it – that's what we've been trying to find out. Thank you.'

He grins. 'My pleasure. Now, do we still need to visit that shop, or can we have a nice day out?'

*

Peggy's beaten us to it. She's stepping out of her car just as we draw up. The car park is really busy, yet somehow we've managed to find a space right beside her Clio.

'Sorry about this,' she says. 'I do hope you've managed to get your shopping done.' At that moment she's joined by another woman, smaller, plump, with a warm, kind face. Peggy introduces her. 'This is Enid, by the way. She's helping with our investigation. Enid, this is Sophie, and her husband ...'

I introduce Ant before adding, 'We were already out Christmas shopping in Grantham, so we just carried on driving – easy peasy. But yes, we're just about finished with our presents, so it's all fine - thanks, Peggy.'

'Well, it's good of you to take time out like this, anyway,' she says. 'Now, what we're needing to do is to get the shop to trace this clock for us. Enid's taken some pictures of it with her phone, so I'm hoping they can find it on their records.'

'We know the date,' I say, blurting it out in my excitement. 'We know the date Ant bought it.'

Pulling thick knitted gloves onto her hands, Enid literally beams at us. 'Do you? Well, that's a good start, then, isn't it?' She has a way of smiling that relaxes you, that makes everything seem all right, even though it might not be.

'Come on, then,' says Ant, leading the way.

The shop is enormous, and very warm. Walking through the door, we make our way slowly through clusters of people, standing, talking, or just clutching their precious items to their chests. I do wonder why the management would take time out to help us when the shop is so busy. But they do.

We take a cursory look around the place before approaching the sales desk. They have some lovely things on the shelves. But once again, Ant leads the way and we approach the sales assistant, who has a willing face, well made-up with a heavy foundation, matt lipstick, and perfect teeth.

'Excuse me, but I wonder if you could help us?' says Ant.

She smiles at his gentle accent. 'Yes?'

'I'd like some information on a Grandfather clock I bought from here many years ago. I'm just wondering if you keep any records at all.'

'We should be able to help you, yes,' she replies. 'We keep a record of everything that goes through our books. I'll just call Mr Briggs, the manager, to see if he can help.'

Minutes later, we're ushered into a small staff room. The room is claustrophobic with six of us in there, so I shuffle off my coat and hang it around the back of my chair. The manager, Alan Briggs, a tall malnourished man in grey pinstripe, introduces himself and asks his assistant to arrange coffee.

Peggy is the one to explain the situation, having full knowledge of the issues at stake. Listening to her, I'm shocked at the stuff going on inside our shop. Sounds like a bloody horror movie, if I'm totally honest.

The manager and his assistant, a pixie-like woman with soft grey hair, are also stunned by the details, as implausible as they sound, but they dutifully begin to check their files. They keep an inventory of each and every item ever sold, thank goodness. Their records were kept on paper at first, but then the data was transferred to an online system in 1991, which makes everything so much easier to trace.

So our clock is easily found. A sigh of relief rattles around the room, and we sit back in amazement.

Alan Briggs shakes his head at the screen. 'Unbelievable.' He scrolls upwards. 'So, the clock was brought to us from a place in Hawes, North Yorkshire. Mainly oak and mahogany, it says here. Nineteenth century. There had been a fire, but thankfully it was rescued and restored. Looks like there was some smoke damage. So we, Burton Antiques, bought it from the restoration warehouse.'

'And then you sold it onto us,' I say.

But he shakes his head. 'Oh, no, no. This was long before that. We bought it in 1965.'

'What?' we all say at the same time.

Checking the notes onscreen, he nods. 'Yep. We've had this clock in our possession a few times. We're quite well-known around these parts, you know. Here, I'll copy the dates onto a document and you can take it away with you. It shouldn't be confidential after all this time.'

'This is very good of you, Mr Briggs,' says Enid, gratefully.

He waves away the compliment. 'Not a problem at all. It's what we're here for. Anyway, I quite enjoy finding out what's happened to our antiques. That's what it's all about, isn't it, the history of the thing?'

At that moment a young girl brings in a tray of coffee, together with a plate of mince pies.

'Here you go,' she says, handing out polystyrene cups. 'Sugar, anyone?'

I accept one gratefully; it's tiring work sitting in that room. 'No sugar, but thank you.'

'So what happened after 1965, then?' asks Enid.

'A good question. I'm just reading about it,' says Alan Briggs. 'Looks like the fire damage occurred in 1964, and the owner died at the same time. Mr Harold Baker. He owned a paintworks factory near Boston, it says. Died rescuing his staff from the fire, poor man. And the sole beneficiary was his wife, a Mrs Dorothy Baker. According to this, they lived alongside the factory at the time, but after his death she sold up and moved away. I can only assume the place was uninhabitable.'

'Is there a forwarding address?' I ask.

'I can't see it anywhere. Not that we wouldn't have taken one, mind. I guess in those days we'd have needed it to send on the money once everything had been valued and agreed.'

'Poor woman,' says Peggy. 'Such a tragedy.'

'So if you sold the clock on, do you know why it came back here for Sophie to buy?' asks Enid, helping herself to a mince pie.

Reading through the notes again, he looks up, his face taut, suddenly pale. 'It looks as if the clock hung around the shop for a year or so. It was the Sixties, and I suppose dark furniture wasn't selling like it had been. People were buying teak, much more trendy.' He gestures towards the screen. 'But in the April of '66, the shop finally had someone interested in buying it. And it looks like we arranged for it to be serviced before we sold it on, something we always do with old timepieces. Apparently, the clockmaker spent five hours on it. It would have been done in what was the old auction room at the back, you know. There's a copy of his invoice here, look. £45, he charged. That was a lot of money for those days.'

'We're in the wrong business, Peggy,' murmurs Enid, smiling.

'But attached to it is a newspaper article,' he continues. 'Looks like he died a few days later. April 29th. Knocked down by a bus on the main road in Gainsborough.'

The room is quiet. Deadly quiet.

'No,' says Enid, replacing the mince pie quietly.

Peggy takes hold of her hand. 'Just breathe, Enid.'

For some inexplicable reason, tears fill my eyes. I mean, it's not as if I knew the guy, is it? But I feel as if I do. I feel so sorry for him and his family.

'So what happens after that?' asks Ant, quietly.

Alan Briggs checks his notes again. 'Then we sell it onto a newly married couple. It's a wedding present from the bride's father, a Mike Butterworth. But they sell it back to us in 1975. Looks like they made a loss on it too, so they must have been pretty desperate to sell. We only paid them £156.'

'I wonder what happened to them,' I murmur.

'All I can tell you is they moved to the US,' says Alan Briggs. 'That'll be why they wanted to sell so quickly, you can bet. So then we sold it to a Mr Robert Whittingham. To an address in Folksbury, Lincolnshire.'

'What? When?' I say. 'What's the address?'

He reads it out. 'May 1975. Mr Robert Whittingham of Folksbury Estate Agents and Whittingham's Haberdashery. He had the clock delivered to his home address, though - 43 Fulbeck Street, Folksbury. Must have been very well-off, this chap.'

Peggy gasps loudly. 'Whittingham's Haberdashery. That was next door to the estate agent's. I remember it. It's your shop, Sophie.'

CHAPTER 16

Enid Mitchell

Monday 17th December
Pepingham

FOR once, our Carol has given me plenty of time to organise. She's usually last-minute with everything, but she actually rang me this morning to say they'll be coming to visit for a few days over Christmas. Which is lovely. I'm so pleased. Even so, I'll need to change the turkey I've ordered. I think the butchers are getting used to me now, though, so maybe I should just order a thirteen pounder to start off with.

Peggy and Sophie are also coming to visit, but later today, after work. They're bringing over the information we collected from Burton Antiques, so we can sit and discuss that damned clock. What a strange day it was yesterday, though. I felt quite shaky after Peggy dropped me off. Harry was upstairs at the time, packing for his quantity surveyors' meeting in Ipswich, but he still knew there was something wrong. Just from my face, he said. He left home this morning - he does the occasional bit of work for his old employers - so we've not really had much time to chat about it. Although I do have Genevieve here. She knows when I'm upset, too.

I tend to do the housework on a Monday, you know. It's a habit from when the children were at school. Well, the weekends were always that hectic, and I never had any time to put anything away. So after dropping them off at school on a Monday morning, I'd set to. I had a much bigger house in those days, of course, what with the Bed and Breakfast side of things. But it was a lucrative business and I enjoyed it, what with the guests coming and going, and me and Peter happy and content.

So I've finished the housework, had a bite to eat and a sit-down, and am just making another cuppa when the doorbell rings. I dash to the door, Genevieve following on behind as usual, and Peggy's standing there, breathing out long clouds of misty air. I usher her inside, out of the cold, and have only just boiled the kettle again when Sophie arrives.

'Come on in, my dear. Peggy's in the kitchen and I've just put the kettle on. Now then, tea or coffee?'

Rubbing her hands together, she steps inside. 'Gosh, it's enough to freeze a brass monkey, as they say. But yes - thank you - tea would be lovely. And I've brought a little drop of brandy to go with it. I hope that's okay?' She pulls a small bottle of Hennessy from her bag.

'Ooh, that'll warm us up nicely. Thank you, Sophie.'

Hanging her coat in the hallway, I show her through to the kitchen. Slim with long golden-blonde hair and smiling blue eyes, she has a lovely aura about her. Warm, trusting, unsophisticated, even though she and her husband are obviously very well-off.

Peggy has already made tea and covered the pot with the tea cosy.

'Thanks, Peggy,' I say. 'Shall we take it through?'

So I busy myself with the tray, and we assemble in the lounge. Peggy adopts her usual position on the couch, long legs stretched out comfortably, her back straight as a die. Sophie sits back into the armchair, looking a little lost and lonely in the company of us two old ladies whom she's only known for five minutes. I try to ease the atmosphere by offering the brandy and pouring it into our empty cups.

'I'm driving, so just a drop, please,' says Peggy.

'The same for me, sweetie,' says Sophie.

'And for me. I have responsibilities,' I say, smiling at Genevieve, curled up beneath the radiator.

'What a gorgeous cat,' says Sophie. 'Such shiny black fur.'

'Thank you,' I say. 'It'll be the omega three in the tuna she likes to eat.'

'What's her name?' she asks.

'Genevieve. But don't make a fuss, please – she's spoilt enough as it is.'

She grins. 'I can tell. She watches you like a hawk.'

'She's used to looking after me, that's why. We lived on our own together for a long time.'

'Right,' says Peggy, taking charge. 'Shall I be Mother?'

So we settle down with our cups of tea, steaming hot and already laced with brandy.

'Just what we need, this brandy,' I say, 'especially on a night like tonight.'

'Forecast is for snow,' says Peggy.

Sophie pulls a face. 'I hate driving in snow.'

'It's not until Wednesday, though,' I say, 'so you'll be fine driving home. Right, shall we get down to business?'

'Well, that's why we're here,' says Peggy, pulling out the sheet of A4 Alan Briggs gave us. 'And I've been having a good old think about Folksbury Estate Agents. I seem to remember there being some kind of hoo-ha before it was sold on.'

I nod. 'Wasn't it the chap at Folksbury Estate Agents that sold up after his wife and kiddie died? And young Chris Haringey snapped it up for a song?'

Sophie turns pale and I hastily regret my words.

'Sorry, Sophie,' I murmur. 'I didn't mean to scare you.'

She shakes her head earnestly. 'No - no - it's all right. I just ...'

'You could do with some more of that brandy,' says Peggy, smiling.

'No. Really. I'm just a bit shocked, that's all. It all seems so unreal.'

Now I'm a hugely sensitive soul - you can ask Peggy. Any little eddies, any disturbances in the air, tend to cause my toes to twitch and my skin to crawl, like termites in the sand. I've always been the same.

And tonight I'm sensing something around Sophie that doesn't quite make sense. Something that maybe she's aware of, or something that maybe she isn't.

First, however, we have to decipher the information we already have.

Sliding herself down to sit on the floor, Peggy lays three sheets of paper onto the coffee table, one containing the list of dates and names, and two that are blank. She then pulls a pen and a pair of reading glasses from her huge carpet bag. How on earth she manages to find anything in there I've no idea.

'Now then, we need to go back to the beginning,' she says. 'Well, as far back as we can.'

I check the dates on the sheet. '1965. That's the first record of the clock being in the antique shop's possession.'

She nods. 'So they buy the clock off someone who dies while rescuing his staff from a factory fire. His wife sells up in 1965, sells the clock to the shop, and moves away with the children.'

'No forwarding address that we can find,' says Sophie. 'Assuming she's still alive, of course.'

Peggy makes notes on one of the blank pages. 'Then the clock hangs around the shop for a year before they sell it on to a chap for his daughter's wedding present. Very nice.'

'First they have it serviced,' I say, 'but the chap who services it dies after being hit by a bus.'

'There's a theme going on here,' says Sophie. 'I mean, not that I'm worried or anything ...'

'Well, no,' says Peggy. 'Because the newly-marrieds sell it back to the shop in 1975 before moving to the US. So they don't die.'

'But then it's sold to Robert Whittingham of Folksbury Estate Agents in 1975,' I say, 'and we know he was also the owner of Whittingham's Haberdashery, the shop that's now Saffron Silk.'

'It has been lots of other businesses, though,' says Peggy. 'Sweet shop, arts and crafts, antiques, deli, et cetera, et cetera.'

'It's had a few incarnations while we've owned it,' says Sophie. 'What's a haberdashery, anyway?'

'It's a craft and sewing shop. Buttons, ribbons, cottons, wool, fabrics,' says Peggy, 'so you can make your own things. You must remember that from when you bought it.'

She shakes her head. 'No - no, I don't. Ant bought it before we met, actually. But what happened to the guy's wife and child to make him sell up?'

Peggy finishes her tea before replying. 'If I remember correctly, they went away on holiday. Portugal or somewhere. She drowned trying to save the little girl when she got out of her depth. Absolute tragedy, it was. He came back alone, a sad and lonely man.'

Sophie looks shocked, pale, still. 'That's awful.'

'I remember the For Sale sign going up outside the estate agents,' says Peggy. 'But he continued to rent out the haberdashery. Must have needed something to live on, I suppose. Poor bloke.'

'He must have sold the clock back to the antiques place, then?' I say, trying to get things straight in my head. 'So then what?'

Peggy checks the notes in front of her. 'No. No.'

'What?' I say.

Uncertain of how to reply, she looks up. 'He didn't sell it.'

'What?' says Sophie, her eyes wide with fear.

'The clock only went back to Burton Antiques when he put the haberdashery onto the market, and they actually had to go and collect it *from* the haberdashery. So I'm guessing that, instead of selling the clock when he sold his house, he moved it into the haberdashery. Maybe he lived there for a while. Although I can't remember much about him.'

Sophie stands up, folds her arms, and begins to pace the floor. 'So then we go and buy it and bring it straight back again a year later. To the very same place.'

'Oh, my god,' I whisper. 'What on earth is going on?'

'I don't know,' says Peggy, 'but we need to find out. Otherwise Indira will be moving those poor children from pillar to post all over again.'

A shiver runs across my shoulders, an unseen hand brushing softly by. Tearfully, I push myself from the couch. 'More tea?'

As I open the kitchen door, Genevieve follows me through. Picking her up, I stroke her dark, soothing fur.

'What are we to do, Genevieve? Just what are we to do?' She purrs softly and I hug her close before settling her back down again. 'Sorry, but I have tea to make for our guests. We've got lots more work to do, as you can tell.'

As I fill the kettle, she nestles against my legs, mewing.

'So if you have any ideas - absolutely anything - you just let me know. Okay?'

She looks up at me, and I know she's understood every word.

Warming up a leftover apple and sultana pie, I place it onto a tray with a knife, bowls and spoons, and a jug of cream.

But then Genevieve begins to mew again, her fur stroking my ankles, her bright green eyes looking up at me knowingly.

'What is it? What's wrong? If it's the cream you're after, you know it's bad for you.'

Suddenly alarmed, however, my thoughts turn to Harry. I know he'll ring me later, but, panicking, I need to check he's all right now. Rushing to the lounge, I pick up my phone and reading glasses and return to the kitchen to text him. Just to be sure.

Are you okay? Just making sure you got there on time. xxx

Picking up the tray, I carry it through to my guests with Genevieve following on behind.

'Here we go,' I say.

Peggy grins. 'Thanks, Enid - that looks delicious. I'm so glad we chose your house, because it would just have been ginger biscuits at mine.'

'Well, it would have been a faff anyway, wouldn't it,' I say, 'seeing as I don't drive?'

'True. Very true. Now then, shall I be Mother again?'

Just then, my phone pings. It's Harry.

Arrived on time. Very busy, so will ring later. Everything okay with you? xxx

I reply immediately.

Of course. Just checking you got there all right. Speak soon then. xxx

Peggy cuts into the pie, passing some to me and Sophie before helping herself. I pour tea into the cups we've already used.

'Now,' says Peggy, sitting back onto the couch, 'I'd actually feel a whole lot better if Indira didn't have to go into the shop at all, but I know she has a business to run. So for now I'd suggest fitting our Duk Raks tomorrow morning. I'm supposed to be working, but we're never that busy in the mornings, so I'm sure it'll be okay. I'll check it out with Ian.'

'Have you thought about removing the clock from the shop altogether?' asks Sophie, thoughtfully. 'I mean, we could just sell it, couldn't we?'

But Peggy shakes her head vehemently. 'No. Absolutely not. All that does is pass the spirit or curse or whatever it is onto the next person. No, it needs dealing with now. Right now.'

Just then, Peggy's phone rings and she picks it up. I catch Genevieve's intense gaze out of the corner of my eye. Something *is* wrong.

Peggy looks up. 'It's Indira.'

CHAPTER 17

Indira Lambert

☆

Tuesday 18th December
Pepingham

IT was just awesome being able to spend time with the children over the weekend. We've not spent time together, not properly, in ages. So we had the Christmas Fayre on Saturday and then went Christmas shopping on Sunday. Although we made sure to set off first thing, to avoid all the traffic.

So of course we got to see Father Christmas twice, the second time at the Christmas market in Grantham. Which was just fab, but very busy, with the scent of food cooking and the sound of carols playing, and some interesting stalls selling hand-made items. In fact, I picked up some good ideas from them. Rishi wasn't too sure about seeing Father Christmas at first, though, because he'd already seen him at the school's Christmas Fayre and this one looked different – shorter and fatter. But after I'd explained they were only people dressed up, that they weren't the real Father Christmas at all, and when Anika walked away with a present wrapped in pretty red paper, he gave in and agreed to talk to him. So I took some amazing photos of them both. I've sent some to Mum and Dad and Harvey. Not that Harvey deserves them.

Then afterwards, the car laden with shopping bags, I treated the children to lunch at this Nepalese place in Ropsley. Which they absolutely adored. The waitresses were dressed in saris of red and gold, and smiled and bowed to us as we pushed open the door, their hands pressed together in greeting. Then one of them took us to our table amid the scent of burning candles and sweet satay sauce, and passed us the menu. Anika and Rishi just loved it, thought it was all so grown-up. But what I loved most was the fact that I was able to spoil them, to give them a day to remember. They've had it so hard since their father left.

After the meal, we did a quick food shop at Tesco's, then drove home to continue the game of Monopoly we'd begun on Saturday. Rishi found the game in the sitting room cupboard while he was looking for his 'hidden treasure', as he calls it. And that game took all Sunday afternoon to finish, but we made the most of it, wrapping ourselves in warm throws, cuddling up in front of the fire, and downing copious mugs of hot chocolate. Rishi's becoming really good at it, though, a proper entrepreneur, and I'm sure it's helping with his reading. But it was a lovely family afternoon, warm and cosy and fun.

Yesterday, however, began just like any other Monday morning, apart from the fact I had to drop the children off at Mandy's instead of school. She'd agreed to take them in for me, to allow me to get on with my baking. So when we called round I took her some of my special veggie lasagne as a thank you, so she wouldn't have to cook later.

But the shop did really well for a Monday. I even sold a couple of sky-blue cushions and the matching throw I made months ago that I thought would never sell. But they did. I made a profit of £90 for them alone, which is amazing. The shop's doing so well, and I know it's Christmas and things will calm down in the new year, but even so I really should try my best to stay on here.

So, once my batch of cinnamon and date cereal bars were in the oven, I had time to sort through the post. There were Christmas cards from some friends in Sudbury, some small packages I'd ordered as presents, and a couple of bank statements. So I saw again the thousand pounds Harvey had transferred across, and that got me to thinking. When he'd messaged me about it, he put nothing in the text about his life and what he was doing with himself, and he didn't ask how I was, or even how the children were. So I just replied with a curt

Thank you. But I sometimes wonder if he's had some kind of breakdown, not just a mid-life crisis kind of breakdown, but a real brain-storming kind of breakdown. Well, what kind of father would just give up on his kids like that? With no communication, no phone calls, no letters, not even a Christmas card? Nothing at all? It's all very strange. And very upsetting.

I guess he must be making a packet out there in Showbiz Land, though. I wonder if he's met someone else. He must have by now. He's not one to let a pretty woman pass by, and there must be plenty of them out there. Not that he's filed for divorce or anything. Which kind of makes me think he might be having regrets.

I wonder if he is.

I have dreams, you know. And I wake up still in the middle of the dream, thinking he's there in bed beside me. So I put out my arm and - he isn't.

I'm grateful to him for the money, of course, but as I worked on my cushions yesterday it got me to thinking. Maybe I should be starting again, too. Maybe I should accept the offer of a meal out with Mark. It would be nice to get all dressed up and go out. And now we were staying at Chimney Cottage, I could always ask Enid to babysit. I'm sure she'd jump at the chance.

So I rang him. I rang Mark.

And now I wish I hadn't.

I really wish I hadn't.

I had two lunches on the go at the time, both lemon-scented Mediterranean couscous, so I was busy in the kitchen. And as I waited for the kettle to boil for the couscous, I took the opportunity to call him.

'Hi, Mark,' I said. 'It's Indira. Are you okay to talk?'

'Hello, Indira. Yes, I'm fine. It's nice to hear from you.'

'You too. Where are you?'

'Peterborough - I'm just in the town centre. I've got a few calls to make and then I'm heading back home.'

'Ooh, lovely. I've never been to Peterborough. Well, yes, I've driven through when there's been a diversion on the way to Dad's, but I've never actually stopped anywhere.'

'Well, maybe we could drive down some time, and I could show you round?'

I smiled. 'Okay. I'd like that. But the reason I'm ringing is that I was actually thinking about your offer of a meal out.'

'Oh, yes?'

He sounded pleased, so I continued.

'I just thought it might be kind of nice to get dressed up and go out, especially with it being Christmastime. And I should be able to get a babysitter quite easily.'

'But that's brilliant. Let's arrange something, then. Tell you what - shall I call round on my way home and we can work something out?'

'Okay, yes. We're actually staying at a friend's house at the moment - long story - but I'm still working at Saffron Silk. I don't close until five, so if you can get here about then it would be good. I'll have the kids to see to, but it'll be okay.'

'No problem.'

'You can meet them, Anika and Rishi.'

'Great. I'm looking forward to it. I'll be there at five on the dot, don't worry. See you later, then.'

But he wasn't.

Five o'clock came and went, and he didn't arrive. I thought maybe he'd been held up by a client. But then, he'd have rung me, wouldn't he? Then I thought maybe there was a traffic jam somewhere and he was moving slowly, unable to call because he doesn't have hands-free. Then I thought me saying he could meet the children might have put him off. Maybe that was a bit pushy?

I waited until a quarter past before I called him. But the phone just rang and rang. So I texted, but again there was no reply. He must just be driving, I convinced myself. He'll be here soon, I thought.

By the time I'd said goodbye to Mandy and sorted out Anika and Rishi, it was twenty-five past five. So I left them to drink hot chocolate in the shop and went through to the kitchen to try again. And this time there *was* a reply.

'Hello?' the man said.

He didn't sound like Mark.

'Mark?'

'Hello there. This is Dr Mason from Peterborough City Hospital. A&E department. I'm sorry to have to tell you, but Mark's been involved in an accident. Are you a relative of his?'

My legs began to shake, and I had to force myself to sit at the table. 'No. No. I'm a friend. We were supposed to be meeting up. Is he okay?'

'He's alive, if that's what you mean, although we don't know the extent of his injuries yet. Do you happen to know who his next of kin is?'

Shocked, my mind whirling, I shook my head. 'No. No - sorry - I don't.'

'Okay. Thank you.'

Then I pulled myself together. 'Actually, he does have an ex-wife. Her name's Jennifer, but that's all I know. And he has a sister, but I don't know her name, but she might have the same surname. You might be able to trace them?'

'That's useful, thanks. I'll get the police onto the job.'

'Can – can I come and see him?'

'He's just about to go into theatre, so you might want to ring Reception in the morning. But if we can't find his next of kin, we may have to get back to you.'

'Can you tell me what's happened?'

'You'll need to check again in the morning. Sorry. Could I just take your name and address for reference, please?'

The first thing I did after that was to gather together my precious children and drive them home. I needed them to be safe. Completely and utterly safe.

Then I rang Peggy Fleming.

*

Peggy and I drove to the hospital this morning. I had to close up shop, but I couldn't have run it properly, anyway. You see, I'm convinced all this has something to do with that clock.

Peggy asked Ian to watch Folksbury Fruits for the day while she drove me down to Peterborough. She insisted I wasn't in a fit state to drive. And I wasn't in a fit state to argue.

The police have managed to track down Mark's sister, Maisie, and she's given permission for us to visit him in Intensive Care.

What a state he's in, though. Sedation, bandages, tubes, wires.

Pale. Fragile. So fragile.

I could hardly bear to look.

Maisie was sitting there at Mark's bedside when the nurse showed us in. I explained who I was, that Mark and I were friends, but that we'd been arranging to go on a date. So she again said we could see him, although Peggy and I just stood in the doorway at first.

'Do you know what happened?' I asked.

'From the sound of it, he was delivering to a pharmacy in Peterborough. Looks like someone was after whatever he was carrying. Or what they thought he was carrying.' She shrugged tearfully. 'Drugs, I imagine.'

'Did they catch them?' I asked.

She shook her head, her eyes dark and intelligent like Mark's. 'No. Must have just run off. Bastards.'

'Are the police checking it out?' I asked.

'There's CCTV, apparently. They're going through it as we speak.'

'Do we know how long he'll be kept under sedation?'

'They're hoping to bring him out in a couple of days. It all depends on how well he responds to the procedure. They've diagnosed epidural hematoma, but they've managed to stop the bleeding, thank goodness.'

'Oh, god,' I moaned, bursting into tears. 'I can't believe this is happening. It's all my fault.'

Maisie stared. 'How is it your fault? You were miles away. And I'm sure you made Mark very happy when he was ...'

She paused, unsure of where her thoughts were heading. Reading her mind, I went ice cold. Without thinking, I sat down, placed my arm around her, and she folded into me, wracked with sobs.

'He's going to be fine,' I said. 'He *will* be fine.'

Nodding quietly, she pulled a tissue from her bag. 'I know.'

Peggy and I stayed with Maisie for an hour or so, then decided we should grab a coffee and drive home.

'Is there anyone we can call?' Peggy asked. 'Someone who can sit with you?'

Maisie shook her head. 'There's my parents, but I don't want them driving all this way. I rang them earlier and they're catching the train. They should be here about six.'

'It's just that we need to get back, I'm afraid,' said Peggy. 'Indira's got children and a shop to see to. Will you be okay? Can I get you a coffee or anything?'

'I'll be fine. There's a canteen downstairs. But thank you.'

'Could I possibly take your number?' I asked. 'Just so we can stay in touch?'

So we swapped numbers, said our goodbyes, and left.

Peggy took me to a local cafeteria and bought coffee and muffins to see us through. I felt so sick I didn't really want them, but I forced them down.

'Peggy,' I insisted, bursting into tears. 'You need to do something. I mean it. I was in the kitchen at Saffron Silk when I arranged for Mark to come over. Whatever - or whoever - is making that awful noise must have heard me.'

'It may have nothing at all to do with it, but we're going to protect the shop and Chimney Cottage anyway - so don't worry,' she said, patting my hand. 'We should have done it sooner, I know. But it will get done, I promise.'

'I'm worried about the children,' I said in between sobs, 'but we can't stay at Chimney Cottage forever.'

'And you won't have to.'

'But look, I insist on paying Enid for all the gas and electricity we're using. She shouldn't have to pay for that as well as letting us stay there rent-free.'

She nodded. 'You can pay her, then. It's fine. As long as you're making a decent profit from the shop. And I trust you are? Now?'

Her eyes looked at me as if to say, *I know your sales have picked up, and I also know why your sales have picked up ...*

Has Peggy done something to help me?

Is that's what's been going on here? Has she actually done something to help increase my sales?

CHAPTER 18

Sophie Dubrowska

☀

Wednesday 19th December
Wells-next-the-Sea

YESTERDAY morning was sunny and beautiful, despite it being the middle of December. Unlike today, which is grey and heavy and bleak. Ant had to dash off early to check out a barn conversion that he says has seen better days, but he's still thinking of bidding on it. It's somewhere out Nottingham way, and it does sound quite nice, with plenty of land and a small village nearby. He does like to get his teeth into things, though, buying cheaply at auction, modernising, improving, and renting out. He rarely decides to sell on, although once or twice he has done. I mean, lonely old properties out in the country aren't always the easiest to rent out, but they can be a lucrative sale once they've been modernised.

I love to get to auction houses myself, as it happens. Even though sometimes we don't get a look-in before someone outbids us. Ant decides on a ceiling price before we go, you see, and we never bid above it. That's how you get caught out, he says; always bid what it's worth and no more. But the thrill of the auction room is addictive. The excitement that builds as you raise your hand, time after time, with the room watching and waiting with baited breath to see how high you'll go. And you do want to go further. You always want to go further. You just want to win the bloody thing. But I know Ant would be furious if I ever paid over the odds.

So with Ant on his way to Nottingham, I pulled on my boots, my red leather ones with the faux fur trims, and climbed into the car. I needed to collect some rents before the Christmas break. Although I quite like calling round in December when everyone's full of the Christmas spirit. I've even had the offer of a brandy or two, which is really nice. Obviously I don't accept because I'm driving, but it's sweet nonetheless.

So yesterday I drove out to Hughes Hand-me-Downs. And as I drove, I listened to the radio, beating time with my hand on the steering wheel and singing along. It really was a beautiful day.

But then I got to thinking about Indira. Peggy rang me on Monday night to fill me in on what had happened to her friend Mark. Such a dreadful thing. Peggy thinks it's to do with the Grandfather clock again, but I'm not so sure about that one. I mean, that kind of thing happens all the time, doesn't it? Pure coincidence, I think. But I did promise to do some more digging, to see what I could find out about the clock's history. I do hope her friend pulls through, though. Dreadful, isn't it, and just before Christmas as well.

Slightly subdued now, I pulled up outside the Hughes' shop. Locking the car, I pushed open the glass door and walked inside. The smell was even worse than usual, and I really wished I could just walk in and turn up the heating. But Mel is such a lovely lady and I would never upset her.

'Mrs Dubrowska,' she cried, looking up. She was stitching the hem of some old trousers she'd obviously been given to sell in the shop. Massive, they were. Brown tweed, about size twenty. Pushing them to one side, she rushed into the kitchen and called for Idris.

'Mrs Dubrowska's here, Idris. Could you come and mind the shop for us?'

'Of course,' he called, his voice warm and kind.

'Come on in, Mrs Dubrowska,' Mel said, as they traded places.

So I followed her through. To find Rowan sitting at the table, as easy on the eye as any girl could wish for.

'Hi,' he said, smiling up at me.

I realised suddenly that he has dimples. Not often you see dimples on a man. My heart fluttered, strangely and quite unnecessarily.

So, to avoid his eyes, I stood where I was and looked around.

'Wow,' I said.

The kitchen was smart, fresh, and clean. The cooker looked state-of-the-art, the silver-grey cupboards added much-needed light, and the worktop was no longer black and stained, but clean and practical. The flooring, too, was lovely; warm and cosy.

I caught Mel watching me as she stood by the kettle.

'Be just a minute,' she called, rushing out to the hall and up the stairs.

She returned with a large bouquet of flowers, white lisianthus and purple freesias. I felt totally embarrassed.

'Oh - my favourites,' I said. 'Thank you, sweetie, it's really kind of you.'

Her brown eyes sparkled. 'Just to say thank you, Mrs Dubrowska. The kitchen is lovely.'

Rowan grinned at my blushes. 'Mum and Dad really appreciate what you've done for them, Mrs Dubrowska. Thank you.'

Smiling, I shrugged my shoulders. 'It needed doing, though, didn't it? But I'm so glad you like it.'

'It was only the floor that needed doing, if we're perfectly honest about it,' he said. 'So thank you. It really does look great.'

He has a curious accent. Slightly-off Norfolk vowels with a Welsh twist. But his voice is soft and deep, as if he could sing for the Welsh Male Choir and get away with it. Very attractive.

Mel made tea in the big brown teapot that reminds me of my childhood, and covered it with the tea-cosy.

'Well, I'm glad they made a good job of it,' I said. 'It does look lovely.'

'Our Ewan came round last night, you know,' she said, picking up a tea towel, 'just to see the new kitchen. Loves it, he does.'

I laughed. 'Don't tell me, you've been showing it off to the entire neighbourhood.'

Rowan grinned. 'You've hit the nail on the head, Mrs Dubrowska. The whole town, practically. They've all been round for a cup of tea and a biscuit.'

Laughing, his mother threw the tea towel at him. 'Get away with you ...'

*

Lunchtime beckoned as I left Wells-next-the-Sea, so I called in at a place in Little Walsingham. It's part teashop, part bookshop, and I've been there before. And it's always warm and inviting, smelling of coffee and toasted teacake and polished wood. Sitting down with a heavy sigh, I ordered soup of the day, parsnip and apple, with a side of hot blue-cheese ciabatta. And, as always, it was delicious. I then had a large Americano, fresh from the bean and delightfully aromatic, and studied a magazine while I drank. It was full of quite useful recipes, and had plenty of ideas for the Christmas season. Then I turned to the fashion pages, just so I could admire the pictures. But if I'm totally honest, I was only pretending to admire the pages. My mind had begun to think of other things. Namely, Rowan Hughes.

Oh dear, I thought, what the hell have I done?

Nothing. Yet.

I left a small tip on my way out and headed for the car, now awash with the delicate scent of freesia. But I had two more tenants to call on before heading home. Both were new tenants, still paying in cash and still needing to know their landlord was interested in them. The first was a young family in King's Lynn. Pregnant at the age of twenty, now with a baby girl, and struggling to save up for a deposit on their first house. The second was an elderly man, newly widowed and wanting a place to live that's not a nursing home, but somewhere he can handle on his own. The flat he's renting is on the ground floor in the middle of King's Lynn, so not too far from the shops. And he seems to be managing quite well, so hopefully will stay a while. But he's kind, very quiet, and seems to be settling in nicely.

The light snow that had been forecast began to fall as I fastened my seatbelt for the journey home. That, plus the fact that I was cold and tired, made me long for a nice cup of tea and a warm bed. So yes, I did call on Radley on the way home. And yes, we did end up in bed.

And yes, I am a woman of low morals.

But honestly, who could resist those gorgeous blue eyes, that shoulder-length hair and that five o'clock shadow? Not me.

But was it worth it.

'So when shall we meet again?' he asked, placing a hot mug of tea into my hands.

'I can't say,' I said. 'I'll be taking a couple of weeks off over Christmas. Like everyone else, I suppose.'

He grinned. 'Talking of Christmas, I've got you a little present.'

I sat up straight. 'Really?'

Popping into the spare bedroom, he returned, holding a small box wrapped in silver paper.

'It's okay,' he said. 'You can open it.'

So I did. It was a mug, a beautiful china mug depicting a snow scene that reminded me of *It's a Wonderful Life*.

'For your cups of tea,' he said.

I kissed him. 'Thank you. I love it.'

'I realise you can't take it home with you, so you're welcome to leave it here.'

For the second time that day, I felt totally embarrassed. Taking his face into the palms of my hands, I looked into his eyes.

'Radley. Don't love me. Please don't love me.'

*

The snow had stopped by the time I left Radley's, which was fortunate as I'd arranged to meet Anyes Brochet at five o'clock, to give her the keys and assist her move into the three-storey in Southwell. But of course, after Radley's little speech, I was half an hour late.

I rang her as soon as I left the house, apologising profusely. And she was fine about it, said she'd been held up herself. She was just pulling up in an Avis van as I arrived.

'Anyes,' I said, closing my car door. 'So sorry I'm late.'

She smiled 'Don't worry. As I said, I've been busy myself. I had to leave school at lunchtime to pick up the van, and then I had to wait around. Nothing ever goes according to plan, does it?'

So I helped carry some boxes and bits of furniture into the house. Some houses we let partially furnished, some completely empty. This one has a table and chairs in the kitchen, a bed and wardrobe upstairs, and a suite and TV in the living room.

I'd popped round on Monday to check the place out, switch on the heating and fridge, and leave teabags and digestives in the kitchen. Now I was bringing a carton of milk with me. We do the same for all our tenants. So I boiled the kettle and made tea while Anyes finished emptying the van.

'Come and sit for two minutes,' I insisted as she placed the last crammed box onto the table.

'Thank you,' she gushed in her wonderful French accent. 'Apologies I have so much stuff. I have already got rid of loads, but it's amazing how much you hold onto, isn't it?'

I smiled. 'You do wonder how we manage with a small suitcase on a two week holiday, but need a huge wardrobe and two massive chests of drawers the rest of the time.'

She laughed loudly. 'Have you ever met a French woman before?'

'Where is it you come from, exactly?' I asked.

So we sat chatting for over half an hour, and then I made my excuses. She needed to return the van, pick up her car, and unpack. I didn't envy her the unpacking. I really hate unpacking.

But she's a nice lady. Smart. Intelligent. About my age, I'd say. And also childless. We'd have a lot in common if we were to become friends. Which we won't. I rarely mix business with pleasure. Unless there's a man involved. But not romantically; that would never do. Or unless there are children involved.

Which is obviously the reason for my becoming so interested in the Folksbury shop. I mean, I'd feel awful if anything bad happened to Indira's children. Apart from the fact it's our shop and I wouldn't want to lose our tenants, either now or in the future. Because when word gets around, which it will, no-one in the world would want to rent Saffron Silk. Also, as I've said before, there's something about that clock that gets to me, that unsettles me. Even though I can't quite put my finger onto it.

CHAPTER 19

Enid Mitchell

Thursday 20ᵗʰ December
Folksbury

THE field running behind Saffron Silk was saturated from the light snow that had fallen, so now the birds were busy, swooping up and down, feasting on its juicy inhabitants. I watched them from the garden while Peggy heaved stones from the rockery to one side, creating a semi-circle to face the garden gate. It was Tuesday, four o'clock in the afternoon, and she'd just returned from visiting Mark in Peterborough Hospital. She said she was taking the rest of the day off and that we had work to do. Luckily, I had no plans apart from present-wrapping, so I was more than happy to help.

In the distance the sun was just setting on the horizon, although a long grey cloud had cast a shadow across it, turning the sky a mysterious shade of purple. It was bitterly cold out there, and I stood rubbing my gloved hands to warm them.

'This thing's getting to be really serious, isn't it?' I said. 'Poor Mark. Such an awful thing to have happened.'

'Yes,' said Peggy, grimly. 'We just need to find out whether or not this - whatever it is - in Saffron Silk, is to blame. It could just be coincidence, I know, but I have a strong feeling about it. And I'm not taking any bloody chances.'

So we were protecting Saffron Silk with Duk Rak.

'Come on, Enid - over here,' called Peggy, walking towards the French doors.

I was helping with the egg-white and pastry brush, Indira having kindly provided us with the red ceramic bowl we'd broken the whites into. Red is a colour of the root chakra, of course, symbolising safety, survival, and nourishment from the Earth energy. A good omen, I thought.

So I painted. Every stone and every gate and every doorway of Saffron Silk that I could find. A pentagram on each one, representing earth, air, fire, water and spirit. Peggy chanted the relevant charm and we envisaged blue light surrounding the property.

'I place you here as protection, by the elements of earth, sky, fire and water, in peace and with love,' she called.

Then it was time to drive round to Chimney Cottage. The end house of a row of four, it was built in 1790, so is very old. And the floors are all a bit wobbly, if I'm honest, but it was just right for me and Genevieve when we lived here. And the road outside is a short cul-de-sac leading onto beautiful woodland, so I like to wander along here sometimes, even now, to soak in the air. I like it best in the autumn when the leaves have turned gold and the air has that musky scent of wood-smoke. Lovely, it is.

Peggy and I called round to get the eggs from my kitchen this time, and I broke them into separate bowls (Harry and I had a nice tasty omelette made from the yolks that night) while Peggy made tea to warm us up. Then we walked over to Chimney Cottage and spent time placing Duk Raks in the back garden and around the conservatory. Tori had offered to come and help, but she hadn't turned up, so I guessed she'd just forgotten.

It was half past five by this time, the sky was dark, the stars were out, and the moon was a soft crescent in the sky. But my back was beginning to really ache, what with the cold and all the bending and lifting. Placing my hand onto the base of my spine, I groaned loudly.

'Here,' said Peggy, 'let me help.'

How she does it I don't know, but all she had to do was touch my spine with the palm of her hand for a minute and I was able to stand upright again. No pain at all.

'Ooh, Peggy - that feels amazing.'

'It's just a balancing of the Qi, Enid – it's nothing. You could do with eating more apples and beetroots. That'd help a bit.'

I nodded eagerly. 'Okay. I will. I do like the occasional apple, but I forget about beetroots unless I see them in the supermarket.'

'Don't worry about it. I'll bring you some over. Ian won't mind.'

Just then Tori came running through the side gate, hair flying and completely out of breath.

'Sorry I'm late,' she said, 'but I've been helping Nan with the shopping.'

'Isn't your mum around, then?' asked Peggy.

'No, she's working.' She looked about us, sadly. 'Have you finished it all?'

Peggy nodded. 'Not quite, though. But we couldn't wait forever. Indira needs looking after, and quickly.'

'So is there anything I can do?' said Tori. 'I'm really sorry, but the bus was late, and then we needed to carry it all upstairs and put it away. I couldn't just leave her to it.'

'There's the bit of side garden and the front to do,' I said, smiling, 'and don't worry about being late. I suspect your nan needed more help than we do.'

I know Tori's grandmother, you know, have known her for years. They all live together in the one apartment on Fulbeck Street – Tori, her mother and her grandmother. Not far from where I live now. Lovely people, they are, even though they've not had it easy. Tori's parents split up when she was only a toddler, and her mother struggled for a long time until they moved in with Christine. So I'm glad Tori's turned out all right, even though she did go through that bad patch.

But we heard Indira's car pull up at that point, so we gathered round to say hello, and the children were as excited as children can be at Christmastime. So Peggy, Tori and I finished up round the back of the house, then we all tumbled inside to drink tea and hot chocolate with Indira and the children. And boy, did we need it.

Indira had already lit the fire, and was busy tidying away the basket of logs and newspaper she'd been using as we walked in. Then as the fire roared into action she made us hot drinks and settled down beside us on the couch.

'I have to confess,' said Peggy, stretching out her long legs, 'I've had just about enough of painting rocks today. I'd much rather be sitting here painting my nails in front of that nice warm fire.'

I turned to Indira. 'So how was business today? Did you manage to get everything done?'

She nodded. 'Well, I only opened up at two, didn't I? But yes, I had a few visitors and it gave me a couple of hours to get everything baked and put away, ready for tomorrow. Mandy picked up the children for me, so I could get on. Honestly, I don't know where I'd be without her sometimes.'

Anika, who'd been sitting on the floor chatting to Tori and Rishi, stood up suddenly.

'Mummy, can I go upstairs to find that picture for Tori?'

Indira smiled. 'Of course, darling, but don't be too long.'

Rishi followed her, and both children ran off.

'It's a picture of Genevieve,' Indira explained. 'She's drawn it herself and wants Tori to have it for Christmas.'

'Ooh, I can't wait to see that,' I said. 'I might get her to do one for me, too. I could frame it, put it on the wall.'

'She'd love that,' she said. 'I'll ask her.'

'So how is Mark doing, do you know?' I said.

She shook her head tearfully. 'I've only just spoken to Maisie, actually. He's still under sedation, she says, and they're keeping him there. He needs another operation, you see - there's some pressure they need to see to or something. They've got him booked in for Friday morning, early. God, what an awful Christmas he's going to have. I still can't believe it's happening.'

'Bless him,' I said. 'So are you going back to see him tomorrow?'

'It'd be better to go and see him after the operation, I think,' said Peggy. 'So what about Friday afternoon? Would that be okay with you, Indira?'

She nodded. 'Yes, no problem. I just pray this one does the trick.'

Tori, still kneeling by the fire, turned to us suddenly, her face deathly white, her eyes wide with alarm.

'Something's wrong,' she whispered.

Pulling herself from the floor, she ran upstairs as if her hair was on fire. Peggy followed on behind, with Indira a close second.

What transpired was frightening, wicked, and downright evil.

My heart thudding, I waited downstairs until the sudden clattering of feet on the stairs told me the children were safe. Indira brought them into the room and switched on the television to keep them occupied. Realising suddenly that I'd been holding my breath, I gulped in some air.

But as Rishi turned to me, I realised he'd been crying, his face pink and blotchy.

'What is it?' I asked. 'What's wrong?'

'It's Peggy,' he cried, bursting into tears again. 'She scared me.'

*

So today we must pat ourselves on the back. We have the information Sophie's dug out, and we now know it's not the Grandfather clock that's cursed – it's definitely the kaleidoscope.

Because on Tuesday evening my lovely conservatory, my herbs and my tools, were soaked in blood. A bloodbath, a scene so morbid and sickening it even turned Peggy's stomach.

You see, after Mandy had dropped off the children at Saffron Silk, and while Indira was still tidying the kitchen, Rishi sneaked the kaleidoscope out of the

Grandfather clock, pushed it inside his school bag, and brought it to Chimney Cottage in the car.

So I kept the children occupied with milk and biscuits, together with a promise to visit Genevieve, while Peggy, Indira and Tori cleaned up the mess. The children never saw it, thank god - they'd been playing in their bedroom at the time. But Tori sensed it. She knew. She ran straight into the spare room, checked the children were okay, then ran back downstairs, straight through to the conservatory. Rishi's coat and bag, still containing the kaleidoscope, were hanging there on the coat hooks, dumped on their way into the house.

After cleaning up the blood, Peggy guessed the kaleidoscope must be somewhere around and asked the children about it. And Rishi confessed. Bless him. He's only a child.

*

Peggy has just popped over to see me. Harry's still busy in the study, so we decide to cosy up in the dining room with tea and my home-made cinnamon shortbread. Cinnamon's full of manganese, you know, really good for us old folks.

'Sophie's managed to track down the owners of the clock,' says Peggy, picking up a biscuit. 'Right back to the lady whose husband died in the fire. She still lives locally, thankfully, so she's arranged to call round on Saturday.'

'But what if she's cursed, or even the one who placed the curse?' I ask. 'She's a complete stranger and we don't know anything about her. Aren't we putting Sophie in danger as well?'

Peggy stares at me as if she's seen a ghost.

'Don't even go there, Enid. Not for one minute.'

'Shouldn't we give her some kind of protection, though?'

Holding her biscuit in mid-air, she nods. 'You're right. It's the Winter Solstice tomorrow. We'll use that to send her some protection.'

Yuletide is celebrated by Wiccans on the day of the Winter Solstice every year. It's a pagan festival marking the death of the Sun-God and his rebirth from the Earth Goddess, when the dark half of the year gives way to the light half. It's the sun's rebirth, because from this time forward the days become longer.

'Excellent,' I say. 'Thank you. But I'll definitely be wearing my thermals again. Both pairs. I'm just warning you.'

She grins. 'I'd expect nothing else, Enid.'

I sigh. 'I still can't get over what happened on Tuesday, though. I just wish we'd finished off the Duk Raks before we went inside. But it was so bloody cold.'

'I couldn't agree more. But really, we weren't to know Rishi had smuggled the thing into his bag, were we?'

'Thank goodness Tori was on the ball.'

'I told you she's becoming a good little empath.' She rubs at her chest. 'Actually, I'm feeling a bit peckish, Enid, even though I've just had two of your delicious biscuits. It's time I was getting off home, I think.'

Nodding, I push back my chair. 'Harry will be feeling hungry, too. Would a jacket potato and half-fat cheddar with salad do you?'

CHAPTER 20

Indira Lambert

☆

Friday 21st December
Pepingham

I'VE spent the past two days just reeling from that incident in the conservatory. Well, who wouldn't? How on earth did that happen? And why? Thank god the walls are glass and easy to clean. Thank god Anika and Rishi weren't in there at the time. And thank god for Enid, Peggy and Tori. Even so, I've given the place a really good bleaching, managed to wash the coats and dry them while the children were in bed, and washed the plants all over again. The only ones that actually absorbed the blood were the aloe vera, so Peggy had to throw them out. But I'll buy Enid some more once I get to the garden centre.

Right now, though, I want to move out of Saffron Silk once and for all. As far away as possible. Really. Seriously. I'm worried for my children. I'm worried for myself, too, to be honest. But Christmas is coming up, the shop is doing really well, and both Peggy and Enid are still trying to convince me to stay on. They say it must be the kaleidoscope that's causing all these weird things to happen, and if it's safely back inside the clock it shouldn't cause any more problems. But nothing about it makes any sense at all. I thought the djinns belonged to the shop, or to the clock. I never thought for one minute they'd follow us to Chimney Cottage.

Peggy asked me about Harvey, actually, on the way back from the hospital. And I know what she's thinking. She's wondering if he's got anything to do with these noises, or if he might have something to do with the attack on Mark. Jealousy, she says. Jealousy is an evil thing, she says, that can't always be explained, and can't always be seen.

But no. He's in Florida. There's no way he could be causing all these incidents, if that's what we're calling them. And there's no way he could be jealous, either. He's the one who walked out on me, not the other way around.

So I assured her once and for all. The answer is no. Harvey is not to blame for what's been happening.

But poor Rishi. He was so upset, and there was no way I could tell him the reason why Peggy took away his kaleidoscope. He'll probably hate her forever. But I've given him the one I bought from Amazon now. It was all wrapped up, ready to put inside his Christmas stocking, but there are plenty of other presents he can have instead. Too many, if I'm honest. But it's nice to be able to spoil him for a change. This kaleidoscope is nothing like the original, though, which I actually prefer. No, this one's more of a child's toy, painted in bright reds and greens and yellows. But Rishi is thrilled to bits, keeps running into the conservatory to get the best light, his face aglow with excitement.

I've given Anika one of her presents, too, just to be fair. It's a lovely set of story cubes and she's having great fun with them, although I think the novelty will wear off once she opens her other presents, especially her Glow Art Board. She's so arty, bless her. I don't know where she gets it from.

So, once the mess in the conservatory had been cleaned up, Peggy took the shop keys and the alarm code and drove straight over to Saffron Silk. No messing. So that awful kaleidoscope is now safely back inside the Grandfather clock. Which is where it will stay. Peggy seems to think it doesn't like being moved, you see. She thinks it's some kind of curse and we need to find out who placed the curse, and why. I asked why we couldn't just burn the thing, get rid of it altogether. But she thinks it's a host, and if we burn it we'd unleash the curse, then we might never be able to destroy it.

It's all very weird, if you ask me.

'We just need to find out its origins, where it came from, who owned it,' she said. 'If someone has put a curse on it, then we need to know why. It's the only way to get rid of the damned thing.'

I don't really know about such things, but the sooner we find out the better, I think. It's really getting to me now and I can hardly sleep at night. I must say, though, I am feeling a tiny bit better since those Duk Raks were fitted. Peggy insists they work, and I do trust her. This Wiccan stuff, though. Really, what am I supposed to think? Apparently, today is the Winter Solstice and there's to be a special ceremony in Peggy's shop tonight. They have one for the Summer Solstice, too, a bit like the one at Stonehenge, I suppose. I should have guessed Peggy and Enid would be into something like that, what with Peggy's patchouli oil and Enid's herbs and everything.

But it's nearly Christmas and I have two very excited children. And if that's not enough to take my mind off things, then I don't know what is. They're running through the school gates right now, ready to start school for the day, and I stand and wave as I always do. The air is bitterly cold, but they don't notice, not one bit. They just wave back, chat to the other kids, and run through the entrance. It's their Christmas party and they're so looking forward to it. They're to have a visit from Santa, and a turkey dinner, and then the afternoon will be taken up with party games and a disco. Anika's wearing a blue dress that literally sparkles with hand-sewn sequins, and Rishi's wearing jeans and a polo neck, also blue. Very smart.

But as I drive back to Saffron Spice, I feel a bit down, a bit depressed. Apart from everything else, Mark's having his second procedure this morning, and that's been on my mind. I do hope it does the trick, makes him completely well and whole again. I just don't want to imagine what kind of state he'd be in if it doesn't work. God, what a mess all this is.

So I decide to ring Mama for a chat. I know she'll lift my spirits - she always does. And I've not yet opened up shop, so I can work on my almond coconut fudge at the same time. It's a little Christmas treat for the café, and people just love it.

Mama's busy, too, she says, baking rose cookies, an Indian tradition, and cleaning, and getting everything ready for the big day. She's spending Christmas with her sisters and their families in Pondicherry this year, but, typical Mama, still feels the need to busy herself with the cooking and cleaning beforehand.

'I'm going over on Sunday,' she says in her sing-song voice. 'Ravi's picking me up early, so I have to make sure the house is left clean and tidy.'

'Oh, that's lovely, Mama,' I say. 'You'll have a brilliant time. Anika and Rishi are really excited, too. It's their school party today, and Santa's visiting.'

'Oh, Indira, that's just gorgeous. Please give them a great big hug from me. I do miss seeing them, you know.'

Now I have to smile at that. Mama has seen my children exactly four times. The first time was when Anika was born, the second time after Rishi was born, the third was when I had them christened in a joint ceremony in Sudbury, and the fourth time was more recently, just after we moved into Saffron Spice. To be fair, though, it's a long journey for someone my mother's age.

'Look, I'll try and save up,' I say. 'We'll come over to see you, next year or the year after. I promise.'

'Really?'

The delight in her voice is too much to bear after these past few weeks, and I find tears rolling softly down my cheeks. Thank goodness she's on the other end of the phone.

'Oh, Indira,' she continues. 'I would just love that. Thank you, sweetheart.'

'The children would love it, too, Mama. It would be good for them to discover their roots. And they'd love to see you, of course.'

'I am thinking of moving in with Adya, though,' she says, thoughtfully. 'She has asked me. And Pondicherry is such a beautiful place to live. Delhi is so noisy these days, I can't hear myself think.'

My parents took us as a family to Delhi three times as we were growing up. And never have I thought of Delhi as being quiet. As far as I'm aware, it's *always* been a noisy hustle-bustle of a place.

But I smile anyway. 'That would be lovely for you, Mama. It's nice to have some company around the place, someone to spend the evenings with.'

'But you could still come and visit, you know. It's a big house, plenty of room.'

'I'll do my best, I promise.'

'But how are you, sweetheart? How are you doing without that dreadful husband of yours? Are you two getting divorced yet?'

I shake my head at the phone. 'No, Mama. But I'm fine. I've made some lovely friends and the business is doing really well. That's why I've not had time to ring you, and I'm so sorry.'

'No, busy is good, sweetheart. But I've not rung you either, have I? I too have been very busy with my mobile beauty, and then I've had my crochet class and my yoga, and the new book club we've set up. What a trouble that has been. But as long as you're okay is all that matters. Are you making rose cookies for the children? You must be making them rose cookies ...'

We talk for a while longer, and then I have to ring off to open up shop. But just hearing my mother's voice has settled me a little, has eased the thoughts that have been chasing around my head for days. How I came to rent a shop with so many issues surrounding it, I will never know. But if I were to believe in fate, as I do, then I'd come to see that it has in fact allowed me to meet some lovely new people. Enid, who treats the children as if they were her own. And Peggy, who, although she would never admit it, has definitely helped with my sales. And that in turn, now I think about it, will allow me to visit my mother. Whom I desperately need right now.

*

It's two o'clock in the afternoon. The shop has five customers, and I'm making cappuccino with a side order of gingerbread cookies. I make mine using coconut sugar and molasses, so they're not too unhealthy. And it is Christmas. But as I'm making the coffee, my phone rings, and it's Maisie. My heart misses a beat.

Pausing the coffee machine, I pick up the phone and place it to my ear.

'Hi, Maisie. Everything okay?'

'It's fine, it's all fine. Mark has just come round and it looks like a complete success. I've just been in to see him.'

My heart settles. 'Oh, thank god. What a relief. How's he feeling?'

'Very groggy, but the doctors say he'll be just fine.'

'Fantastic. That's awesome news. Thank you so much.'

'Are you still coming over today?'

'Yes, of course. Peggy's bringing me, although I'm quite capable of driving myself.' I smile. 'I think she quite likes to mother me.'

'Aww. But that's nice. Any idea what time you'll get here, then? Because I'll be calling back later on.'

'Peggy's said to leave at four thirty, so about quarter past five?'

'Okay. I'll be here.'

'Lovely, and thanks for letting me know about Mark.'

'No problem. It's great news. I'll see you later, then.'

Happy now, and so relieved, I ring off, serve my cappuccinos and gingerbread cookies, and return to my sewing. I sit on the chaise longue in the shop to sew. People like to see the artist at work, and it's nice for me when they stop to chat. It's company.

I've made some cotton shopping bags and am currently sewing buttons onto them. They're a bit different to my usual products, but I hope they'll sell. I'm using the same pattern as the silk bags I usually make, because although they are very attractive they're not really strong enough to withstand the weight of food shopping. But my cotton bags are also eco-friendly and will, I hope, encourage people to use fewer plastic bags. I'm really pleased with them so far, though. They're hand-finished, strong and durable. The buttons are remnants from my button tin, in various sizes and colours, and I'm placing them at odd intervals. Just to add a little something.

It's four-thirty now and I've closed up the shop and set the alarm. Peggy's outside in her car, a white Clio, so I jump in quickly. Mandy's collecting the children from school for me and taking them home for a play-date. But I know from previous experience they'll be so excited with it being the last day of term, and I kind of regret not picking them up myself. It is what it is, though, as Mama would say.

We manage to park in the hospital car park and I wait while Peggy pays the parking fee. She's being so good to me I decide to buy her flowers as a thank you.

The place is heaving with activity as we approach the hospital entrance. Lights blaze from every single window. Cars and ambulances pull in and out, and in and out, seemingly non-stop. Members of staff in blue or white coats walk the pavements, chatting on their phones or to each other. A nurse waits just outside the main entrance, holding the handles of an empty wheelchair. Obviously awaiting the arrival of her patient, she smiles as we walk through the doors.

Mark's face lights up as we arrive, and we sit and talk for a while. But he's very sleepy, so we decide not to stay long. I've brought him a box of my avocado fudge brownies, which makes him smile, even though he's not too hungry just yet.

Maisie pops in for fifteen minutes. She doesn't live far away, she says, so can pop in and out whenever she likes, and fifteen minutes seems to be about all Mark can take at the moment.

'I work for myself, so I can come and go whenever,' she explains.

'What is it you do?' asks Peggy.

'I'm a composer. I write music - jingles for ads - that kind of thing.'

'Wow, that sounds interesting,' I say. 'What have you done recently, then? Anything we'll have heard of?'

She laughs, her eyes dancing. 'Don't worry - it's not as exciting as it sounds. Baked beans?'

I smile. 'Okay ...'

'So what do you do for a living?' she says. 'And how did you two get to know Mark?'

CHAPTER 21

Sophie Dubrowska

☼

Saturday 22nd December
Callythorpe

AS promised, I've been spending much of my time researching Whittingham's Haberdashery.
Haberdashery is such a quaint word, don't you think?

I've done quite well, actually. I've discovered that the owner of the haberdashery moved down to Norfolk after he sold Whittingham's Haberdashery to Ant. Ant found the sale documents last night, and they have Robert Whittingham's new address on. I mean, he may not still be there after all this time, but it's a start. And we have to start somewhere.

So I've now been sitting here, googling, for hours. Googling. Not such a quaint word. But I googled for phone numbers, possible relatives, possible businesses. Admittedly, many years have passed since Ant bought the property, and this guy must be getting on a bit by now. After all, he first bought the shop in 1975. So maybe he's retired. Maybe he's dead. Who knows?

But then I had a complete stroke of luck. Because I discovered that Robert Whittingham does no longer live at the address on the sales papers. I've spoken to the current owners, who told me that a Mr Whittingham sold the house to them five years ago, although they don't know where he moved to. And that got me to thinking. Maybe he didn't like to tell them where he was moving to. Because, if he's getting on a bit, which he obviously is, might he have moved into a care home, or some kind of care-assisted place? Just saying. So I decided to ring the care home in nearby Happisburgh.

It took me a while to explain things to the nurse, but eventually they agreed to give me some information. And yes, they do have someone there by the name of Robert Whittingham, but as I'm not a relative they can't grant me visiting rights or allow me to speak to him. But when I insisted, they reluctantly gave me the number of his niece, Sharon, the person in charge of his care. So I called her.

'No,' she said, after I'd given her the details, 'that's not my uncle. He's never lived anywhere near Grantham. He comes from round here, has lived here all his life. Sorry.'

Discouraged, I was about to thank her and ring off, when she said, 'But there is a Rob Whittingham lives near me, not far away, actually. He owns the corner shop. Now *he* used to live up Grantham way. I don't know if that's much help, love.'

'It is. Thank you, that's brilliant. Could you give me the address, please?'

Talk about serendipity. This Robert Whittingham lives in Aldborough and is about mid-sixties, she said, and may just be the person I'm looking for. So I drove out early yesterday morning. It takes two and a half hours to reach Aldborough, but this thing needs sorting and I am determined, as ever, to get the job done. Peggy insists there's a history to this clock, you see, something that needs looking into, and that something or someone is still attached to it.

And it still gives me the bloody shivers when I think about it.

So I arrived in Aldborough just before ten. The shop is a Spar franchise that looks out over the village green. A nice position. So I parked up nearby and walked in.

Rob Whittingham is a friendly guy, warm and welcoming, with soft grey eyes. He offered me coffee from the Costa machine, then we retired to the rear of the shop to chat while his young assistant took over the till.

'So you're now the owner of the old haberdashery?' he said, patting a stool for me to sit on while he stood, leaning against the wall.

'My husband bought it, actually, just before we got married. So, technically, he's the owner. We don't actually live there, though – we just rent it out. But I help look after the business side of things, and we've a tenant who's having some problems with the place.'

'And you want some information?'

'If that's okay? It's just - there have been things happening there that we can't quite explain.' Embarrassed, I laughed. 'Sounds a bit far-fetched, doesn't it?'

His eyes serious suddenly, he shook his head. 'No. It doesn't. Life does have a habit of kicking you in the butt, so to speak. And who's to know what's behind it all?'

I looked down at my coffee. 'I heard what happened to your wife and child. I'm sorry.'

He sat down then, his back seeming to curl over. 'It's not your fault. It was an accident. Lily got out of her depth, that's all. I just wish I'd been there.'

'I am sorry.'

He sat upright. 'So how can I help you?'

'This is good coffee - thank you. Actually, what I need is information about a Grandfather clock you used to own. Apparently, you bought it from Burton Antiques in 1975 and then sold it back to them in 2000. Is that when you moved to Aldborough?'

He nodded. 'That's when I bought this business. I actually had two shops in Folksbury, you know. I also ran the estate agency next door. I'm a qualified estate agent, but I didn't have the heart for it once Natalie and Lily died.'

'Do you happen to know anything about the clock? I know it's a long shot, but ...'

'Actually, now I come to think of it, I do. It had belonged to a couple from out Lincoln way, and the reason I know that is because they sold their house through me when they moved to the States. Sold up, lock, stock and barrel. Said they'd bought the house so they could bring up a family there, but it just never happened. Poor mites.'

'Oh, bless,' I murmured.

'But I saw the clock in their hallway when I went to value the property, and I remember admiring it. Then, later, I saw it again in this antiques place we used to go to out Gainsborough way. And Natalie loved it, so we bought it. Actually, the couple who'd owned it before were planning on some revolutionary new fertility treatment over in the States, so hopefully it worked out for them.'

Smiling, I nodded. 'Do you know anything about a kaleidoscope being hidden inside the clock?'

'I do, as it happens. Yes, Lily found it, was playing with it just before we went to the beach that day. She loved it, insisted on taking it on holiday with us. I brought it home again afterwards and pushed it back inside the clock. She loved the bloody thing, but I just didn't want to see it again. Too many memories.'

'The couple from Lincoln, then. You don't happen to have their details, do you? I mean, I know it's years ago, but ...'

'The only link I have with them these days is the girl's mother, Jean Butterworth. She and Natalie happened to be friends. They knew each other from some school or other. Natalie was a teacher, you see.'

'Would it be okay if I got in touch with her, do you think? Would she mind?'

He stood up. 'Tell you what - I'll give her a ring and see if it's okay. She's quite fragile these days, so I'd need to warn her. Give me your number.'

*

The drive home was fairly easy and I got back at one thirty. By which time the temperature was minus one and I was starving.

As I listened to some music - Celine Dion - I pulled a box of home-made veg soup from the freezer and placed it inside the microwave to heat up. Then I made cheesy toast with some old Roquefort from the fridge, and dipped it into the warm soup.

Ant was in his Do Not Disturb mode in the study. Tax returns, he said. Because, even though we have accountants to do everything, we still have to accumulate our receipts and invoices and send them on. So the new kitchen and cooker in Wells-next-the-Sea will be claimable against tax. As will any clearing out and updating of properties I've had to arrange.

Ant had already had his lunch, going on the state of the kitchen, so after I'd eaten I took him in a cup of tea and let him know how my morning was going.

'Have you thought about checking old newspapers on microfiche or something?' he said. 'They might have something about that fire, but you'd have to go up to the library to find them.'

I grinned. 'That's a brilliant idea. Thanks, Ant.'

I didn't quite fancy visiting the library, not in that weather, so I decided to search the internet instead. So while flakes of snow swirled gently down outside the living room window, I sat before my laptop and a roaring log fire, and I googled.

I found it. A short piece in the Lincolnshire Echo, dated 10th July 1964. Alongside an article telling us how 300 people were injured after the Beatles' return to their home city.

LINCOLNSHIRE. A Two-Day Fire. Lincoln Fire Brigade Work in Relays.
A fierce fire has been raging in the workshop of Mr Harold Baker's Paintworks factory at Wyberton, Boston, since Wednesday afternoon, and members of the Lincoln Fire Brigade have been working there in relays. Unfortunately, Mr Baker himself perished in the fire while rescuing his labourers. A true hero, he will be sorely missed. He leaves behind a wife and two children.

After that, it was easy. I actually found Mrs Baker's details in the telephone directory. She's listed as Mrs

Harold Baker of The Grange, Little Lane, Horbling. I checked Google maps to find it's only twenty minutes away from Wyberton, so thought it was highly likely to be her.

'No time like the present,' I said to myself, pulling my phone from the coffee table and pressing in the number.

'Mrs Baker?' I said, quietly.

'Yes?'

She sounded suspicious, as she should be. I've had more than a few hoax callers myself.

'My name is Sophie Dubrowska. I live in the area, and I'm just wondering if you could help me at all.'

'What is it?'

After a quick discussion, she seemed quite happy to see me once I'd discussed the case, once she knew I already knew about the fire. So we agreed to meet up at her house on Saturday morning - today - assuming the snow hadn't settled.

So, satisfied with my afternoon's work, I rang Peggy with an update, then sat with a coffee and my laptop, and googled dogs. We really need to get a dog, maybe a cockapoo or something, easy to look after, someone to take out for walks, someone to make a fuss of. But as soon as I saw their lovely warm faces staring at me from the screen, I began to think of all the times I wouldn't be at home, all the times it would be sitting here, all by itself.

Which got me to thinking. Maybe we should buy two dogs?

Suddenly, my phone rang. It was an unrecognised number, but I answered anyway.

'Sophie here.'

'Hi, Sophie. It's Rob Whittingham.'

'Oh, hello, Rob.' Then I hesitated. 'You don't mind if I call you Rob?'

He laughed. 'No, of course not. It's fine.'

'Well, it's nice to hear from you.'

'Thank you. But I'm just letting you know, Sophie, that I've spoken to Jayne's mother. She wouldn't give me Jayne's number or where they live, but she did say they're both fine and that they now have three children, ranging from the grand old age of forty-three down to thirty-four. They even have a couple of grandchildren out there. And no, in answer to your question, nothing untoward has happened.'

'Well, that's a relief, isn't it? But thank you for that, Rob - it's really useful.'

'So maybe that old clock theory isn't what we think it is, after all?'

'It doesn't quite explain everything else, though. But it's good news, nevertheless. Thanks, Rob.'

*

Mrs Harold Baker is in fact Mrs Dorothy Baker. Thank god for women's liberation. But she's very sweet and, even though she poo-poos Peggy's theory about the clock, is happy to fill me in on exactly what happened all those years ago.

Mrs Baker's house is set in a wonderful garden, though, full of pine trees, with winter jasmine growing along the trelliswork at the side of the house. And inside, it's homely, tidy, with the scent of orange oil and washing powder. Mrs Baker, who insists I call her Dorothy, shows me into the living room and I sit back onto a plump peach-coloured sofa.

'Tea?' she asks.

While she makes tea in the kitchen, I take a look around. The place is spotless, and there are photos of children and grandchildren on the long dresser. She's obviously very proud. Bless. She's never remarried, though, going on the name in the telephone directory. And she's living alone, by the looks of it. But she doesn't seem lonely at all; you can tell these things.

'We chose that clock the week we got married,' she says, bringing the tea through. 'The man said it had belonged to a member of the aristocracy, although I'm not really sure about that one. It was beautiful, though. I loved it, but I sold it after the fire, sold all the furniture. I took my children and our personal things, and we moved away. Went to live with my parents in Leek, up in Staffordshire. I needed the peace and quiet, you know.'

'I can understand that,' I say. 'It must have been such a traumatic time for you.'

'My parents were amazing, though. They looked after the two boys for me, so I could grieve, so I could get it out of my system. And I did. Eventually.'

'I'm so sorry about what happened, Dorothy. But where did you buy the clock from, can you remember?'

She smiles, her eyes clear and bright, her skin smooth and well cared for.

'I most certainly do,' she says. 'It was this little place near Boston, a second-hand furniture shop. It's not there anymore, of course, but I know the man who sold it to us. I know him by sight, anyway. He lives not too far away, and it's strange, but I only met him again a few months ago. July time, it was. Outside the chemists. I'm amazed he recognised me after all these years.'

I'm not that amazed, personally. She looks the type of person who doesn't change that much with age.

'Is there any way I can get in touch with him?' I ask.

'I'd imagine so. He told me where he works, actually. He helps out in a charity shop over in Lincoln. I think it's Help the Aged, but don't quote me on that.'

CHAPTER 22

Enid Mitchell

Sunday 23rd December
Folksbury

IT was the Winter Solstice on Friday, so we celebrated as we always do, at the back of Peggy's shop. Folksbury Fruits is part of an old row of cottages, a bit ramshackle but serviceable, with a dilapidated cart outside for display purposes. The cart's kept inside at night, so we have to push past it to get into the shop, but other than that there's just about enough room for us all. Ian had already brought round an old table for us to use and is fine about our meetings, he says. As long as we're not putting spells on him, he says.

Peggy, wrapped in her long purple cloak, was just opening a bottle of chilled white wine as I entered the shop. The table was already laid with food and drink, plates, glasses and cutlery, and tall white candles, their flames flickering in the soft breeze that permeated the shop walls. I'd brought a basket containing mushroom quiche, a carrot and walnut salad, some buttered baguettes, and a bottle of low alcohol wine for the drivers. We'd all brought something.

To begin with, we stood in a circle, all nine of us, while Peggy passed us each a glass of wine. There was myself, Peggy, Wendy, Heather, Susie, Joan, Katie, Marie, and Tori, our latest recruit. The number nine represents faithfulness, gentleness, goodness, joy, kindness, long-suffering, love, peace and self-control, and we in the Sleaford coven agree to use it for our number.

'May Bright Blessings be upon you all. And welcome to the fiftieth Solstice Night celebration of the Sleaford Coven,' said Peggy in her huge theatrical voice, the aroma of patchouli heralding her every word. 'Tonight is an evening of celebration, of rebirth. Of joy. Bright blessings to you all.'

We murmured in agreement, lifting our glasses to the air.

'So let us begin,' she said.

Breaking the circle, we helped ourselves to food. Peggy made tea for those that wanted it, and we stood eating and drinking, chatting to each other quietly.

Afterwards, we gave thanks for the joy of life, and Peggy made a wish for Sophie and Indira and their families. To keep them safe.

'Bright blessings,' we said, this time to each other.

Then we headed to the woods near Peggy's house. We always spend an hour in quiet meditation on the Solstice, although we were in a party mood tonight, laughing and joking as we carried our cushions to the woods and sat down around the fire. Peggy had set it alight earlier, and as we gathered together she threw rosemary and lavender oil onto the burning embers to help us relax. The scent was delicious, and we breathed in deeply as the flames grew higher, our faces reflecting the colours, the logs spitting and crackling and speaking to us. Words of peace and love. Tranquillity.

Now I have to be honest here. Meditation around a roaring fire in the freezing cold is all well and good if you're a youngster like Wendy and Heather. But me and my old back. And if it's snowed, well, you can imagine. So I tend to wear my thermals for the Winter Solstice. Two pairs. As Peggy well knows. But they do the trick.

Peggy then took charge. Holding up the pentacle she'd brought, she walked around our circle, pausing now and again to speak, her words filling the air, her strong aura of blues and greens calming us, settling us.

'I call upon the element of earth to bless this circle. May it protect us with its grounding force as we perform our works here tonight.'

Our meditations are quiet, calming, peaceful, and I always look forward to them. They bring us together as a group, as a family.

So I closed my eyes.

We began with some deep breathing, in through the nose for a count of four and out through the mouth for a count of eight.

'Imagine a tiny spark of shiny golden light, right at the centre of your heart,' said Peggy.

'Allow it to expand,' she continued. 'Allow it to expand slowly, filling the body, the arms, the legs, the throat and the mind.'

'Allow it to expand beyond your body, beyond the woods, and out, into the village and beyond. As far as you can possibly imagine.'

'And while your golden light expands, send with it your love and your peace. Send it out as far as you possibly can, until it can go no further.'

I did. I allowed it to spread, far beyond the woods, far beyond the village, and out. Into the world. It centred me, calmed me, relaxed me. And such a wonderful feeling of stillness and peace, of quiet, rested itself inside me.

After a few minutes, Peggy encouraged us to breathe deeply again, to sense the trees around us, to feel the heat of the fire, to hear her voice.

'Come back, back to these woods, back to your bodies, your thoughts. Carry that peace within you.

Take it away, into your lives and the lives of the people you love.'

Slowly, I opened my eyes.

Such a wonderful feeling.

We'd usually head back to the shop after our meditation, just to collect our things, but tonight Peggy had a surprise for us.

'Before we leave, there's something I'd like us all to do,' she said. 'As you know, group meditation is so much more powerful than individual meditation. And there's something I'd particularly like us to meditate on.' She pulled out a pair of gloves, tiny black lace gloves, shining a torch onto them so we could see properly. 'These were found inside an old Grandfather clock, along with this kaleidoscope.' She showed us that, too. 'And I think there's some kind of a curse, so that when they're moved away from each other something bad happens.'

I gasped loudly. When did that happen? When did Peggy find those gloves? Why had she never said anything?

She looked at me. 'I'm sorry, Enid. I wasn't sure quite what I'd found and I needed to look into things a bit before I said anything. But please don't say anything to Indira.'

I nodded. 'It's okay, Peggy, don't worry. But can we please be quick about it – my backside is freezing.'

We all laughed at that, but then became serious again as we began asking questions.

'Whereabouts is the clock?' asked Marie.

'At the moment, I'm unwilling to say,' said Peggy. 'All I know is that black gloves can be a symbol of death. On the other hand, they could simply be a pair of gloves. But they're very old and very tiny, and I can't understand why anyone would hide them inside a Grandfather clock.'

Wendy spoke up at that point. 'How do you know there's a curse? Has something happened?'

'It may not be a curse – it may be something else. But yes, some bad things have been happening and we need to put a stop to them.'

So we sat and we meditated again, praying for help, for assistance in our quest.

*

There was frost on the ground this morning as Harry and I sauntered along to the woods behind Chimney Cottage. The air was crisp and clear and you'd have thought there was nothing at all wrong with the world. Well, how could there be when Harry was holding my hand?

'I've wrapped everything,' I said. 'It's all under the tree, ready. There's just the cake to ice and the beds to make.'

'And the turkey to collect,' he said. 'I'll see to that. And I'll do the beds - you need to watch your back. So you just concentrate on making everyone comfortable when they arrive.'

'They'll be fine, Harry. Genevieve will make sure to keep the children entertained, won't she?'

He grinned. 'She will, but I'm quite sure the Netflix will help, too.'

'Oh, I'm so looking forward to them arriving. I'm going to make gingerbread men later, and I need to defrost my mince pies.'

He became serious suddenly. 'You do know I've put on weight since I married you, don't you? And that Bill died of a heart attack?'

My heart missed a beat. Two, in fact. 'Oh, Harry, I'm so sorry. No - you're right - I shouldn't be feeding you pastries and cakes and things.'

He smiled. 'Darling, it's fine, it's what you do. It's part of your nature. But maybe in the New Year I'll go on a diet. What do you think?'

'That's a good idea, and I'll join you. I could do with losing some weight myself. I'll look up some recipes – nice, healthy ones.'

I do love to see my Carol and the kids, you know, but it's so difficult nowadays, now she and Richard are working, and little Rosie and Adam are at school. And I only see my Jonathan occasionally, when he takes a break from travelling the world, working in all kinds of temperatures. It must be in the genes, all this travelling. Because I never stopped as a child – it was one place to another and back again.

Letting go of Harry's hand, I bent down to collect nettles for my nettlespud soup. It's one of my favourite recipes, and so nutritious. So I tend to bring plastic gloves and a bag when we come out in case I want to collect some.

'That's enough,' I said, knotting together the handles of the bag. 'Come on, let's carry on walking.'

It really was a beautiful morning, but if I'm honest my mind was on other things. I'd stayed behind at Peggy's shop on Friday night, after the others had gone home. Harry was picking me up, but I'd delayed him so I could help Peggy drive everything over to her house and wash up.

We'd carried the last of the crockery into the kitchen, so Peggy closed the boot and locked the car door. Then, heading back inside, we began to wash up. We discussed the black lace gloves, of course. Because I was amazed she'd never said anything about them.

'I knew you'd be upset,' she said softly. 'I only found them that night Indira gave me the keys and I took the kaleidoscope back to Saffron Silk.'

'It's fine, Peggy – don't worry about it,' I said.

She turned to look at me. 'Do you know anything about bioluminescence, Enid?'

'Why - what is it?'

'Well, in layman's terms, it's the emission of light by a living organism. You can find it in marine animals like jellyfish, and it occurs in fungi and bacteria. A firefly is a good example, though.'

'Okay, yes. But what does this have to do with the gloves?'

Placing a wine glass onto the draining board, she sighed heavily. 'When I went to replace the kaleidoscope, just after that little incident in the conservatory, there was a very faint glow at the back of the little cupboard in the clock. I think I'd not seen it before because the light had always been on. But I didn't bother switching it on that time because I was only going to be a minute. Anyway, I put my hand inside and felt around to see what was there.'

'Ooh, Peggy!' I exclaimed. 'It could have been anything.'

She carried on washing up. 'Nothing I can't handle, not with my copper bowl at the ready. Anyway, I found those little lace gloves, tucked into a tiny ball at the back of the cupboard. So pretty, they were.'

I shivered. 'They are pretty, but we don't know anything about them. And why were they glowing? That's spooky.'

'I've seen that kind of thing before, though. When something's been sitting around that long, it can develop a form of bacteria that becomes luminescent. It's fairly unusual, but it can happen.'

'So if it hadn't been for the bacteria and the light being off, you'd never even have seen those gloves?'

'You're right. Lucky or what?'

'But what do you think it's all about, Peggy? It's getting a bit out of hand, don't you think?'

'As I said earlier, I think maybe there's a curse. I honestly can't think of any other explanation.'

But I was sceptical. 'But who would do something like that?'

'Well, as you know, a curse is just bad vibes, a kind of prayer for evil. The opposite of praying for something good. It might have been put there by a witch, someone able to perform magic spells. Or just someone with a grudge, who wished harm, but didn't realise just how much harm they'd wished for.'

I'd dried a few plates by this time and placed them onto the table. Peggy's kitchen is small, with an old rickety table against the wall and very few cupboards. It's only a small cottage, two-up, two-down, and there's the scent of oregano oil, a kind of disinfectant, around the place. I use it myself in the wintertime. In fact, it'll be my home-grown and home-made oregano oil that Peggy's using. But Peggy doesn't really need a big kitchen, living all by herself as she does. Well, she's busy at work six or seven days a week, so she doesn't really spend much time at home. And her main occupation when she gets home is just sitting with her feet up and a G&T. Or so she says.

'Will it be an easy thing to sort out?' I asked. 'There must be something we can do.'

She looked at me, her eyes tired, her face grim. 'There's always something we can do, Enid.'

CHAPTER 23

Indira Lambert

☆

Christmas Eve
Folksbury

IT'S Christmas Eve, and the children are unbelievably excited. Rishi could hardly eat his breakfast this morning, so I had to bribe him, promising him a visit to the ducks in Ruskington after Christmas. And sure enough, that did the trick – porridge and raisins disappeared in a flash.

  I've actually brought Anika and Rishi to work with me in the shop today, as Mandy looked after them all day Saturday. But I intend closing at twelve, once my coffees and snacks are out of the way. Then we're going back to Chimney Cottage, filling the car with the rest of our gear, then driving down to Dad's for Christmas. It will be nice to just relax, watch Disney films, and spoil my precious, gorgeous children.

But I've been thinking. In a strange way, I think things have become a little easier for me just lately. When I first moved to Folksbury, it was as if the universe had taken my whole life and thrown it up into the sky. Then when it landed again, all the bits were in the wrong place, and I didn't know quite how to get to them or how to handle them. But now I feel so much stronger, so much more in control, despite having to live in Enid's cottage, and despite that awful sound. Because, once Peggy and Enid have sorted it all out and everything's back to normal, I know I'll be fine. Me and the children – we'll be just fine.

Harvey wouldn't recognise me.

And yes, I'm keeping an eye on Rishi while I work. There's no way he's going anywhere near that clock. In fact, I'm keeping them both in the shop where I can watch them. Rishi's sitting on the rug, colouring in, and Anika is helping me in the café. She's taking orders for me, so I can get on with my work in the kitchen. She's a good little waitress, I have to say, although her spelling needs some work. But it's teaching her exactly why we need neat handwriting and correct spelling, so that's good. And when we're not busy with the café, I'm teaching her to sew, both of us sitting there on the chaise longue.

It makes me feel nostalgic, though. It makes me remember how Mama taught me to sew. How she first sat me down with a needle and thread and a button, showing me how to place the needle in just the right place, and how to pull the cotton through taut so it doesn't become knotted. And I remember sitting there beside her while Dad helped Diti with her piano, both our tongues stuck out in concentration. Then laughing at each other when we looked up and realised, and how funny it all looked. I was stitching this big button onto a tiny silk bag at the time. It was only there to fasten down the cotton loop at the top, but Mama gave me the bag once I'd finished. But it was my very first handbag, and I loved it. Red silk, with a bright orange button.

It'll be nice to have some time off, though. I've been so busy, what with the shop and the children, and having to drive to Chimney Cottage and back all the time, and with visiting Mark in hospital.

Mark. He's not doing brilliantly, if I'm honest. He's back under sedation as he's not responding well to treatment. It's just awful, the whole thing. But Maisie's keeping me up to date and he has his parents with him, so I've not been to visit since Friday. Although I am calling in this afternoon on my way to Sudbury. Just briefly, as I'll have the children with me. I've explained to them what's happening, and for now I'm just calling Mark my friend. Well, that's what he is, really. And I'm still not sure he's anything else, to be honest..

So I watch from the chaise longue as Anika takes an order. She's a pretty little thing, even if I say so myself.

And she smiles and nods her head and writes everything down like a real pro.

'And tell your mummy you're a very good waitress and to give you extra pocket money,' says the lady. She's elderly, local, her hair just so, her clothes pristine and her shoes perfect. We've spoken before - her name is Imelda and she's lived in Folksbury since her marriage forty-odd years ago.

So I stand up, take the order from Anika, and make a large Americano, plain - no milk and no sugar. Choosing a large white china cup and a flowered saucer from my charity shop collection, I place a chocolate cigarillo onto the saucer and carry the coffee to the table myself.

'Here you go, Imelda. And I will give Anika extra pocket money, don't worry. The coffee's on the house, by the way, just to say thank you for your custom this year. I really appreciate it.'

Her powdery skin wrinkling ever so slightly, her pale eyes smile up at me. 'Thank you, it's very kind of you. But I will leave a tip, just for your lovely young waitress there.'

I grin. 'Thank you. I'm sure she'll appreciate it.'

'I do like to come here, you know. This shop has a kind of presence about it, a kind of melancholy feeling I can't quite explain. A bit like the inside of a castle, or a very old church.'

Alarmed, I step back. 'Oh. I'm so sorry about that.'

But she shakes her head. 'Oh no, you don't understand. I'm a writer. I used to write papers on psychology, but recently I've begun writing thrillers. It helps with the writing, puts me in the right frame of mind. It's actually a good thing.'

Relieved slightly, I smile. 'Oh, okay. Well, you're always very welcome, whenever you feel the need.'

She leaves two five pound notes beneath her plate and I allow Anika to clear the table. Excitedly, she finds them, gives one to Rishi, still playing on the floor, and keeps the other for herself.

'Mummy - look,' she cries, showing me the note.

Bursting with pride at her generosity, I smile. 'It's only because you're working so hard, darling. You deserve it.'

But Imelda's comments unsettle me. Maybe she's just highly sensitive, because no-one else has ever said anything. I hope she is, because I wouldn't want to put people off. So maybe there is something here, something awful that's causing all these things to happen. But what? And why?

We definitely have to move away. We must move away.

I've started looking for shops again. I actually began after the incident at Chimney Cottage, although I've not said anything yet to Peggy. Haringeys, the estate agents next door, have promised to keep an eye out for me, and they do keep sending me details, but so far I've found nothing suitable. Haringeys is an interesting old shop in itself, though, not your usual run-of-the-mill estate agency. No. It has deep wool carpeting and antique leather armchairs and old-fashioned oak desks. Not like the estate agents in Sleaford and Grantham, but more in keeping with the age of the property itself. The great big red door looks like it's the original, although I think Saffron Silk's door is the original, too. It really needs replacing at some point, to be honest, and maybe I should mention it. I mean, Dad just painted it with an exterior paint in Golden yellow when we moved in, and okay, it took a few coats, but it does look attractive. And I love the name I've chosen. Mama helped me with it. She says it describes my Indian heritage, that it would interest people. And then of course after I'd begun selling my silk cushions and things it became even more appropriate. Good old Mama. Okay, less of the old. She'd hate that.

I guess I could always call my next shop Saffron Silk. Once I've found it.

*

The drive to Peterborough only takes forty minutes, but then we'll have a two hour journey to Dad's. That's taking into account the traffic, which will be horrendous, and the toilet stops, knowing Rishi.

Our first toilet stop is near Market Deeping, only twenty-five minutes into the journey, but admittedly I need to go too. So we all three of us trundle into this small café at the centre of town. We visit the loo, all at the same time, then I buy ginger tea and two milkshakes, we drink them up, and leave. And it's as we're leaving that I hear my phone ping.

It's Maisie.

Ring me? xx

I assume she's calling about when and where to meet, so I call her as we're settling back into the car and I'm fastening Rishi's seatbelt.

'Hiya, Maisie.'

'I didn't ring. I didn't know if you'd be driving or not.'

She sounds like she's choking on her words, and my stomach does a somersault.

'What? What is it?'

'It's Mark ...' and she begins to cry.

Quietly, I close Rishi's door and sit back into the drivers' seat. 'What?'

'He's – he's gone,' she sobs. 'An hour ago.'

'Oh, Maisie – no ...'

'He just never pulled through, not properly.'

My throat tightens and tears stream down my face.

'Mummy?' cries Anika from somewhere behind me. 'You okay, Mummy?'

I turn. 'He's died, Anika. He's died.'

'Listen, there's no point in you all coming to visit now, is there?' Maisie's saying.

But I nod at my phone. 'Yes - yes, we should visit. We'll come to see how you are, to make sure you're okay. We're only twenty minutes away.'

'All right. But only if you're sure.'

'It'll be good to see you. I need to talk to someone who knew him ...'

'I'll be in the café downstairs.'

'Okay. See you there.'

Stunned, I pull a tissue from my bag and wipe my face.

'Mummy?' asks Anika, undoing her seatbelt and rushing round to my door. 'Are you okay?'

I open the door so we can hug one another. 'I'm fine. Just a bit shocked, that's all. I thought he was getting better.'

'Aren't we going to the hospital now?' asks Rishi, disappointed.

'Yes, we're still going,' I say. 'We just won't be able to see Mark.'

The drive there is awful, I'm so upset. But eventually we pull into the car park, pay the fee, and walk inside, past the charity shop and into the café.

Maisie sits there with a coffee, her face tear-stained and raw. She stands up to greet us, but I just burst into tears and hug her. The children throw their arms around me, too, and we all four of us stand there, silent and morose.

Eventually, we pull ourselves together and get drinks and snacks. I buy fries for all of us, something the children rarely have, and we all sit there, dipping them into pods of tomato ketchup.

'Mum and Dad are sitting with him,' says Maisie. 'We were all here when – when it happened. The hospital rang first thing this morning. He'd had a really bad night ...'

Instinctively, I take hold of her hand. 'I'm so, so sorry, Maisie.'

We sit and talk for over an hour, much longer than I mean to. But we need it. We need to let go of our feelings, get everything out, cry and hug and talk and regret. If only we'd done this, or that, if only I'd arranged to meet him earlier. Or later. Or not at all.

But my children are so patient through all of this, and I am so very proud of them. They just sit and listen and chat, even though Rishi is usually so fidgety after the first ten minutes. Admittedly, I have to feed them rubbish like fries, but once in a while doesn't hurt. Maisie and I just drink coffee by the gallon, but by the time we've finished I feel as if we've known each other for years.

Checking my phone for the time, I stand up. It's four forty-five.

'Sorry, but we should be going,' I say. 'We need to get to Sudbury in time – Dad's making dinner. But I'm really sorry, Maisie, I just hate leaving you ...'

She smiles. 'It's fine, don't worry. But look, let's stay in touch, shall we?'

'That would be great, yes. I'll call you once we're back home.'

She bends down to hug the children. Which, despite the fact that they've only just met her, seems like the most natural thing in the world.

'Happy Christmas, you two. Have a lovely time, won't you?'

'I'm really sorry about your brother,' says Anika, hugging her back.

Rishi just stands there, unsure of what to say or do. So I give him a cuddle, then hug Maisie myself.

'You have a nice Christmas too, Maisie. The best way you can.'

Tearfully, we take our leave, visit the loos again, climb into the car and drive down to Dad's place.

The snow is just starting to fall. It's set to cover the earth in a deep muffled robe overnight. Quiet. Peaceful.

CHAPTER 24

Sophie Dubrowska

☼

Christmas Day
Barnet, North London

WE drove down to Barnet yesterday afternoon, Christmas Eve. It took us a good three hours, what with all the traffic, but it's great to be spending time with my parents again. Sounds like Mum's her usual self, too, walking around in her dressing gown until ten in the morning. But it's thinking time, she insists. Inspiration time. Then she showers, dresses, spends an hour over brunch, and begins to paint. Fair enough. She does very well with it, so she must be doing something right. And Dad – he's just Dad. Busy, busy, busy. On the phone, on his laptop, or just working with pen and paper.

It's now eight o'clock in the morning, and I awaken to Mum knocking on our bedroom door.

'We have a white Christmas,' she calls. 'It's snowed. And breakfast is all ready for you, my lovelies. Your dad's making mushroom omelette specially, seeing as Ant's here.'

Dad and Ant have always got on well. They're similar ages, I suppose. And they're both businessmen. And they both like ruling the roost. Which is fine for Mum. I mean, she likes a man to have power over her, especially if he's a toy boy. But I'm not like that. Oh yes, Ant thinks he rules me, but he doesn't. No. If I'm being completely honest about it, I do just as I like, whenever I like.

'Won't be long, Mum,' I call. 'I just need the loo.' Dashing to the en-suite, I sit and pee whilst coaxing Ant to get up.

'It's eight o'clock,' he moans. 'Don't they know we're on holiday?'

'It's Christmas,' I call. 'Come on. Father Christmas has been.'

There's the sound of children outside the bedroom door, so I hurry, flushing the loo and washing my hands. Knowing them, they'll be chasing me to be quick so they can open their pressies.

They're my brother's children. Ethan and his wife Sonja arrived late last night, so Lisbeth and Erika were fast asleep in the car. Ant and Ethan had to carry them into the house and then straight up to bed, bless. Which means I've not yet had the opportunity to say hello. They're such beautiful girls, too. Well, they would be, wouldn't they, seeing as they're half-Swedish. Actually, that's not quite fair. There must be some Swedish women who aren't that beautiful.

So Ethan and Sonja are happily married with two beautiful girls and a home to die for. Ethan runs a small accountancy firm that's doing very well, and Sonja's a qualified dietician who works with the local surgery and pharmacy in Barnet. So why they had to arrive that late last night is beyond me. I mean, they only live ten minutes away. Anyway, it was great to see them, and we stayed up 'til the early hours, catching up and drinking vodka and tequila.

Which is why Ant wants to stay in bed this morning.

'Ant,' I call again. 'Lisbeth and Erika want to open their pressies and you're delaying it all.'

'Okay, okay. I'm getting up.'

I return to the bedroom and peek out of the window. The garden is deep in snow. The sun is just rising in the distance, and the pine trees lining the fence cradle the snow with their lovely spiky branches. It looks beautiful, a winter wonderland with a pinky-orangey background. Quickly throwing on some clothes, I make my way downstairs, followed slowly by Ant in his dressing gown. Way, way too much vodka was consumed last night.

'Morning, lovelies,' murmurs Mum, pecking us both on the cheek. She's up and dressed for a change. Her hair is perfect and her makeup just so. She always has perfect makeup, my mother, but I think, especially today, she has tried a little harder. Maybe at her age she needs to do a little more repair work after a heavy night of vodka. Especially with Sonja in the house, who is so blonde and so beautiful I'd no doubt do the same if I could be bothered.

The mushroom omelette is washed down with freshly-squeezed orange juice and coffee, and is delicious, as always. Once Ant has satiated himself and woken up, he makes his way upstairs to get showered. The rest of us sit around with more coffee and toast, and chat. But then there's a pull on the sleeve of my cardigan and I look down to find Erika, five years old, tugging at me.

'Auntie Sophie?' she says. Her pale green eyes are as wide and innocent as a newborn kitten's.

I know exactly what's coming next, but I feign ignorance. 'Yes?'

'Have you seen all the presents under the tree?'

I smile. 'I have. They look beautiful, don't they?'

'Yes. And we opened the ones from Father Christmas, but I think we really need to open the other ones too.'

She pronounces open as om'pen, which is so cute. Pulling her onto my knee, I place my arms around her. She's soft and warm and smells of bubble gum. And she's so tiny.

'What did you get from Father Christmas, then, sweetie?'

She smiles, and I see that two of her front teeth are wobbly. 'Do you want me to show you?'

'Mm, please.' I nod and she climbs to the floor.

'Come on, Lisbeth,' she calls. 'We need to show Auntie Sophie our presents.'

We move to the living room, now a haven of calm and tranquillity after last night's drinking session. And there's the heady scent of pine coming from the tree in the corner, heavy with decorations, lights and tinsel.

Pulling my hand, Erika runs forward. 'Come see.'

She proudly shows me their scooters, bright pink and complete with tassels, leaning against one of Mum's classic green Chesterfields.

So I stand and admire while Erika and Lisbeth scoot round the room, out into the hall, through to the kitchen, then back again. They are so excited and truly besotted. There's a small pile of pressies on the floor that they must have opened earlier, so I sit and admire these, too, as they show them to me, one by one.

Mum calls us through for more coffee, so it's eleven o'clock by the time I'm showered and fully dressed. I'm wearing my green velvet dress and thick purple tights, and am so looking forward to opening my own pressies. I just love surprises.

*

Mum and Dad have done us proud. Christmas dinner was delicious and the post-dinner brandy went down a treat. We've had the usual turkey and cranberry sauce sarnies for tea, and numerous cups of tea and coffee, and now the men are playing snooker in the library while we girls play with the children and chat. But now the girls have scootered out to the library, Sonja has begun a conversation around whether or not to have another baby. Because now Erika has started school she's feeling broody again, and wonders whether next time she might make it a boy.

If only, I think. If only. Just the one child would be enough for me. Boy or girl. I wouldn't mind. I wouldn't mind at all.

Unexpectedly, sudden, stupid tears fill my eyes, and I make my excuses, rushing out to the cloakroom. Sneaking upstairs, I fix my face before I return to the living room, happy and smiling, and offering to fetch more drinks.

'Nothing for me, lovely,' says Mum. 'I'll make us all a cuppa once the girls are in bed.'

'I'll take them up now then, shall I?' says Sonja. 'They are really tired. They were up at the crack of dawn and haven't stopped since.'

'Bless their cotton socks,' says Mum, softly. 'Go on then, take them up and I'll put the kettle on.'

They know, I think. They know I was upset. Damn it.

Having said goodnight to the men in the library, Sonja carries Erika through to us, with Lisbeth following on behind. So I kiss both girls in turn, swallowing hard to avoid more tears. But the truth is I don't think I've ever realised before how much I miss having children.

It's Erika. It's Erika who's brought this on. I'll be fine once I get home and away from all of this, I think. Once I'm back out there, busy working, busy organising, I'll be fine. Maybe we *should* get a dog, a puppy. A cute, adorable puppy.

Ant goes up to bed at ten o'clock. It's been a busy day and he's tired. Mum and Dad go up not long afterwards while Sonja, Ethan and I sit watching *The Holiday* with gin and tonics.

I've already seen this film twice, so just after Cameron Diaz meets Jude Law, my mind begins to wander. Back to Saturday afternoon. Back to my lunch with Rowan.

You see, after leaving Dorothy Baker's house, I drove straight out to Lincoln. I'd promised to check out the clock's history as quickly as possible, so that's what I was doing.

Help the Aged is now called Age UK, and Lincoln is not a huge city, so I was able to find their shop quite easily. Even so, I felt a bit nervous because Dorothy Baker hadn't been too sure about it. But I googled the shop, which is one of a row on Newark Road, parked up nearby, and walked in. I confess I wasn't really expecting anything to come of it. The guy might have taken the day off, he might no longer be working there, he might not even remember the bloody clock. But a promise is a promise.

So I pushed open the door. To the aroma of damp clothes. Again. I seem to make a habit of visiting charity shops. I mean, they're a great idea, don't get me wrong – I just wish they'd put the heating on sometimes.

Unsure of just how to approach this, I pretended to browse. There was a coat in lime green that looked interesting, but as I got closer I realised the wool had bobbled, as if it had been put through the washing machine. Big mistake.

Just then, saving me from my misery, the woman behind the till looked up.

'Looking for anything in particular, duckie?'

Best be honest, I thought.

'I'd actually like to speak to one of your employees, if that's okay?' She looked troubled, so I put her mind at ease. 'No, no, it's nothing bad. It's just that he used to work in a second-hand furniture shop near Boston and I'm trying to track down a Grandfather clock he sold.'

She smiled. 'Ooh, that sounds interesting. It'll be Derek you're after, then. He actually owned the furniture shop. Second-hand *and* new, I think it was. He talks about it a lot.'

'Great. Thank you. Do you know where I might find him?'

She nodded. 'He's just popped out to the bakery. He won't be long if you want to wait.'

'I will. Thank you.'

Derek didn't keep me waiting long, and luckily he did remember the clock. But only because it had in fact belonged to a member of the aristocracy.

'Sir Samuel Hicklin. I remember the name because I've heard of him since. Had something to do with steel and ironmongery or something. He bought the clock for his daughter, you know – a wedding present?'

'That's great news - useful. Thank you,' I said. 'Do you happen to know who owned it before that?'

He shook his head. 'No. Sorry, love.'

'So where was Sir Samuel from, can you remember? Was he local?'

'No, no, not at all. It was up Derbyshire way - the Dark Peak. If you know the area. A chap I used, a kind of middleman, had it stored in his warehouse and I bought it off of him after he had an accident. Fell off the ladder, broke his back, poor chap. I got it at a good rate, though, considering.'

I went cold. Ice cold.

'Considering what?' I asked.

'Well, considering it had belonged to Sir Samuel Hicklin, of course. If that's the truth. It was Bill, the storage chap, told me. From what he said, it had had a few owners, that clock. He actually bought it off of a woman whose husband was a boot and shoemaker, over in Barnsley. He was killed in action just after the war began. I think he was something quite high up as well, an officer or something.'

'So after you bought it, can you remember what happened then?'

Taking another bite of the sandwich he'd bought, he shrugged. 'Got rid straightaway. A couple bought it. They'd just got married, too, as I remember. Nice couple, from round here somewhere. Funnily enough, I bumped into her, the missus, a few months ago. Lovely and sunny it was, then.' He indicates the grey weather outside.

'Mr and Mrs Baker. She remembers you - that's how I tracked you down. But that was it, was it? You just sold it on? Nothing else happened?'

He looked puzzled. 'No. Why? Should it have done?'

I smiled. 'No, it's fine. But thank you for taking the time to chat.'

He waved his sandwich at me. 'Given me time to eat my buttie, hasn't it?'

Satisfied with my morning's work, I left to drive home for my own lunch. But as I was opening the car door, I heard a shout.

'Mrs Dubrowska.'

I knew who it was, even before I turned my head. Rowan. I closed the car door.

'Rowan, how nice to see you. And it's Sophie. Please.'

He smiled that lovely, dimpled smile. 'Sophie. Sorry.'

I smiled, too. 'How are you? Are you out to do some Christmas shopping?'

'Yep. A new kettle for Mum and Dad, to go with the new kitchen. Silver grey or navy blue, probably. What do you think?'

'That's so nice of you, sweetie. But - have you had your lunch yet?'

CHAPTER 25

Enid Mitchell

Boxing Day
Pepingham

OUR Carol and Richard did their usual thing of taking us to the Drunken Duck in Folksbury on Christmas Eve. It's becoming an annual event, actually. But wonderful it was, just being able to sit there with my family around me, the log fire blazing, and everyone smiling and happy. We really do need to make an effort to meet up more often. I miss them.

So Rosie and Adam didn't get to bed until ten thirty, which is very late for them, and I was hoping for a lie-in on Christmas morning.

But there was no chance of that. Harry and I nearly jumped out of our skins when they ran in at six o'clock, calling at us and shaking the covers.

'Nannie - Harry - come and look what we got,' cried Adam.

Rosie is seven years old, so the big sister. Adam's only four, so he looks up to her, follows her lead. Thus the two of them bouncing up and down on the edge of our bed at six in the morning.

'It's okay, love. You go back to sleep,' I told Harry.

So he rolled over and did as he was told, which made me smile. My kind of man.

'Come on, Nannie,' insisted Adam.

Pulling a dressing gown on over my nightie, I followed the children into the bedroom next door, where two Christmas stockings, emptied of their contents, lay on Rosie's bed. There were penny whistles, books, chocolate oranges, tiny jigsaw puzzles, felt pens, chocolate pennies and a box of dolly mixtures.

'Gosh,' I exclaimed. 'Haven't you done well?'

Taking hold of my hand, Rosie encouraged me to sit down. 'Would you like something, Nannie? You can have one of my chocolate pennies.'

So for the next half hour, I sat with my grandchildren and ate chocolate and read stories and built puzzles. But I absolutely banned them from the penny whistles. Much too much noise at that time of a morning. Besides, Harry was only next door and he'd agreed to cook the turkey, so the last thing we needed was a sleepy chef.

But I needn't have worried, because dinner was delicious. Prawn cocktail to start with. Turkey with every trimming imaginable, including my favourite - cranberry sauce. Then we had roasted parsnips, potatoes, carrots and red onions. Green beans and peas. Stuffing made from roasted chestnuts that I prepared two weeks ago and froze. And thick, succulent gravy.

We'd invited Peggy round, as always. I've always invited her for Christmas dinner, ever since Peter left. Well, it was silly us both being on our own over Christmas. And she knows Carol and Richard, and of course Harry now, so it's all fine.

Peggy caught me on my own in the kitchen, actually, just before dinner.

'Sophie rang me last night, and she's been on the case nicely - managed to get some useful information for us.'

'Lovely,' I said. 'So what's she come up with?'

'Well, she's making a list of the shop's previous tenants, so we can hopefully get some information from them. And one chap she's spoken to has said the clock might have belonged to a Sir Samuel Hicklin, which we think was before the Second World War.'

I smiled. 'That is impressive.'

'The trouble is that many of the records will have run out by now, and we're not going to get much information from just talking to people, because they'll be long gone.'

I felt slightly dispirited. 'So what do we do, Peggy?'

She shrugged. 'We dig deeper, Enid. We dig much deeper.'

But first we had Christmas to celebrate. After the turkey, there was supposed to be Christmas pudding and brandy sauce, but we were much too full. And Rosie and Adam had eaten that much chocolate they could barely eat their main course, let alone pudding. So the pudding stayed in the cupboard. But all in all we did have a wonderful meal.

We'd just finished watching the Queen's Speech afterwards when Sam, my brother, rang. But if I'm honest, Christmas wouldn't be Christmas without Sam ringing. He lives in Snowdonia now, on one of these residential caravan sites. It has a lake and a golf course, and he just loves it. He and Jackie used to be teachers, you know, so when they retired they sold up, bought the caravan, and used the spare money to travel. They've been everywhere, even out to visit my Jonathan in Dubai. Seems like Sam still has the travel bug.

'Sam,' I said, smiling. 'Merry Christmas.'

'Merry Christmas, Enid. How are things?'

The sound of his voice was like birdsong to my ears. Memories. Sam riding Sonny like a madman along the beach. Sam falling off his bike and fracturing his wrist. Sam bringing home his first girlfriend, an older American woman that Mum never approved of. Sam going off to college, me in tears, me missing him like crazy and running away from home. Until Dad found me, hiding in a barn, using an old toilet roll to wipe my eyes ...

'I'm fine, we're all fine,' I said. 'When are you coming to visit, then? I've not seen you since the wedding - you're always busy flying off somewhere or other.'

'I'm afraid it's Jamaica this month, Enid. We're desperate for the sunshine. But how about we come over the end of March? We're not doing anything then.'

I smile at the phone. 'Yes, March would be lovely. Let me know when, and we'll arrange some days out.'

'Great. So how are the kids, and the grandkids?'

*

I've bought tickets to see the panto at Sleaford Playhouse tonight, but first we're doing our usual thing of taking a Boxing Day stroll through the woods. I know - we're creatures of habit, but it's comforting for folks, isn't it, doing the same thing, year in, year out, especially at Christmastime.

So we get all wrapped up against the biting wind with coats, hats and scarves, and leave Genevieve curled up beneath the radiator while we traipse outside. The morning air hits us like a frozen glove, but we continue our walk along the Peterborough Road before turning right, past Chimney Cottage, past the old streetlamp and into the woods. Despite the cold, I'm really looking forward to strolling along the rough tracks and breathing in that earthy smell you get from rotting leaves.

So we carry on, through the long grass and the shivering nettles. Pausing, I pull on my plastic gloves and fill a cotton bag with nettles for soup. Rosie waits patiently before taking my hand, then pulls me along to catch up with the others. She is so like Carol as a child, the way she skips along, chatting away, her eyes delighting in all she sees. Makes my heart sing, it does.

Once we've caught up, the ground becomes bumpy, so we walk carefully, with Carol holding onto Adam's hand. Five minutes in, there's a clearing surrounded by trees, evergreens and a huge oak, and we pause to let the children run round. Richard and Carol play hide and seek with them while Harry and I stand and watch. But we laugh so much at the way Adam runs that our sides start to ache. He's such a character. A born entertainer, says his mother.

We continue our walk for another half hour, show the children the old quarry, then go home for hot chocolate and marshmallows. Carol makes a lunch of salmon and tuna bake, and we eat ravenously. But the fresh air has worn Adam and Rosie out and they'll have another late night tonight, so we take them upstairs for an afternoon nap. It doesn't take long before Harry and I have joined them, but we always sit upright in the lounge for our afternoon nap. So Carol and Richard stay out of our way, playing with my old game of Scrabble in the dining room.

The panto this year is Goldilocks and the Three Bears, and the children are beside themselves with excitement. So while everyone goes upstairs to change, I stay in the kitchen to make turkey sandwiches and salad for tea. And it's as I'm carving up the turkey that my phone rings. It's Peggy.

'Enid?' she says.

'Yes?'

'I have something to tell you. Indira's just rung.'

I know it. I just know it. Whether it's the tone of Peggy's voice or my own gut feeling, I don't know, but I just know it.

'It's Mark,' I say.

Peggy's voice wobbles. 'Christmas Eve.'

My stomach tumbles to the floor. 'Oh, god. Poor Indira.'

'She didn't ring yesterday. She didn't want to spoil our Christmas.'

'Oh, bless her. What an awful thing. But wasn't she going to see her father?'

'They still went to see him, but they didn't stay long, came home this morning. She wasn't really in the mood for Christmas, she said.'

'I'll call round.'

'You've got the pantomime on, haven't you?'

'I'll have time – don't worry.'

Pulling the family together, I explain the situation and they understand immediately.

'No, you need to go round, Mum,' says Carol. 'Look, how about I make the sandwiches? Then we can pick you up from Chimney Cottage, and you can eat yours in the car on the way there.'

'Lovely,' I say. 'Thanks, love.'

So I rush upstairs, change into my smart navy frock and cream cardigan, push a small jar of organic honey into my bag, and walk round to Chimney Cottage. I don't do running, not at my age.

It still feels strange, knocking on the door of what was once my home. But at least I still own the place.

Indira answers, her face swollen with crying, a tissue in one hand. 'Enid. Come on in.'

I do so, and am met with children's arms around my legs.

'Hi, you two,' I say, hugging them. 'Did you have a nice time at Grandad's?'

Anika nods quietly and I immediately regret my question. But Rishi smiles enthusiastically, pulling at me to follow him through to the lounge.

There's a woman sitting here, trim and attractive with red wavy hair. The light from the fire roaring beside her illuminates her face, which looks raw and puffy and tearful.

Standing up, however, she smiles and comes to shake my hand. 'Hullo.'

'Hi,' I say. 'I'm Enid, a friend of Indira's.'

Indira scoots the children upstairs to play, then introduces us. 'This is the lady I was telling you about, the lady who owns the house, who's letting me stay, and who's also a very good friend. Enid, this is Mark's sister, Maisie.'

I'm not quite expecting this. 'Hello, Maisie. I'm - I'm truly sorry to hear the news about Mark. I've only just heard about it, or I'd have come round sooner.'

'Come in and sit down,' says Indira. 'Would you like some tea or something?'

'Get her a G&T,' says Maisie. 'She could probably do with one. In fact, we could all do with one.'

At that, soft tears roll down her cheeks and she crumples back onto the settee. Indira sits down beside her, hugging her with one arm while shushing her and stroking her hair with the other. I sense a connection between them that at first shocks me, I must confess, old fuddy-duddy that I am. But then I see it as it is. Two people. In love.

'I'll just see how the children are,' I say, allowing them time together.

Indira nods, so I climb the stairs to find Rishi there, absolutely dying to show me his toy robot. And it is a wonderful thing. It rolls along the carpet and sings and dances and rocks, and is just enchanting.

'He's lovely, Rishi. Who bought him for you?'

'Father Christmas. He came all the way to Grandad's house for us.'

'Did he? Well, you must have been very good for him to do that.'

He smiles cheekily. 'I am very good.'

Then Anika shows off the painting she's made with her new pens. It's a white unicorn with beautiful blue eyes and the longest eyelashes I've ever seen. And I genuinely admire it, because I've never been able to draw for toffee.

'Would you like something to drink, you two?' I ask. 'I'm going to put the kettle on and make some tea for Mummy and Maisie.'

'Orange juice, please,' they say in unison.

The kitchen is a mess, as if I've interrupted Indira's cooking. But I just ignore it and make tea, leaving it to mash while I carry beakers of orange juice up to the children.

'You're being very good, you two. Thank you.'

'It's okay,' says Anika. 'Mummy's upset, isn't she, so she needs to talk.'

Such a perceptive child.

'You're so right, and so clever. I think she's lucky to have such adorable children.'

So I return to the kitchen, pour the tea, and take it through to the lounge.

'Here we go. Nothing like a nice cup of tea. And I've put some honey in there to help calm us – I hope that's all right.'

Maisie wipes her eyes. 'Sorry about before. I just ...'

'There's no need to apologise, my dear. I can't imagine for one moment how you must be feeling. Such an awful shock.'

I pass her a mug of tea, the edge of my cardigan sleeve laced with sweet orange and frankincense. Calming. Uplifting.

CHAPTER 26

Indira Lambert

☆

Thursday, 27th December
Pepingham

I'VE never thought of myself as gay. I am not gay. But there's something about Maisie that fills my soul. That makes me need her. It's the sweet tenderness in her eyes, the warmth of her touch, that connection we have.

We connect.

And I've realised something else over the past few days. I've realised that love is not just about being attracted to someone physically. Although I am, and she is. Attracted to me, I mean. But it's more than that. It's respecting someone. It's giving them space to be themselves. And at the same time, it's about placing two arms around them and never wanting to let go. But being willing to do so if that's what they want.

I don't think Harvey ever respected me. Well, he respected me because I had a good job, a responsible job that allowed me to earn good money. And now I look back, I think that's all he wanted. Someone to help him have a good lifestyle. So when I had Anika and stopped working, that's when it all began to go wrong.

I do think he loves the children, in his own way, even though he's not seen them in nearly three years. But then I suppose the industry he works for is twenty-four seven, so it's probably not that easy for him to fly out here and visit, anyway. Then again, he's never rung them either, or facetimed them, or even written them a card. Not one single card. As if he's disappeared from the face of the earth. Apart from the money. The occasional flurry of money that appears in my bank account. Guilt money.

Mama is trying desperately to get me to divorce him. And I should. But until now I've not wanted to. I keep wishing he'll come back, you see, that he'll be sorry, that we can start again. Not just for me, but for the children.

But now. Now I'm not so sure.

Christmas Day was very strange this year. It was really difficult to cope with Mark's death, with the awful circumstances, and I still feel that somehow it's all my fault and it could have been avoided. I mean, I was nowhere near the place, knew nothing about it, but something's telling me I shouldn't have asked him where he was that day, because someone or something was listening. And even as I say those words, it sounds ridiculous. I know it does.

But Dad, who is lovely really, just couldn't understand why I was so upset over someone I barely knew, someone who only came into the café and bought coffee and cake once a week. I think I was in shock, to be honest, although I did try my best to make Christmas Day a good one, especially for the children. And I think I succeeded. Anika understood, of course, being the little mother she is. And Diti was there for me to talk to, but she had a shift that began at midnight on Christmas Day, so she had to leave early. She's an airline hostess, had to get across to Gatwick for half past ten. But she has such an exciting career it's no wonder she's not interested in marriage and children. She did understand my distress, though. She knows what it's like to lose someone, having made her way through numerous relationships. But let's face it, holding onto a guy when you're flying halfway round the world every few days must be like holding onto a bar of soap with wet hands. Difficult.

'So how long had you been seeing him?' she asked, as we sat down to a cuppa on Christmas Eve. The children and Dad had gone up to bed and we were having a quick catchup before heading there ourselves. Although Diti had already bagged the third bedroom, so I was sleeping downstairs on the sofa-bed. Now, snuggling down beneath the duvet, I fought desperately to hide my yawns. It had been a long, terrible, week.

'We weren't actually dating,' I said. 'Not dating-dating. He used to come into the café, that's all, and we'd chat about stuff.'

She smiled. 'Nice.'

'Then he asked me out to dinner, but I wasn't sure, said I'd have a think about it.'

Her brown eyes sparkled. 'Why?'

'Because I've not ...'

'You've not been with anyone since Harvey? That lowdown scumbag that's not even worth the ground you're actually walking on?'

Soft tears filled my eyes. 'I loved him, Diti.'

Rolling her eyes to the ceiling, she sighed. 'I know.'

'I just needed time. And the idea of seeing someone else ...'

'I know, but now look what's gone and happened. The first guy you fall for, and ...'

'Oh, Diti,' I cried, 'it's all my fault.'

She sat bolt upright. 'What?'

'I can't explain it now, but I really wish I'd accepted his invitation when he asked me. I was so stupid. I really wish I'd just said yes, straightaway.'

'But Indira, you weren't to know what would happen. You weren't to know some bloody clown would hit him over the head and steal his drugs. I mean, if you think about it, with the job he had, it was an accident fucking waiting to happen.'

I'd never thought about it in that way before. Maybe it was. Maybe he was courting danger, carrying drugs in his car, delivering them to pharmacies with no protection whatsoever and no means of defending himself.

I wiped my eyes. 'Thanks, Diti. You're always the voice of reason.'

She patted my arm. 'And I'm always here. But we need to see each other more often. Ring me. Any time.'

I laughed. 'I do, but you're always on a plane, or sleeping it off, or something.'

*

Dad's new friend, Ellie, came round on Christmas morning, just as we were unwrapping our presents on the floor by the tree.

'Indira,' she gushed, hugging me. 'I've been really looking forward to meeting you. And the children. It's so lovely to finally see you all.'

Ellie is the woman Dad's planning on taking to Hawaii. She was born in Portree on the Isle of Skye, and there's a soft airy lilt to her voice that actually conveys a picture of the island, even though I've never ever been there. But it's supposed to be very beautiful, and Ellie's not bad-looking, either. Late-fifties, I'd imagine, with dyed brown hair and clothes that, admittedly, date her. But she seems kind and caring, and Dad's face just lit up as she walked through the door. Without knocking, I might add. No. I hope she'll make him very happy.

She only stayed a short while, unfortunately, as she was on the way to visit her own parents. But I'm glad I was able to meet her. I'll stop worrying about Dad so much now. I'm sure he's in very capable hands.

The children and I left, too, on Boxing Day. I felt really bad about it, but Dad did understand in the end. You see, I'd spent most of that night stretched out on the sofa-bed, just staring at the ceiling. The children were upstairs in the spare room and I knew they were safe and sound, but even so I was on edge, worrying about what was going to happen next, and what I'd do if anything did happen next. Then, in desperation, I texted Maisie at three o'clock in the morning.

She arrived at Chimney Cottage just after lunchtime. We needed each other.

But I seem to have the whole world worrying about me. Enid came round last night, then Dad rang me, then Mama rang. She's still at Auntie Adya's and is having a wonderful time. So it's looking like she will be moving there, which is fine by me. And she's such a social creature, she'll fit in beautifully. She says she'll send me some money once she's sold the house, so we can take a trip over there and visit. Which is wonderful, awesome, something we can all look forward to.

Maisie and I did have a good Boxing Day afternoon together, despite all the upset of Mark's death. We took the children for a walk through the woods and then explored the village, even though everything was closed.

Pepingham's a pretty little village, I have to say, but it's not Folksbury.

Then, back at the cottage, we made tea together (my own roast cauliflower and lentil stew with pitta bread and pumpkin hummus), and sat and chatted with the children before they went up to bed. They were just fascinated by the tales Maisie has of her travels and her work. She's worked all over the place, even as far as Australia, and has pictures on her phone of kangaroos and koala bears and wombats.

'Can you get a job like that if you play the piano?' asked Anika, enthusiastically.

'Well, obviously, you have to be able to read music if you want to write it,' said Maisie.

'Cool,' said Anika. 'So when will you be going back again?'

Maisie smiled. 'I only go to places when they have work for me. A lot of the time, they send me work to do from home, so I don't get to go anywhere. But if it's a big project, like a film, then they'll invite me over.'

'Where's your house?' asked Rishi.

'It's in Tansor, not far from Peterborough. The house I live in used to be a blacksmith's, so it's nearly as old as the cottage you're staying in now.'

Rishi frowned. 'What's a blacksmith?'

Once the children had finished with their questions, we took them up to bed and read them a story before making our way back down to tidy the mess in the kitchen. So I was busy washing up dishes and chatting away when Maisie suddenly turned to me, took me in her arms, and kissed me. Full on the lips.

I was shocked, had never thought of her in that way before. But suddenly it felt right. It felt amazing. Laughing, I kissed her back, my wet Marigolds hugging her close.

Then later, as we sat before the roaring fire with a glass of wine, she turned to me.

'I want us to be a couple,' she said, 'a proper couple.'

I took hold of her hand. 'I do care about you, Maisie. I care about you a lot. But I'm not sure. Just at the moment, I think I'd like to take things slowly.'

'There's no rush, baby,' she said, kissing me gently.

'I have the children to think about, you see, and I have so much on. And I'm thinking of moving out of Folksbury, and there's so much to think about, so much to do ...'

'But that would be ideal,' she said, smiling. 'You could come and live with me. There's loads of room. I have four bedrooms and a study ...'

I laughed. 'Maisie, don't be so impulsive. We've only just met.'

'We have. And as I've just said, there's no rush.' She grinned persuasively. 'But the schools around me are just awesome.'

Maisie drove home late last night. After she'd gone, the house was very quiet, a plodding kind of quiet, as if a blanket had been thrown across its roof. I knew I wouldn't get to sleep if I tried, so I stayed up until two, making pumpkin casserole in batches for the freezer, and listening to the radio.

The children are now watching *Paddington* (is this the fourth time - I'm losing track?) and I'm in the kitchen preparing veggies for the café tomorrow.

Suddenly, the doorbell rings, so I wipe my hands and dash through to answer it, expecting it to be Enid. But it's not. Tori is standing there, a large canvas bag slung across her fur-trimmed coat, a purple bobble hat perched upon her head.

'Hello?' I say, surprised.

She smiles. 'I'm sorry to interrupt anything. It's just that I heard about your friend Mark, and thought I might be able to help.'

'Come on in,' I say, waving her through to the kitchen. 'Cup of tea?'

She nods. 'Mm, please.'

I switch the kettle on and move some of the clutter from the table. 'Come and sit down, Tori.'

Removing her gloves, she sits, pulls a laptop from her bag and places it onto the table. She wears a ring on seven of her fingers, all vintage, I think, with a different coloured stone on each. She's a curiosity, that's for sure, with her long dark hair and her so calm demeanour.

'So how do you want to help, exactly?' I ask.

'Well, I've been discussing it with Peggy and we've decided to look at everything - the facts - methodically, each thing in turn. So I'm going round getting information from everyone, and writing it all down.'

'Okay?'

She looks up at me. 'If that's all right?'

'Well, yes, I suppose so.'

'Great. Thanks, Indira.'

'So just what is it you need to know?'

*

Going through everything with Tori has dragged up the fear, the insecurity, the stuff I've been trying to push away. We really, really do need to move away from here, just leave them all to it. There's no need for me to be around, is there? We could just leave and let them sort out the problem for themselves. It's not my shop, after all – I'm only renting the place.

So I finish preparing the mixture for my avocado fudge brownies, infuse a cup of warming ginger tea, make hot chocolate for the children, then take that and my own laptop through to the sitting room. While Anika and Rishi watch CBBC, I check out every website and every empty shop I can find. I look at Grantham, Sleaford, Peterborough and Newmarket, fully aware that I need to ensure good schooling for Anika and Rishi.

But the only shop I can find that has facilities for a café with living accommodation above is way beyond my price range. I'm currently paying £950 per calendar month and that's just about achievable. Folksbury is only a small village and I think that's a reasonable kind of rent. But the one in Newmarket is £1400. Ridiculous. I don't even bother checking out the schools.

What I can do, though, and what I do, is to put my details onto all the estate agents' lists. So if anything comes up, I'll be among the first to hear.

Closing the laptop, I look around me. The fire is roaring, my children are sprawled on the Chinese rug gazing rapturously at the TV screen, and I am warm and fed. And suddenly, for the first time in such a long time, I feel loved. Truly loved. Because Maisie is the kind of person my heart has been desperate for. I'm so lucky to have found her. But I need time to come to terms with the idea of us being a couple. I need to be careful not to rush into things too quickly. So, sighing heavily, I carry my laptop upstairs to its place in the bedroom.

Chimney Cottage is charming. Of course it is. It's warm and homely, and I'm so grateful to Enid and Harry for allowing us to live here. Although I am paying them for gas and electricity, and I buy my own logs, of course. But Saffron Silk is also a great little place and I'm missing it. Well, all our things are there, aren't they? Obviously, we've brought some of our stuff to Chimney Cottage, but it's not the same, is it? And I love Folksbury, particularly at Christmastime. With the arty little cupcakes in the baker's window, the stuffed toys in the craft shop next door, and the jewelled colours of the nativity scene in the churchyard. Folksbury does seem to come alive at Christmastime. I love it, and I don't really, really, want to leave.

But I must. If whatever that thing is - the curse or ghost, or whatever Enid and Peggy think it is - if it can kill Mark, then what could it do to me, to my children?

CHAPTER 27

Sophie Dubrowska

Friday, 28th December
Callythorpe

I haven't so much as spoken to Rowan since Saturday, not even to wish him a Merry Christmas. Because, for the first time in my life, I feel incredibly guilty.

And I feel guilty because I've fallen in love. With him. With Rowan.

Oh, my god.

But I still love Ant.

Is it actually possible to love two people at the same time? If so, then how is it possible?

We sat in the Pentola del Pesto and ate spiced chicken soup. And spaghetti puttanesca. And warm chocolate brownies. With rich brandy cream.

We talked and we talked and we talked. We kissed. We held hands. We went back to his apartment, the one he bought after his wife cheated on him.

Oh, my god.

What the hell have I done?

Why couldn't I just have done what I usually do with men? Make love and leave. No, scrap that. Have sex and leave.

Now don't get the wrong impression. Rowan and I didn't have sex. No way. We just sat and talked, and drank tea, and became closer than I would ever have thought possible.

He was so kind, so patient, so absolutely beautiful.

But I can't do this to Ant. I just can't.

So that settles it. I must never see Rowan again. There's no way I can see him again.

But you do know what this means? It means I can't have fun. It means I can't sleep with Radley and any other tenants I might take a shine to. At least not for a while. It would be too much, would remind me of what love is really all about, of what I've been missing all these years.

Oh, my god.

So yesterday I determined to take my mind off things. I agreed to meet up with Enid, Peggy and Tori to discuss the next plan of action. Tori has made a compilation of events leading up to the clock being purchased by Ant and myself. Which gets me to thinking, actually. I mean, why hasn't anything awful happened to me and Ant? Why are we so different? He did buy the bloody thing, after all.

We'd agreed to meet up at Enid's place again. Peggy drove over after work and I planned on arriving at about the same time, having had a fairly lazy day of hanging around the house, cleaning, washing, playing music, and googling for dogs. It's called moping about.

So I arrived at Enid's at five on the dot. But as she opened the door with a flourish of her gold bangles, I caught the distinct scent of patchouli from behind her. Peggy had arrived early.

'Sophie,' she said, ushering me in. 'We've been waiting for you, my dear.'

So we settled down in the dining room, a wonderful space of memories and trinkets, with photographs of parents, children, and grandchildren. Which made me feel a bit melancholy, if I'm honest. The dining room at our house is the complete opposite, full of holiday snaps, just the two of us, and that's only when I can be bothered to frame them.

There was a welcoming tray of tea and shortbread on the table, so we helped ourselves while Enid fussed around, making us feel at home. I noticed Genevieve stretched out beneath the radiator again, watching.

Tori, bless her, took charge of everything, opening up her laptop and pointing at it with a pen. She's such a lovely young thing. Such a calming presence.

'So here we have the list of people who bought the clock,' she says, 'and the purchase dates.'

I went cold. *Our* names are on there. Mine and Ant's names are on there. At the top of the list, obviously, because we still own the thing. As Tori scrolled down, the list continued in descending order, the last name being Sir Samuel Hicklin's daughter. Date unknown.

'We need to get in touch with these people if we can,' said Peggy. 'We need to know exactly what happened before their lives were turned upside down by that clock. If they were turned upside down, of course.'

'Or by the kaleidoscope,' said Tori. 'We're not quite sure yet which one is causing the problem, even though it was obviously the kaleidoscope that caused all that mess at Chimney Cottage.'

Peggy nodded. 'True. Very true.'

'Shall I make a list for us all?' offered Tori. 'If we could each get in touch with someone, it would speed everything up. Obvs.'

'Good idea,' said Enid, patting her hand. 'We'll need names, addresses and phone numbers.'

'I can help,' I said, pulling the laptop from my bag. 'Give me the first name. Not mine, of course.'

Tori laughed. 'I know. That must feel so totally weird.'

'It's strange you've had no incidents yourself, Sophie,' said Peggy. 'So the only people who've suffered, or we think may have suffered, are the shop's tenants?'

'That's right. I have a list of them here.' Opening up the laptop, I found the document I'd put together. 'I can get in touch with them if you like. It would be better if I rang them myself, I think.'

Peggy nodded. 'Okay, yes. Thanks - that would do nicely.'

'So if you do that,' said Tori, 'I can do more research and maybe get some more names to look into.'

'I don't do online, as you know,' said Peggy, 'but I can help with phoning people.'

'And I'll do what I can,' said Enid. 'Just let me know.'

Tori nodded. 'Okay. Awesome. Thanks. I'll let you know what I find out.'

'Great,' said Peggy.

'There's just one problem,' said Tori, pointing to her screen. 'We don't know much about this man yet. Sir Samuel Hicklin. We've been told he may have bought the clock for his daughter as a wedding present, but we don't really know where he got it from, or when. And I've googled him, but I can't find anything about his daughter at all.'

'That's strange,' I said.

She nodded. 'All I can find is that he was born in May 1868 and had something to do with manufacturing steel. That's how he made his fortune.'

'When did he die?' I asked.

'1922. So he'd have been, what, fifty-four years old?'

'Do we know where he was from?' asked Enid.

'There's not much information at all,' said Tori, 'but I have looked up steelmaking. At that time it was made in only two places - Middlesborough and Sheffield. So I guess we could start there.'

'I know where he lived,' I said quickly. 'I spoke to the guy who sold the clock to Dorothy Baker. He told me the clock had belonged to a member of the aristocracy up in Derbyshire. I mean, it may not be the same person at all, but if it was, then he lived in the Dark Peak. Sounds a bit scary all by itself, doesn't it?'

Peggy smiled. 'It's just part of the Peak District, that's all. I've a cousin lives there.'

'Brilliant,' said Tori. 'So at least we've got something to go on.'

*

The period between Christmas and New Year is always wishy-washy, a bit dead, a bit drab and dull. But this year it's like a zombie that's actually died. And stayed dead.

I miss Rowan so much it hurts. That's a cliché, I know. But it's real pain, physical and deep. Unrelenting.

Ant has been good company, of course he has. He always is. But after the first flush of discussing the news; the government, the US president, and the state of the NHS, all I've really wanted to do is curl up and go to sleep in the hope it will ease the pain.

'Get a grip, girl,' I say to myself. 'It's just a crush, you'll get over it. And it's not like you've slept with him, so you've not really done anything wrong.'

To be honest, I don't know whether that's a good thing or a bad thing. Maybe if I had slept with him, maybe if I'd released all that pent-up emotion, I wouldn't be feeling so bad.

Today, however, Ant is back in his Do Not Disturb mode, so I stretch myself out on the sofa and pull my laptop towards me. It's time to get down to business.

We've had nine tenants renting the shop that's now called Saffron Silk. That's a quick turnover, it has to be said. The first one was a Sally Montgomery. She ran it as a sweet shop, one of these mock-up Victorian sweet shops. That shop's ideal for something like that, though, and I seem to recall she also sold toys on the side. She seemed to be making a tidy profit, if I remember correctly, but she only stayed for eighteen months. So I need to find out why.

Hoping her number hasn't changed after all this time, I press it into my phone.

She answers immediately and I introduce myself. Luckily, she remembers me, so I continue with the conversation.

'I'm just wondering, Sally, and I know this sounds a bit strange, but could you tell me why you left the shop when you did?'

She hesitates. I can hear the uncertainty in her breathing. But then she says, 'If I'm honest, there were some strange goings-on. Unexplained sounds, things going missing, lights switching on and off by themselves.'

I'm puzzled. 'Oh, I'm sorry about that. But why didn't you say something at the time? It might have been a fault with the electricity, something we could have sorted.'

'I - I don't know. But I don't think it was the electricity, and there was other stuff going on as well - weird stuff. I just thought you'd think I was losing it.'

'Well, I am sorry. Sorry you had to move out. But can I ask you something else?'

'Yes?'

'Did you disturb the Grandfather clock in the living room at all? Did one of the children acquire a new toy while you lived there?'

'The kaleidoscope, you mean?'

So it's real. This enigma is bloody really real.

'Yes. The kaleidoscope.'

'Imogen found it. She pulled it out of a kind of door at the base of the clock. I think that's when everything started to happen, if I'm honest. It was strange, and I kind of lost my grip on everything. But once I'd realised the connection, which admittedly took a few weeks, I pushed the horrible thing straight back inside the clock and rang you. To give you a month's notice.'

'Okay,' I reply, thoughtfully.

'Why, though? Why are you asking me all this?'

'It's just that we've had some similar things happen recently, and I just thought I'd see if it had happened before.'

'Wow. Sorry about that.'

'No, it's not your fault. But thank you for your honesty. I hope you're doing okay?'

'We're fine thanks, yes. Actually, have you spoken to a guy called Nick Whiteley? He rented the shop just after me. Ran it as a barber's shop, but gave it up after his wife left him. He ended up needing psychiatric treatment, you know, was in hospital for a while. Rumour has it he tried to kill himself – ran his car into a tree with no seatbelt on. He's lucky to be alive, really. I think he's all right now, though, but it's all very sad.'

I'm shocked, physically shocked. 'What? I never knew that.'

'I think it was all brushed under the carpet. But that's why he gave up the shop – couldn't cope with it anymore.'

I do remember Nick, actually. He and his wife. They were a really nice couple, but I think their little boy was somewhere on the Asperger's scale and that probably caused some friction between them. Bless.

But Sally and Nick are not the only tenants to have had such problems. I managed to get through to a few of the others - not all of them answered - but they were just as open and honest, giving me their reasons for moving, their doubts about the history of the shop, the area. That row of shops is very old, you see. 1838. Anything could have happened between now and then.

But it's interesting how we can just accept the fact that an object or even a building can hold onto energy like that. I mean, surely energy dies with us when we go. You see, I've never been able to understand this idea of ghosts or spirits. Although there are plenty of tales around, especially in this area, with its history of warplanes crashing and of ghostly apparitions being seen near the site. Lincolnshire had so many airfields during the Second World War it was known as 'Bomber County'. Forty nine, to be exact. And the number of stories about ghostly airmen exceeds even that.

But Peggy thinks it's a curse, this thing, which would suggest someone placing an evil spell of some kind and just leaving it there. Again, that doesn't really make sense to me. Or maybe I'm too logical a person to buy into that kind of thing.

Thoughtfully, I make tea for myself and Ant, and carry it through to him.

'Had a good day?' he asks.

'Yes, thanks. A strange one, though.'

'In what way?'

So I sit down and I interrupt his work, and I tell him everything. About the shop, I mean. Not the fact that I've fallen in love with a man who's five years younger than me. No. That would not do.

'It's all very strange,' he says, 'but if there is something going on there, have you thought about an exorcist? Maybe we should get an exorcist.'

Surprised, I nod in agreement. 'That is a possibility, I suppose. I'll chat it over with Peggy.'

But as I head back to the sitting room to phone her, my phone buzzes and there's a message from Rowan.

CHAPTER 28

Enid Mitchell

🐈

Saturday, 29th December
Pepingham

GOLDILOCKS and the Three Bears was an excellent production, right up my street, and the children were full of it, laughing all the way home. Until they fell asleep in the back of the car, that is. Then Rosie spent most of Thursday pretending to be Goldilocks, while Adam acted out Baby Bear. Bless their cotton socks. But they make my day, they do, when they're at their best like that. And even when they're not, when they're being naughty and obstreperous and won't do as they're told, I still love them. But that's kids, isn't it? They shouldn't be doing everything they're told, not to my mind, anyway. They should be learning to question authority sometimes.

But today they're going home. I'll miss them, of course, but we're planning on visiting them Easter week, when they're on their school holidays.

So I make Carol and Richard a flask of tea for the journey, and another one full of hot chocolate for the children, and tuna mayo sandwiches. Then we hug them all goodbye and thank them for coming.

'Just put me down for next year,' says Carol. 'I know we're always last minute, so just assume we'll be coming up for Christmas every year. Richard's parents go to Cyprus at Christmastime, so it'll be fine.'

I smile gratefully. 'You're on my list. Can't wait to see you again.'

So we hug and kiss and they wave from the car as it drives off, and I am left forlorn. But I have Harry beside me now, and Genevieve of course, and I have work to do. Harry returns to the kitchen to tidy up and make coffee, and says he wants a nice, relaxing day. He's not used to children running round, you see, even though he has really enjoyed himself. He and his ex never had any children, so I guess it must be a shock to the system, especially at his age. But I'm meeting up with Peggy, Sophie and Indira today, so he'll have the space he needs. We're getting down to business, Peggy and I. We need to see off this thing before someone else dies.

*

So we're driving out to the Dark Peak. Hathersage, to be exact. A quaint village at the edge of the Peak District, and the home of Sir Samuel Hicklin when he was around. Sophie's driving, Peggy sits beside her, I sit behind Peggy, and Indira sits beside me. It's a lovely comfortable car, mind – an Audi. Tori's staying at Chimney Cottage for the day to look after Anika and Rishi, Sophie's brought jelly babies for us to munch, and we've all brought a packed lunch.

On the way there, Sophie fills us in on what she and Tori have found out about Sir Samuel.

'There's something called the Peak District Family History Network, located in Buxton. Tori rang them.'

'Good old Tori,' I say, smiling.

'They told her that Sir Samuel's only child was a daughter called Grace. His wife died in the 1918 flu epidemic, so Sir Samuel and Grace were the only family left living at Hicklin Hall.'

'But then she got married and that's when her father bought her the clock?' asks Peggy.

Sophie nods. 'I suppose.'

'So she must have left him there to live all on his own,' says Peggy. 'Poor chap.'

'No,' I say. 'They had servants and maids and suchlike in those days, so he wouldn't have been on his own.'

'So do we know who she got married to?' says Indira.

'A Charles somebody,' says Sophie. 'It's in my bag on the back there.'

But we leave the bag for now because we're just coming into Hathersage. There's a car park opposite the outdoor swimming pool, so we park up near a trio of small recycling bins. The village itself is beautiful though, set among wonderful moorland and gritstone edges, with houses built of the same stone. Completely different to Pepingham, with its flat landscape of farms and woodland.

We quickly find a kiddie's park that's not far from the pool, so we can sit on a bench and eat our sandwiches. I've brought egg mayo and cucumber.

'It all looks lovely, doesn't it,' says Peggy, 'but it used to be an industrial village, making millstones and pins and needles. Sounds idyllic, but the workers suffered dreadfully from lung disease after inhaling bits of metal and grindstone. Didn't live beyond forty, most of them.'

'Gosh,' says Sophie. 'Thank god we know more about such things nowadays.'

A chill wind begins to blow, and we huddle inside our coats and hoods. A small boy runs across the grass in front of us, followed by his mother, and we watch as they head towards the play area.

'Come on,' I say. 'Let's get some hot coffee in that there Deli we passed, then we'll head on up to the churchyard. It's the best place to look for dead people, I find.'

So we have our coffee, which is delicious and warms us up no end, then we walk back out into the freezing cold air. The churchyard is along School Lane, past the school and the pub, and up a very steep road. I have to stop every now and again to catch my breath, clinging onto the metal rail at the side, but at least by the time we've reached the top I'm lovely and warm again.

So we walk through the wooden lych gate, which is beautiful, with carved roses hanging above. And there's an ancient cedar tree on the other side, so we walk beneath it, checking each gravestone for the name of Charles Braxton, Grace's husband. There are four of us, so it shouldn't take long.

There's a bouquet of purple anemones that's been placed upon a grave near the path. I pause. I feel the grief, for some reason, as if it's a new death. But it isn't - the gravestone dates from 1963. I am glad, though, that someone's still here to care for it.

'It's all so peaceful,' murmurs Sophie. 'What a beautiful place.'

'Come on,' says Peggy. 'There's a sign here for Little John's Grave. You know, one of Robin Hood's Merry Men. We can't leave without seeing that.'

So we look at Little John's grave, which only Peggy finds really interesting, and we continue on our way. There's a small stone building to our left - the door is open and a man stands there, holding a watering can.

'Can I help you, love?' he asks Peggy, who's been leading the way.

She nods. 'We're looking for the grave of a Charles Braxton and possibly his wife and child. You wouldn't happen to know where it is, would you?'

'Do you know when he died? They're all in some kind of order, you see.'

'He died in 1929 and she died in 1923.'

Putting down his watering can, he motions for us to follow him. 'This way, then.'

'Thanks,' says Peggy.

He turns as we follow him. 'Is it the Charles Braxton that was married to Miss Grace, Sir Samuel's daughter?'

She nods. 'It is, yes.'

'Do you know the story, then?' He stops and indicates a gravestone.

Charles Braxton, his wife Grace, and Alice, their daughter, are all here, buried together. But then we see another name, below Alice's but above Charles's.

'Rose Grace Braxton,' I read out. 'Born 24th December 1923. Died 27th December 1923. Three days old. The poor little thing.'

Peggy turns to the gardener. 'No, we don't know the story, but we'd be very interested to find out, if you wouldn't mind.'

'Such a sad story it is, an' all,' he says. 'He bought himself a new car, you know, then ran over the missus and the little girl with it. Killed 'em both. He went a bit mad afterwards. Hung himself. They lived up at Braxton Hall, you know – well, that's what it was called in them days.'

'What's it called now?' asks Sophie.

'Gritstone. It's Gritstone Hall now.'

'Can you tell us anything more about it?' I say.

He stares at me as if he's only just noticed I'm there. I get that sometimes.

'Here, my wife works at the nursing home in the village. Why don't you go and visit?'

'Why do we need to see her?' asks Peggy.

'Well, that's where his maid's daughter is living - Charles Braxton's maid. She'll fill you in on the story if you want. She's a hundred years old now, though - had her birthday a few weeks ago - so I'm not sure she'll remember that far back. But you can always try.'

Peggy smiles. 'That would be really useful, Mr ...'

'Geoff. Geoff Sowerby. Church warden.'

'Thank you very much for the information, Mr Sowerby. Do we need to make an appointment or anything?'

'Here, come on. I'll take you down there myself.'

There's a much gentler route back down to the village that takes us through fields and sheep and mud, with the most wonderful views. So we amble along behind Geoff, chatting as we go.

'So you're investigating a Grandfather clock that Charles Braxton used to own?' he says. 'My, it's a long time ago now though.'

'It is,' says Peggy, 'and we're only here for the day. But we're hoping to find out where Sir Samuel bought the clock and who owned it before he did.'

'Interesting. So just what is it with this clock, then?'

*

Margaret Booth is frail and a bit deaf, despite her hearing aids. So as not to crowd her, Peggy and I have decided to visit on our own while Sophie and Indira take a walk around the village. Geoff Sowerby introduces us to the senior nurse, a large lady called Sheila Pearson, and leaves. Sheila excuses herself for a few minutes before showing us into a side room, bright and airy with the scent of lavender.

As she leaves, we settle down to the tea and biscuits she's brought, and introduce ourselves to Margaret. She recognises Charles Braxton's name immediately, so we're hoping she can remember what happened to the clock, too.

'I understand your mother was a maid at the house,' I say, loudly.

Drinking from her sip-cup, she nods. 'She only just missed being killed herself, you know. And if Charles had never bought that silly car, little Alice would probably still be alive today. She had another one on the way as well.'

'How old was she, his daughter?' asks Peggy.

'Alice? A couple of years younger than me, she was. I was only five at the time, but I remember it like it was yesterday. She ran out, she did, followed her mother, out to see the new car. We'd never seen anything like it before, you see. Didn't have such things, not in them days.'

'So what happened, exactly?' I say.

She shakes her head sadly. 'Raced up the driveway like a dragon, it did. But it was snowing, you see. And it was as if the wheels just kept on going. And it just couldn't stop, and ...'

She's obviously becoming distressed, so I take hold of her hand and send calming thoughts.

'Margaret, don't get upset. Please. It was a long time ago.'

'I remember it like it was yesterday,' she repeats. 'There they were, laid out on the ground, and nothing to save them.'

'Was there something wrong with the car?' asks Peggy.

'No. Nothing. It just couldn't stop. The snow - that bit of snow - it had only just settled. Pretty, it was. But poor Miss Grace, she was only a slip of a girl herself. And poor little Alice.'

'So what happened afterwards?' I ask. 'You say there was another one on the way? Did she give birth to the child?'

She seems to go into a daze at that point, so I pour more tea and encourage her to drink.

'Margaret,' I say, 'can you remember what happened to Grace Braxton after the accident?'

She nods. 'She was just about still alive, so Charles carried her into the drawing room, even though she was bleeding quite badly. But the shock sent her into labour, so when the doctor arrived he was able to deliver her. Had a little girl, she did, before she died. Rose, they called her. But she wasn't a well thing when she was born, very tiny.' Tears fill her eyes, even now. 'She died a few days later.'

'So what happened to Charles after his wife's death? We've been told he went off the rails,' says Peggy.

'Went mad, he did. Went round telling everyone he'd killed Miss Grace's father so he could inherit the house.'

'And did he? Did he kill him?' asks Peggy, looking at me as if she knows something I don't.

'Well now, no-one can know that for sure, can they? Sir Samuel was dead and gone by this time.'

'So Charles could have killed his wife's father, but no-one was able to prove anything one way or another?' asks Peggy.

'That's right. And then, of course, there was the uncle.'

'Whose uncle?'

'His uncle. Charles's uncle. He went telling everyone how he'd poisoned him, but slowly, so no-one would know. So he could inherit. But no-one believed him, silly sod.'

'Why not?' I ask.

'What? Kill two men and not get found out? No. He went mad after killing his precious wife and daughters, that's all. Poor Miss Grace. He went and hung himself in the end.'

'So before he inherited, how *did* Charles make his money?' says Peggy.

She smiles slowly. 'They say he was a magician.'

Peggy looks shocked. 'Pardon?'

'A member of the Magic Circle, he was. It was the talk of the village, according to Mother. He was always taking the train down to London, she said.'

'Was he now?' says Peggy. 'Interesting.'

'He inherited the house and the money from his uncle too, of course. Mum used to say he'd done well, managed to drag himself up from his bootstrings. I think what she meant by that was that he was lucky, hadn't had much of a life before that.'

'So what *did* he do for a living?' Peggy asks again.

'Like I say, he was a magician. Never needed to work, not that I know of. Except when he went off to war, of course.'

'Okay.'

'So when he inherited, that's when he met Miss Grace and they got married. She moved in with him then, into his uncle's house. It's still there, you know, just across the road from the school. But after Sir Samuel died, they moved up to Hicklin Hall.'

'Is that when he changed the name to Braxton Hall?'

She nods. 'Such a beautiful place to live, it is, especially for a child. I loved it there.'

I smile. 'So do you know what Sir Samuel and Charles's uncle did actually die of?'

'So sad. Sir Samuel died after a riding accident. Mother used to talk about it all the time. But the uncle I don't know much about. Sorry.'

She's beginning to look tired, but I have one last question.

'Margaret, do you know anything about a kaleidoscope? Did Alice have one, can you remember?'

She smiles. 'Oh, she loved it, she did. Her father brought it home from London one day. She wouldn't part with it, carried it everywhere.'

'Okay. That's really useful. Thank you.'

'It was on the ground beside her, you know. When she died. Such a tragedy.'

It's time to go now, so we thank Margaret profusely, find Sheila to thank her too, and leave. As we walk along the main road, I ring Sophie to arrange to meet up. But there's no reply, so I call Indira instead.

'Indira?' I say.

'Hi, Enid. How did it go?'

'Well, we've got more information to go on, that's for sure. So where are you two now?'

'Isn't Sophie there with you?' she asks, suddenly anxious.

'No. Why?'

'She said she was going to come and find you - she'd had enough of walking round.'

'Where is she, then?'

'Well, I've no idea.'

'She's probably sitting in her car, out of the cold,' I say. 'Let's meet up there.'

So we meet up at the car park, check Sophie's car, which is empty, and then ring her. And only then do we begin to panic, because there's no reply.

It's four o'clock by this time, and it's dark and cold.

'A café, that's where she'll be,' says Peggy. 'A nice warm place to sit and wait.'

So Indira keeps ringing and texting Sophie's phone as we walk round, asking people, searching for her. But there's no reply. And no-one remembers seeing her.

'Right. We split up and we keep looking,' says Peggy.

'No,' says Indira, shaking her head. 'I can't - I can't be on my own. Sorry.'

'No,' says Peggy. 'You're right. Sorry, Indira.'

'We'd be better off staying in one place, anyway,' I say, 'then if she's looking for us, she'll find us.'

'Okay,' says Peggy. 'We go back to the Deli, we sit in the window, and we keep a lookout.'

CHAPTER 29

Indira Lambert

☆

Sunday, 30th December
Hathersage, the Dark Peak

I awake to the sound of rain pattering against the windows. Rolling over to check my phone, I see that it's nine o'clock. Suddenly the horrendous events of last night rush through my head, and I groan loudly. Not wanting to think about them, I throw back the covers (sheets and blankets, quaint and old-fashioned) and put my feet to the floor. I need the bathroom.

The house is homely, with soft carpeting and the scent of aged pine. And Barbara made sure we had a quick meal before we went up to bed, omelette with spinach and smoked salmon, and crusty bread with butter. But it lay heavy on my stomach, so I didn't get to sleep for ages.

We didn't leave the hospital until gone midnight, but Sophie was absolutely fine, they said. She'd had a CT scan and there was no damage at all to the brain. Thank god. So, apart from the severe bruising she'd sustained, and an awful headache, she was fine.

We'd found her lying in the corner of a short cobbled street, just behind the restaurant on the high street. She was actually sitting on the ground near the wall that makes up the Deli's car park, so we were nearby all the time, drinking coffee and talking. And it was as we were leaving the Deli that we heard her. A soft moan behind the wall. I heard it before the others, so ran over to take a look. There are three little cottages just there, and an old-fashioned street lamp that shone its light onto her. So I rushed forward.

'Sophie ...'

Leaning against the wall, one arm supported by a large plant pot, she was holding her head in her hands and crying with pain. I rushed to pull her up off the cold ground, but Peggy stopped me.

'Best not to move her, Indira. Here, Enid, call an ambulance, and be quick about it. I'll get the police.'

So we covered Sophie with our coats to keep her warm, and waited patiently until the ambulance arrived twenty minutes later.

'Can you remember what happened?' I asked as we waited. 'Who on earth would do something like this?'

'No idea. I just kind of felt someone behind me, and when I turned round they hit me.'

Her voice was weak, grey, tearful, and I guessed she was still in shock.

'I feel a bit sick,' she said.

'Here,' said Enid, fishing a bottle from her bag and shaking it. 'Have some of this. It's my rosa canina remedy – dog rose. It'll help calm you down.' She used a dropper to place three drops onto Sophie's tongue. 'There you go, love,' she whispered gently.

'Crazy, isn't it?' said Peggy, grinning. 'You come to Hathersage for a nice day out and this is what happens.'

Enid smiled. 'Can you credit it, Peggy?'

Sophie smiled weakly. 'Don't make me laugh, you two. Please.'

'Sorry,' said Peggy. 'But look, love, can we borrow your car? We'll have to take the risk with the insurance, but we'll follow you into hospital, make sure you're all right. We won't leave you alone.'

Sophie nodded towards her handbag, and Peggy pulled out the keys.

'They weren't after your money, then,' she said. 'Looks like everything's here. And they weren't after the car, either, nice as it is.'

Sophie smiled at that, but her face was white and she was obviously in a lot of pain. So we sat on the cobbles beside her and chatted, to try and take her mind off things.

When the paramedics arrived they said she was probably okay, but would need a scan just to make sure. Then they gave us five minutes with the police, who took a statement and asked for the paramedics to try for some DNA.

'Can I come with her?' I asked, as the two paramedics prepared to move her.

They were fine about it, so I stepped up to the ambulance, climbed inside, and held Sophie's hand all the way there. The hospital is the other side of Sheffield, so it was a half hour trip, but she was warm finally, and safe. The police came and took another quick statement from her once she'd had her CT scan, then we all drove back to Hathersage to stay with Peggy's cousin, Barbara.

So this morning Sophie's stretched out in the bedroom next to mine, Enid and Peggy are sharing the next room along, and Barbara is on the sofa downstairs.

After visiting the bathroom, I return to my room, pick up my phone, and call Tori. She's looking after Anika and Rishi for me, so I rang her last night to let her know what was happening and that we'd be staying overnight with Barbara.

'Morning, Tori,' I said. 'Sorry, I've only just woken up. It was a bit of a night, as you can imagine.'

'Fuck, you're telling me,' she says, and I pray my children aren't in the room. 'Oops - sorry, Indira. I'm just so glad Sophie's okay, though. It could have been something truly bad, couldn't it?'

'It could have been, yes. But how are Anika and Rishi? Are they all right?'

'They're fine, don't worry. Harry brought Genevieve round last night for them to play with, so that's what they've been doing. They're in the sitting room now, and I'm sorting them out some brekkie.'

'Thanks, Tori. This is really good of you.'

'Not a problem. And they're fine, really, so no need to worry.'

'Thank you, anyway. I'll let you know when we're on our way home.'

So, satisfied everything is all right, I wash and dress and head downstairs. Barbara is already awake and is busy, making tea and toast.

'You want some?' she asks.

I smile and nod. 'Mm, please – that'd be lovely.'

Despite being Peggy's cousin, she doesn't look at all like her. She's shorter and broader, and has thick wavy hair. But there's something in her demeanour that does remind me of Peggy. A kind of confidence, I guess. A strength. I can't quite explain it, but it's there.

'Did you sleep all right?' she asks.

Pulling back a chair, I sit at the table. It has a covering of oilcloth, white with small purple flowers.

'I did – yes, thank you. Am I the first one up, then?'

At that moment, Sophie walks into the kitchen. She still looks very pale, but she smiles and sits beside me.

'How are you feeling?' asks Barbara, kindly. 'You want some painkillers?'

'It's okay, thanks - they gave me some at the hospital and I've just taken them.'

'Here then, I've a nice warm lavender bag you can put around your neck.' Pulling it out of the drawer behind her, she folds it up. 'Always helps with headaches. I'll pop it in the microwave.'

Enid and Peggy appear at that point, so we sit and chat and eat and drink. The kitchen is warm and the conversation light, and I start to become sleepy. I'm so used to being busy all the time, what with the children and the shop and the housework, that when I stop I truly stop.

'Are you okay?' asks Enid, staring at me.

I realise that I've actually closed my eyes, so I open them, apologise, and join in with the conversation. Then Barbara brings us hot, strong coffee, and I begin to come round nicely.

'Do you remember anything at all about last night?' Peggy is saying.

Sophie looks puzzled. 'I'm not sure, not really. I just caught this shadow out of the corner of my eye, and then ...'

She looks upset, her eyes filling with tears, so Enid touches her hand gently. 'It's fine. Don't think about it now, love.'

'I wonder what they were after,' says Peggy. 'They didn't take your bag or anything.'

'Maybe they were disturbed,' says Barbara.

But Peggy shakes her head. 'No. If they'd been disturbed by someone, surely that person would have rung for an ambulance.'

'The police think it was a spur of the moment thing, that they just took advantage,' says Sophie.

I suddenly realise something. 'It seems weird, I know, but all this is ringing bells. It just reminds me of when Mark was attacked, only it's not quite so bad.'

The room turns cold as a shiver runs through us all, and we stare at each other.

*

Peggy helps ease Sophie's headache with some gentle pressure on her scalp and forehead, so she feels well enough to drive us home. And that's what we do. I can't wait to see my children again, and Enid is anxious to get back to Harry, to safety and to some kind of normality. What a weekend it's been.

Sophie drops me off at Chimney Cottage and is just pulling away when Maisie rings me. I pull the phone from my bag, but then Anika and Rishi rush through the door enthusiastically, noisily, excited to see me. I've never been away from them before, you see, other than when Rishi was born, of course. But it's a very strange sensation, and they must feel the same as I do.

'Maisie, can I call you back?' I say.

'No probs, Indira. Speak soon, then.'

Genevieve is sprawled beneath the radiator in the kitchen and I bend to stroke her as Anika and Rishi fill me in on what they've been up to.

'I've made a dinosaur, Mummy – look!' says Rishi, proudly displaying a purple dinosaur, which is massive, a whole metre across and made from papier-mâché.

It's not like Rishi to get excited over art, so I'm very impressed. 'Wow, that's brilliant,' I say. And it is.

'And I've made some embroidery, Mummy,' says Anika, showing off her plain white tee-shirt, now with a pink and yellow flower embroidered onto its chest.

'Well, I never knew I had such clever children,' I say, turning to Tori. 'Thanks, Tori. Thank you for this.'

She's busy filling the kettle. 'No. I've loved every minute. Thank you for letting me look after them. You want tea or coffee?'

'Listen, any time I need a babysitter, you'll be first in the queue. And yes, coffee would be great, thanks. I could do with it.'

So I sit with my coffee and my children, and I ring Maisie back. I last spoke to her on Saturday, just before we set off for Hathersage.

'How was the trip?' she says. 'Did you get the information you needed?'

'It wasn't that brilliant, to be honest. Sophie had an accident and ended up in hospital.'

'My god, no. What happened?'

'She was hit on the back of the head in an alleyway. It took us ages to find her.'

'You're joking.'

'No. I'm not.'

The line goes quiet.

'Maisie?'

'You don't think this has anything to do with Mark, do you?'

'I did wonder that myself for a second. But it can't be. There's nothing to relate them.'

'There is. There's you.'

But I can't even think about that. I don't want to think about that.

'Don't, Maisie. There's no connection. It's just pure coincidence.'

'Okay. If you say so. But please - be careful, baby.'

'Look, Peggy and Sophie are meeting up soon to go through everything again. If the two incidents are related, then we need to find out what's going on. Because it's all becoming a bit too dangerous for my liking.'

'The police in Peterborough rang me yesterday, by the way,' she said.

'Really? What about?'

'The CCTV results. All they can get from it is a shadowy figure, but it looks like a woman. Long hair, long skirt. A druggie, probably.'

'Wow. She must have had some strength, then, to do that to Mark.'

'My thoughts exactly. But I suppose if you're desperate for a fix ...'

'Did they find any DNA?'

'No. Nothing. They say he was hit with a blunt instrument, but they've no idea what it was. The strange thing is that they found his delivery box in a nearby alleyway, complete with half the delivery. So the girl must have been disturbed or something.'

'Wow. That's very strange. You'd think she'd have taken the lot, wouldn't you?'

'Well, they're looking into it, obviously.'

'But how are your parents doing, Maisie?'

'Mum's still in floods, but they're bearing up. They know they have a funeral to arrange.'

'Oh, bless them. And how are you?'

'The same as Mum, really. But I'm trying to keep busy, to keep my mind off things.'

'Look - next weekend - why don't you come over? It would be great to see you.'

'Okay, yes. Thanks, I will. And I have more news. I may have found a property for you to rent. I'll send you the link.'

I smile at the phone. 'Really? Whereabouts?'

'Not too far from me, but far enough in case you get fed up.' She laughs. 'It's out the other side of Stamford. A smallish shop with three bedrooms and a garden. But there's parking across the street and it gets really busy with tourists, especially through the summer. I guess that's the kind of thing you're looking for?'

'Wow. How much?'

'Ah. Well. Look, I can help with that, just until you get some regular custom. Which will happen really quickly, I'm sure.'

'No. Sorry, Maisie. I couldn't do that. Really. But thank you for the offer. It's very kind of you.'

'Please, Indira,' she says. 'Just have a think.'

'Really. I mean it. Sorry, Maisie. You can send me the link, though, and I'll take a look.'

But I'm nearly in tears as we say our goodbyes.

What's wrong with me, I think? Will I ever be able to trust anyone again? Has Harvey ruined the rest of my life for me?

This all feels right. So right. And yet it doesn't.

Locking myself in the bathroom, I lean against the wall and I sob and sob. I think about all the hours I've spent crying since Harvey left. Wasted hours. Hours of loneliness, of hurt, of recrimination.

Will it ever stop?

CHAPTER 30

Sophie Dubrowska

New Years' Eve
Callythorpe

IT'S New Years' Eve today, but I don't feel much like celebrating. I have a head that's as sore as a clown's when no-one's laughing. And Ant is upstairs, busy packing, ready for a business trip to Edinburgh on Wednesday. So why he has to do it now, I've no idea. But at least it keeps him occupied, so he's not asking how I am every two seconds. Bless.

He does love me, I know he does. But it's not the kind of love I need. It's not complete. It's more like a brother's kind of love, or even a father's. Maybe that's it. Maybe he's too old for me, treats me more like a daughter.

Now Rowan, on the other hand, treats me like a goddess.

Yes, I did reply to his text on Friday. And yes, I did meet up with him, under the pretext of popping round to see Enid. And yes, I did sleep with him. And yes, it was amazing. Absolutely. Amazing.

So travelling out to the Peak District on Saturday was a welcome distraction. I felt so bad cheating on Ant in that way, I could hardly look him in the eyes. I know, I know, I've cheated on him a lot over the years. But not like this. Not when there's the danger of my actually leaving him for someone.

Oh god, what have I done?

But Peggy and Enid are calling round soon, so I'm busy plumping up the cushions and defrosting an M&S chocolate log I bought before Christmas. I always buy three, just in case of visitors.

I'm switching on the coffee machine just as the doorbell rings, so I rush to answer it.

'Hi,' I say. 'Come on in.'

It's a cold, grey day out there, so I usher them into the warmth, take their coats, and hang them up. They make a fuss of me as we gather together in the kitchen, admiring the house, asking how I am, saying how awful the whole thing is, and then Enid gives me peppermint oil to spread across my forehead. At which point Peggy offers to rub it on for me, and I accept. She wants to balance the Qi, as she calls it, and I have to say it feels wonderful.

Then I make coffee and offer Florentines and slices of chocolate roll.

We settle in the living room, where I've already set up my MacBook. Because we have some serious work to do.

Peggy sits down, stretches out her long legs, and sighs. 'What a week. One murder and one near-miss. We really need to get down to business.'

'Indira rang me yesterday,' says Enid, 'because the police have been in touch with Maisie. They're saying it's a woman, a girl, on the CCTV cameras. But they've got no DNA and nothing about the murder weapon. So, unless it is just a junkie after drugs, we have absolutely nothing to go on.'

'Except we have more information about our friend, Charles Braxton,' says Peggy, helping herself to a second Florentine.

'What's that?' I ask.

'Well, I'm wondering if our search stops with him. You see, I picked up on the fact that he might have been a member of the Magic Circle - something Margaret Booth told us. So I rang an old colleague of mine, Tom, this morning. Now he did say that members of the circle promise not to disclose magic secrets, and anyone breaking the rules can be expelled. But it only relates to the magic itself, so he could confirm for me that Charles Braxton was in fact a member of the Magic Circle between 1918 and 1920. But then he was expelled, due to his association with an occultist named

Aleister Crowley. I have heard of him, actually. He was a heroin addict who, amongst many other evil deeds, was a double agent during the First World War. So not a very nice man at all, truth be told.'

'Wow,' I say. 'But I thought the Magic Circle was something that was around centuries ago.'

Peggy shakes her head. 'No, it's still alive and kicking. In fact, Prince Charles and Stephen Fry are members.'

I'm truly astounded. 'So what did this guy tell you about Charles Braxton?'

'He said Charles came to them after the Great War, determined to make a name for himself. He'd lost his father to the War, he and his mother were destitute, and there was only one person left to look after them. His uncle, on his father's side. So, according to their records, Charles and his mother moved in with him. Shortly afterwards, the uncle died and Charles found he was a rich man with a house and money to his name.'

'So Margaret could have been right,' says Enid. 'Maybe Charles did poison him.'

She nods. 'Tom said the Dark Peak, where Charles came from, is known as the UK's Bermuda Triangle, home to tales of witchcraft and ghosts. So if there have been some goings-on up there, it doesn't surprise him in the least.'

'They've not been going on up there,' I say. 'Apart from what happened to me and Mark, they've been going on around here.'

'That's true,' says Peggy. 'But what's even more interesting is that, if Charles was telling the truth about murdering his uncle, was he also telling the truth about killing his father-in-law?'

'Wow,' I say.

'So if we can, we need to see if there's anything on that there computer to show us how he died. He was a prominent man in his day, so you'd think there'd be something on it.'

'But Margaret Booth said it was a riding accident,' says Enid.

Peggy nods. 'She did, but it may not have been. Or something might have spooked the horse and Charles might have orchestrated something to cause the accident - you never know.'

So we google Sir Samuel Hicklin.

'Look. There,' says Peggy, pointing with her long fingers.

'Sir Samuel Hicklin,' says Enid. 'Born Hicklin Hall, Hathersage, Derbyshire, 15th May 1868.'

'So he inherited Hicklin Hall from his family, by the looks of it,' I say. 'I bet it's beautiful. Maybe we should have gone and taken a look while we were up there.'

'Didn't have time, did we, not with you getting yourself knocked on the head,' says Peggy, smiling.

'Here, let's google Charles Braxton,' says Enid, excitedly. 'It'd be interesting to see his background, too.'

'Let's just concentrate on Sir Samuel first, though,' I say.

We don't find anything at first, so we change the search to Hicklin Hall. We have to look quite a way down the results, but eventually we find a short article on the death of Sir Samuel Hicklin.

'Sir Samuel Albert Hicklin of Hicklin Hall. Died 30th November 1921, aged 53 years,' I say. 'Looks like the cause of death is a fall from a horse.'

'So it was an accident, then,' says Enid.

'You'd think if he'd been riding most of his life,' I say, 'he'd have been proficient, would have had enough experience to avoid an accident like that.'

But Peggy looks thoughtful. 'There are ways and means, Sophie. The thing is, if Charles was telling the truth and he did kill him on purpose, he could have done something as simple as cutting through the stirrup a bit. Just so it would come apart when he was out riding. Or he could have spooked the horse somehow, as we've said before.'

'Like placing a scarecrow somewhere, or something he knows the horse won't like?' I say.

She nods. 'Could have been anything. We'll probably never know.'

'Come on, let's take a look at Charles Braxton,' says Enid. 'Is there anything about him or his uncle?'

So I put his name into the search engine. Very little comes up, but what we do find is quite revealing.

'Charles Braxton,' I read, 'born Bamford Mill, Bamford, Derbyshire, 13th March 1893. Died Braxton Hall, Hathersage, Derbyshire, 24th December 1929.'

'Christmas Eve,' says Peggy. 'Probably couldn't stand the pain any more, probably couldn't face Christmas without them, his poor family.'

'Let's see if it says anything about his wife,' I say.

So I google her, too.

'Grace Victoria Braxton, née Hicklin. Born Hicklin Hall, Hathersage, Derbyshire, 23rd June, 1898. Died Braxton Hall, Hathersage, Derbyshire, 24th December 1923.'

'The same date as Charles,' says Peggy. 'Christmas Eve.'

Enid looks up. 'The same date as Mark.'

'Oh – my god,' I say.

*

It's one thirty, and for lunch we've eaten the remainder of the chicken I cooked last night. I made sandwiches with it, adding a green salad of spinach, avocado and green beans, with French dressing. But the denouement is meringue coated in chocolate, and a dollop of fresh double cream. From the bakery in the village. Delicious.

And Enid definitely has a sweet tooth, because she just laps it up.

'This is lovely, Sophie,' she says, scraping the plate with her fork to pick up the last few crumbs. 'Thank you.'

'My pleasure,' I say. 'I'll leave the clearing up until later, though. We have work to do.'

Ant pops his head around the door.

'Sophie - I'm popping out for a pub lunch, so I'll leave you ladies to it.'

'Sorry, sweetie,' I say. 'I didn't think it would take this long. But I'll see you later.'

As he leaves, we pick up our coffee and return to the living room. It's warmer than the dining room, and I feel the need for warmth as my head is starting to pound again.

Peggy looks at me kindly. 'Are you okay, love?'

'Just my head,' I say.

'Here. Sit down.'

I sit back into the sofa, and she skirts around the back. Good job she's slim, I think, as she begins to rub my scalp. But it feels so tender that I pull away.

'Sorry,' she says. 'I'll be careful.'

Now I don't know quite how she does it, but it's worked. I can still feel a dull ache from where I was hit, but there's no actual pain any more. Amazing.

'Wow. Thanks, Peggy.'

'No problem,' she says, sitting down beside me.

Enid sits on the other side of me and I open up the MacBook.

'Now then,' I say, 'where were we?'

'I'm interested to know more about Aleister Crowley's cronies,' says Peggy. 'Was Charles actually able to use their knowledge to his advantage? What I mean is - did he use it to get rid of his uncle and his father-in-law?'

And so I google.

Mr Crowley is described as "an English occultist, ceremonial magician, poet, painter, novelist, and mountaineer. He left Cambridge University in July 1898, having not taken any degree at all despite a First Class showing in his 1897 exams."

There's page after page of information, but as I scroll down Peggy spots something.

'Look – there,' she says. 'He placed a curse onto one of his friends. If that's the truth, what was to stop our friend Charles learning the same thing, and copying it?'

Then Peggy starts to talk. And she makes sense. Complete sense.

'So if we follow Charles's life, we can see he was born in a mill. So does that suggest his family was poor, maybe mill workers? And then he's sent off to war at the age of – what?'

'Twenty-one,' I say, quickly working it out.

'Twenty-one. So then he comes home at the age of twenty-five, twenty-six, and his father is dead, and he and his mother have to move in with his uncle as they're destitute. But then he meets Grace.'

'Maybe he gets a job, maybe he doesn't.' I say. 'But he's in love, so he needs to ask for her hand, but she's rich and he isn't.'

Peggy nods. 'So he hatches a plan. He knows he'll be the sole beneficiary when his well-off uncle dies, but he can't wait that long because he wants to marry Grace. So he speeds up the process.'

'So does he learn how to administer poison from his set of cronies?' asks Enid.

'Possibly,' says Peggy. 'So he kills him off and inherits, then asks Grace to marry him, and all three of them live in his uncle's house.'

'But then he begins to run out of money,' I say, 'I don't know - from gambling or from losing his job, or ...'

'Margaret Booth said he used to travel to London a lot,' says Enid. 'That might have been to do with gambling, or visiting call girls, or some other such thing he didn't want his wife to know about.'

'Exactly,' says Peggy, 'or even just visiting his occultist pals and whatever they might have been up to. So then, of course, Grace says she's expecting and he realises he has to provide for all three of them, plus his mother.'

'So, because he got away with killing his uncle, he hatches a plan to kill Sir Samuel.'

But I shake my head. 'You know, this is all circumspection. And really, it's got nothing to do with why Mark was killed, or why I was hit over the head last night.'

Peggy nods. 'Unless there's some kind of connection with that clock.'

CHAPTER 31

Enid Mitchell

Saturday, 9th February
Hathersage

IT'S six weeks exactly since that fateful night Sophie was attacked. But we're all four of us back here again, sitting in the Deli in Hathersage. It's warm and cosy, and smells of coffee and toast and melted cheese. We've just finished our warm ciabattas and Peggy's now treating us to coffee. She's already arranged for us to stay overnight at Barbara's place, so we've been invited there for dinner later. Which I'm quite looking forward to, it has to be said. So all told it's going to be a good weekend.

'Right,' says Peggy, placing a tray of coffee onto the table. 'Let's warm ourselves up with this little lot before we trundle up to the hall.'

I pull a face. 'Doesn't sound very welcoming, though, does it? Gritstone Hall?'

'No, but at least it's not named after the owner these days. What would that be like? Gelly Hall?'

Indira smiles. 'My kids would love that, though. They'd be calling it Wibbly Wobbly Gelly Hall.'

'I don't think Peter Gelly would quite appreciate that,' I say.

'We're not walking up there, are we?' says Sophie. 'It looks like quite a trek, you know. I think it would be better if we took the car.'

Peggy nods. 'Of course, and there's plenty of space for parking. I checked with him, with Mr Gelly.'

Indira laughs. 'Mr Gelly. You'd think with all that money he'd have changed his name by now.'

My cappuccino has a lovely heart-shape etched into the surface, so I sip it, and it tastes as good as it looks.

'So why exactly are we having to bury the kaleidoscope and gloves?' asks Sophie.

Peggy sits back. 'Yes, I've been meaning to mention this.' She turns to me. 'Enid, you know you said we'd never had a case that involved a curse before?'

'That's right,' I say.

'Well, I have had one. Before you and I were a team.'

'Oh?'

'Over in Anglesey, it was. It was the case of a young man dying in a car accident, leaving behind a wife and baby boy.'

'Oh, bless,' I say.

'Well, the wife consoled herself by always wearing her dead husband's watch, said the leather strap smelled of him. But every night, when she removed the watch to go to bed, she'd fasten it around the handle of her hairbrush to keep it safe.'

'That's so sweet,' murmurs Sophie.

'Then many years later,' Peggy continues, 'the wife took ill and died too. But by this time the son Matthew had got married and it was his wife who came to me, looking for answers to the strange sound that had begun to fill their home every night.'

'No,' says Indira.

'You're joking,' adds Sophie, suddenly pale and drawn.

'What happened was that when the family home was sold up, the watch was taken by Matthew and placed into a drawer in his own house. Luckily for him, he remembered what his mother used to do with the watch at bedtime. So when we got round to investigating the noise, which took a while, we discovered that when the watch was wrapped around the hairbrush again, the noise stopped.' She pauses to sip her coffee. 'The lucky thing was that he'd kept both his mother's items.'

'Wow,' says Indira.

'So what I'm taking from this is that if we make sure the kaleidoscope and the gloves are kept together and never moved again, the noise should stop, and hopefully all the other issues we've been having.'

'Fingers crossed,' I say.

'I think Charles Braxton placed a curse on them on purpose,' says Peggy, 'through his occultist cronies.'

'But why,' asks Indira, 'and wouldn't he be upset if we just buried them?'

Peggy shakes her head. 'Because he was an evil man, that's why. And I don't think it would upset him, because they'll be where they're meant to be, in the grounds of what was once Braxton Hall. Peter Gelly has given us permission to dig deep into the edge of his farmland, somewhere that will never be touched. And he's making a note on the Deeds for future owners of the property.'

'Well, I'll be glad to get it all sorted,' says Indira. 'But what I don't understand is why Mark and Sophie were attacked. Or do you think that was just coincidence?'

'Given that no DNA has ever been found, and that the CCTV only came up with a mere shadow in Mark's case, I do personally think the attacks were something to do with the curse. But, unfortunately, it's something we'll never be able to prove.'

We all went to Mark's funeral, even though not all of us actually knew him. We felt the need, somehow, but it was a very sad affair. He was so young, had so much to live for, and he and Indira had been getting on so well.

'Come on, let's drink up,' I say, miserably. 'We've got some work to do.'

So we grab our coats and head outside. The sky is heavy with snow and the street busy with weekend shoppers. The Indian restaurant next door has already started their cooking, so all I can smell is the tang of curry, delicious as it is.

Crossing the main road, we walk behind the petrol station to reach the steps that take us through the small community garden, up past the Methodist church, and along to the car park. Climbing into Sophie's car, we drive through the village, turn right onto Jaggers Lane, then right again onto Coggers Lane.

'Wow,' says Indira, as we reach the next junction, 'it's beautiful. Stop the car, Sophie.'

Pulling into the side of the road, we tumble out of the car, admire the view, and take lots of pictures. And it is beautiful. The hills in the distance are white with snow, and the clouds above them have turned crimson with the sun. Then we notice the sheep grazing in the nearby field have stopped their chewing to stare at us, so we wave at them, laughing, before returning to the car.

'Come on, let's get this thing done,' says Peggy, 'before the snow catches us.

So we drive on to Gritstone Hall, parking up not far from the house. It's an imposing three storey place built of old battered stone, with leaded lights and interesting battlements at the top. The long driveway is actually quite steep, so I can imagine Charles Braxton having to put his foot down to get to the top. Maybe that's why the car slipped, I think. Maybe tyres didn't have so much grip in those days.

'It's what's known as a tower house, sixteenth century, millstone grit,' says Peggy, climbing out of the car. 'Thus the name, I suppose. I bought a book on it. Lord knows what's gone on since it was built, what other tales it has to tell.'

I stand and stare. I'm sensing the horror Charles Braxton must have felt as he drove that car into his beautiful wife and daughter. How awful it must have been for him. And then to lose his newborn baby, too. No wonder he put a curse on everything.

'You okay, Enid?' asks Peggy, pulling open the car boot.

'I'm fine, Peggy. Let's just get this over with, shall we? I'm ready for a nice warm fire and some comforting food.'

She grins. 'Barbara makes a mean meat pie, I'll give her that.'

Pulling her carpet bag from the boot, she produces a large brass bowl, and I recognise it. It's the bowl she used to heal herself the night we stayed at Saffron Silk. But today there's a lid on that wasn't there before.

'What are you doing with that, Peggy?' I ask.

'It cost me an arm and a leg, this bowl,' she says, 'but we need it. We'll be burying the kaleidoscope and gloves inside it.'

When she removes the lid, I see that both items are already there. The beautiful kaleidoscope - and it is beautiful in its way - and that tiny, tiny pair of black lace gloves.

There's a lump in my throat. I'm feeling such a strong connection between these two items, between their owners, and can only guess at why they were hidden inside that old Grandfather clock.

'So sad,' I say, quietly. 'Such a sad story.'

'Apart from the fact Charles Braxton killed his wife's father and his poor old uncle,' says Peggy. 'Not a very nice person, all told.'

Sophie digs around inside the car boot, too, pulling out a large garden spade.

'I came well prepared,' she says. 'I've brought gardening gloves as well – four pairs,' and she pulls them from her bag.

'Come on, then,' I say. 'Let's get this over with.'

So, wrapping my old red scarf around my neck, I follow Peggy and the others, away from the house and back down the road. There are two brand new gates here, one for cars and one for walkers. But just yards away, to the right of the walkers' gate, we find a tiny patch of land the owner has already dug over for us.

'Just here,' says Peggy, quietly.

We wait as she places the bowl onto the ground.

Sophie begins to dig. The soil is still loose from being dug over, but it's heavy from the overnight rain. So she and Indira take it in turns.

Eventually we've dug deep enough and wide enough to be able to bury something and ensure it is never, ever, seen again.

Peggy picks up the bowl, ready to lower it inside.

'Bloody hell, Enid,' she says, 'you'll have to help me with this. I'm scared of the damned things falling out and having to scramble after them.'

So I take one side of the bowl while Peggy takes the other, and between us we manage to lower it into the ground safely.

But before we can replace the soil, Peggy stands back. 'I'd just like to say a few words, if that's okay?'

'That's fine,' says Sophie.

So, standing there, tall and spirited, Peggy folds her hands and closes her eyes. Assuming this is some kind of prayer, we all follow suit.

'I wanted to come here this week for a reason,' she says. 'This Friday is what is known in the Wiccan calendar as Lupercalia. It's the day we celebrate purification, fertility, and the coming of spring. I feel it's appropriate. A new beginning, a cleansing of the curse. A whole new start, really.'

'I'll second that,' says Indira.

'Me too,' says Sophie.

'And me,' I say, opening my eyes.

So Peggy picks up the spade, takes some soil and pitches it into the hole.

'Away with you,' she whispers. 'Darkness and evil, be away ...'

Suddenly, smoke begins to rise. Green smoke that curls into the air. I stand back to avoid it, but not before I've seen the crescent moon on the side of the bowl.

It's green, a bright putrid green. The same colour as when Peggy burnt her hand and placed it inside to heal.

'It's okay,' says Peggy, nodding. 'It's just doing its job.'

'What's that?' says Indira, looking petrified.

'It's taking the evil from the bowl and sending it to the sky. Out of harm's way.'

Sophie smiles. 'Wow. Some bowl you've got there, Peggy.'

*

Barbara's house is lovely and warm and cosy after our excursion to Gritstone Hall. Carrying our bags upstairs, we freshen up quickly and scurry down to the delicious aroma of mulled wine and chicken stew.

'The stew's been on the go all day,' says Barbara, dressed in a pair of paint-splattered dungarees and a sweater, 'so it should be lovely and tender. And there's little or no alcohol in the mulled wine, so if you want something alcoholic, just ask.'

'It all smells lovely,' says Indira.

'And excuse the attire,' Barbara continues. 'I've been painting. The artistic kind, not the decorating kind. There's an exhibition on in the memorial hall next week, and I like to dabble. But I've been so busy I've not had time to change.'

Peggy chuckles. 'Now I'd never have noticed it if you hadn't pointed it out, Barbara.'

But she merely waves us to the table. 'Come on now, sit down and we'll have a glass of wine, shall we? Just the right temperature, it is.'

'And there's definitely no alcohol?' asks Sophie.

Folding her arms, Barbara nods. 'It's been warming up that long, I doubt there's a drop left in it. But there's red wine on the table, if you fancy it. I opened it so I could put a drop or two into the stew.'

Peggy turns to Sophie. 'What's wrong, Sophie? Are you not feeling well?'

Sophie hesitates, but the look on her face says it all.

CHAPTER 32

Indira Lambert

☆

Saturday, 9th March
Folksbury

PEACE and tranquillity. There's nothing like it.

So we're staying. We're staying in Folksbury. I'll be running Saffron Silk, the children will be attending Folksbury C of E, they'll be seeing the same friends, having the same piano teacher, visiting the same parks and …

Life. Back to normal.

It's exactly one month since we buried Peggy's bowl, along with that awful kaleidoscope and those tiny black gloves. Exactly one month since I found my freedom again.

The children are outside playing in the back garden, and I've just locked the shop for ten minutes to come and play with them. They have diablos that Mama sent over for Christmas, a spinning toy that you throw into the air and catch again on a length of string. But they're great fun, and I watch as Anika throws hers to the sky and catches it, still spinning. Like a pro.

Breathing in the fresh air, I look around. There's a tractor at the far end of a distant field, a tiny little red thing moving slowly along, churning up the ground ready for the spring crops. They tend to rotate their crops around here, so I've no idea what they're growing from one year to the next. Which sounds nice, doesn't it. Sounds kind of permanent. Sounds like we're definitely staying.

Above us, the sun comes out and there's a cool breeze that blows gently through my hair. As if the clouds above me are sighing with relief, too.

No more noises, no more blood, no more pictures going missing, or stairs disappearing, or any of the other weird things that went on after Rishi found that kaleidoscope.

In fact, I feel so good I've decided to take a holiday. I only booked the tickets last night, but we'll be taking the train to London Gatwick, then flying out to Delhi. In September, for a whole four weeks. Well, it's a good month to visit India, the children will only miss two weeks of schooling, and I can close the shop and not lose too much business. But Anika and Rishi are so excited, I just can't tell you. Me, I'm cool as a cucumber. Not.

Tori keeps on at me to trade online, actually, which would be quite useful for whenever I'm away from home. I could post everything once I got back. It would mean making lots of extra stock and storing it somewhere, of course, but I'm sure I could manage that. Anika's keen to help with the sewing, too, so we could make things together. Not that it will interfere with her schoolwork. Oh, no. They have to grow up strong and bright, my children. Their education will always come first.

But it's good to be able to work, with no worries cramming themselves into my head. No money worries, because the shop is still doing very well. And no worries about ghosts and apparitions and people dying.

Anika is still catching the spinning diablo. Time and time again she throws it and catches it, and I'm just applauding her when Rishi pulls at my hand.

'Mummy. I'm hungry.'

Boys. Always thinking of their stomachs.

I hug him close. 'Come on then, let's go and make you something.'

Pulling open the door, I hear my phone ring. It's Maisie. So I pick it up and talk as I follow Rishi into the kitchen.

'Hi, Maisie.'

We're getting on really well now we've decided to just be friends. Admittedly, we did go through that patch when we thought we were madly in love. Which is quite understandable, really. Because I was on the rebound and Maisie was cut up about Mark.

We just weren't thinking straight.

'Indira,' she says. 'I'm just on my way to see you. Is that okay?'

'Of course, no problem. But you weren't supposed to be coming over until next Sunday. Is it something special?'

It was in fact the weekend we went away together that made the decision for us.

We'd missed each other over the New Year when I was up in Hathersage, and afterwards too, while I was moving out of Chimney Cottage. Maisie was too busy with a contract to come and help me pack, although Enid and Harry did help, and they were brilliant. It was great to just get back home again, to know we were all safe and sound.

So we decided on a weekend away. Well, actually, it was Maisie who decided on it. Enid and Harry were wonderful, though, offering to look after Anika and Rishi for me, and checking on the empty shop. And obviously the children were thrilled at being able to stay with Genevieve.

But as excited at being away from home as I was, having not been on holiday in such a long time, I did feel a little nervous at the prospect of sleeping with another girl. Well, I'd had no experience of anything like that. Ever. I'd only slept with a man, and just one man at that.

So on the Saturday I closed up shop, kissed my children, and trundled off. Maisie had booked us a small cottage in Sheringham, a lovely seaside town on the Norfolk coast. It was just outside the town but overlooking the beach, and we intended going for long walks and eating pub meals, even though the kitchen at the cottage was more than adequate.

It did take me a couple of hours to reach the cottage, but it wasn't too bad a drive, and Maisie was there to welcome me, with a log fire and tea and toast. And that first day we walked miles and miles. But first we had to walk to the nearest pub, The Lobster, for a delightful lunch of prawn salad, fresh bread, and cold beer. Then we walked out to the beach and along the sands. The wind was howling and the waves were high and choppy, so we had to keep running away to avoid being splashed. But it did make us laugh.

'I dare you to get as near as you can without getting wet,' called Maisie, running on ahead.

'I'm not getting my boots anywhere near wet,' I said. 'No way.'

'Go on. I'll buy dinner tonight if you do.'

So I did. I ran down to the waves and came within an inch of them before I had to race back, only stopping once they'd stopped chasing me, and when I was completely out of breath.

'Chicken!' she shouted.

'I'm not chicken. I just did it.'

'Do it again, then. I didn't see.'

I laughed then, a great big belly laugh I'd not experienced in ages.

'You did see it,' I called. 'You were watching. I saw you.'

She ran off then, and I followed.

When I caught up with her, we laughed and giggled and laughed again until tears ran down my cheeks. And I can't tell you just how good that felt.

The evening, however, was not so much fun.

We ate dinner in the local restaurant, about twenty minutes' walk from the cottage. It offered a traditional cuisine and was quite expensive, although Maisie insisted on paying. But I sensed a slight resistance in the air that made me uncomfortable. I don't know if it was the colour of my skin, or the fact that we were two women on holiday together, and maybe enjoying each other's company a little too much. But I'd never experienced it before, and it wasn't nice.

But then prejudice is not a nice thing. Not in any place, and not at any time.

My children will grow up to see people as they truly are. Good or bad. Strong or weak. To see people, regardless of the colour of their skin or the people they choose to love. We are all different, yet we're all the same.

So the evening got off to a bad start, although Maisie was fine about it and understood why I felt so awkward.

'Come on, let's get back,' she said. 'I've got a nice bottle of white chilling in the fridge.'

I grinned. 'That'll make me forget everything, then.'

The cottage was cold when we got back, so we lit a fire and sat there with cushions and blankets in order to warm ourselves. Then Maisie put on some music and poured the wine, and we huddled together, cosy and warm and sleepy, our faces pink from the sea air and the fire.

'I thought we could visit the town tomorrow,' she said, running her hand through her hair, now a messy bundle of curls after being washed by the wind. 'There are some lovely arty crafty shops along the high street. You'll love it.'

'Now I wonder why you'd think that,' I said.

'Because I know you. Because, even though we've only known each other for two minutes, I feel like I've known you forever.'

I smiled. 'Aww - that's sweet, Maisie.'

'Don't you feel the same?'

'Of course I do.'

'But you don't really know me yet.'

'Why do you say that?'

She moved her head to one side, thoughtfully. 'I don't think you do. I think you're still in love with your husband.'

I gulped down some wine. 'Why?'

'I think you do love me, but you're scared of getting close. There's some kind of blockage there.'

My heart began to pound. She might be right, I thought. Damn, damn, damn it. So, leaning forward, I kissed her. Gently.

'There,' I said. 'Does that prove you wrong?'

Putting down her glass, she rose to her knees. 'Not quite. But this would.'

She began to undress me. First, my jumper. Then my top and my bra. Then she kissed me, pushing me slowly to the floor. Unzipping my jeans, she placed her hand inside them.

'I do love you, Indira. So much,' she whispered.

Her touch was amazing. I hadn't had sex since before Harvey left. The last time was the night before I dropped him off at the airport for his flight to Palm Springs. Me in tears in the car, and him as cool and calm as ever.

But I couldn't do it. I just couldn't do it.

Pulling her hand away, I sat up and burst into tears. Whether they were sobs of rage or despair, I have no idea. But I was really, really upset.

'Sorry, Maisie. I'm so sorry ...'

Taking me into her arms, she held me while I cried. 'It's okay, darling. Just let it out. I don't mind. I just needed to know, that's all.'

So that was it. The end of a beautiful romance. But we decided to remain friends. Which we have. And the rest of that weekend was awesome.

*

Maisie has just arrived, complete with flowers and chocolates. It's dark outside, so Anika has put away her diablo and is now upstairs, painting. Rishi's lounging in the sitting room, his nose stuck inside a storybook.

But the flowers are beautiful, a massive bouquet of roses in gorgeous pinks, lilacs and creams. And there are boxes of chocolates, too, for Anika and Rishi.

I smile. 'Have I missed someone's birthday?'

But Maisie shakes her head. 'I just wanted to bring you something. I may not be seeing you all for a while, that's all, and I'm gonna miss you guys.'

My heart lurches. I feel slightly sick. 'What? Why? Where are you going?'

'Come and sit down,' she says, 'and I'll explain.'

So she does. But I don't sit down, I make tea instead. While Maisie explains she's had a job offer that will take her to Mumbai for eight months. That will allow her to use her talents in Bollywood. That is an opportunity she can't possibly turn down.

'But that's amazing,' I say, excitedly. 'I've just booked flights to go and see Mama in September. We'll be there for four weeks. We could meet up.'

Turning me to face her, she takes both my hands. 'That would be wonderful, darling. But if I've met someone else by then, you mustn't mind.'

I haven't thought about that. I haven't thought she might meet someone else, fall in love with someone else. I obviously need to make a decision, one way or the other. But I just nod and carry on making tea.

'I know,' I say. 'But I'd still want to come and see you.'

'And I'd love you to – you know that.'

My throat tightens suddenly and I blink away the tears.

'When do you leave?' I ask.

Standing behind me, she hugs me, her head leaning into mine. 'Tuesday, the midday flight. But don't cry, darling. I'm only on the other end of the phone.'

'I know. I'm sorry. I mean, it all sounds amazing and I should be so happy for you.'

'I know it's a bit of a shock, but that's why I've come up here to tell you. I didn't want to tell you over the phone.'

'Come on,' I say. 'Let's go and drink some tea. That stuff they have in India is dreadful.'

CHAPTER 33

Sophie Dubrowska

☼

Easter Sunday, 21ˢᵗ April
Ruskington, Lincolnshire

INDIRA'S children are so beautiful. Adorable, in fact. Such lovely skin, such huge brown eyes. Dressed in delightful rainbow shades, they laugh loudly at the mallard ducks while their tiny fingers throw chunks of bread onto the grass at the edge of the beck. Then they run away, screaming, as the ducks become overenthusiastic and they're surrounded. But Indira takes charge, pulling the children back to where we're sitting, so she can keep an eye out.

'How about we leave it a while,' she says, 'then you can throw more bread once they've settled down a bit?'

Look, the ice cream van will be here soon - we could go and get some if you're good.'

'Yes!' they shout, both at the same time. And for the next ten minutes they're as good as gold.

It's Easter Sunday and we've gathered together in Ruskington, a tiny village just north of Sleaford. The sun is out, the sky is blue, the fragrance of primroses fills the air, and all is well with the world.

If I'm honest, though, not everyone is happy. Because I've had to tell Ant the truth. About everything. He'd already guessed about the tenants, though, about my sleeping with them. I mean, Ant's not stupid, as we well know. So he's known about it for a while, and wasn't a bit shocked when I confessed.

But he *was* shocked by something else. By the fact that I'd actually fallen for someone. By the fact that I was leaving him for someone. He thought he had me as his wife forever and ever.

We didn't use a condom, you see, me and Rowan.. That afternoon, that first time, we didn't use a condom. I wanted all of him. I wanted to welcome all of him into me. Every last bit of him. And now I'm pregnant with his baby. Now I've had to tell Ant. Now I've had to leave.

I mean, I do feel bad, of course I do. I still love Ant - just not like that. Not as a woman should love a man. But now he's free to find someone who can love him properly. Because life's too short for anything else.

Poor Ant.

It's just that some days I feel so guilty. Ant isn't a bad man. He's lovely, really. Intelligent, nice-looking, very successful. And he will find someone else, I know. But until he does, a tiny, tiny part of me will continue to feel very sad.

Today, however, I'm happy. Rowan is kind, thoughtful, caring. A man who fulfils me completely. Someone I can spend the rest of my life with.

I am very happy.

I'm sitting on a bench - there are two here, opposite each other, essentially pieces of oak set against the two iron fences that form a short bridge across the beck. Rowan's here with me, as are Enid and Harry, newly returned from their week with the grandchildren. And of course Peggy, Indira and the children sit on the seat opposite. Rishi and Anika are finding it hard to sit still, but the promise of ice cream definitely does the trick. I must remember that one.

But such a lot has happened over the past few months, since Rishi found that kaleidoscope. Some dreadful things, but also some very good things.

Mark's sister Maisie has gone to work abroad for a few months, to try to come to terms with her loss, but also because she's been offered an amazing contract. She's very talented, by all accounts. And her parents have decided to retire, to move to the coast, so they can lick their wounds in peace. Losing a child is such a dreadful thing, but at least we think we know why Mark was killed now. At least there's some kind of reason for it.

It was a couple of weeks ago when I had the thought. I'd moved into Rowan's apartment by then, and was standing at the sink washing up. Such a simple task, but it gives the mind freedom to roam, doesn't it? And I got to wondering about why Mark and I had been attacked in the way we were. But it was only as I was drying my hands that I remembered something. The young couple who moved to the States to try for a baby, who actually ended up with one. Actually, three, to be exact. So what if ...?

On the spur of the moment, I picked up my phone.

I rang Rob Whittingham.

'Rob, it's me, Sophie Dubrowska. I came to see you in December about Whittingham's Haberdashery. Do you remember?'

'Oh, hello? Yes, of course I remember you. How are you?'

'I'm fine, thanks. I hope you are, too.'

'Yes, yes, I'm doing very well. So how can I help you?'

'Well, something's just occurred to me, and I wondered if you could help me out with it.'

'Of course,' he said. 'Fire away.'

'Well, you know the young couple who left to go to the States after selling the old Grandfather clock?'

'Yes?'

'When you spoke to their mother, did she happen to say whether or not they used that new fertility treatment they told you about? What I mean is, did she say anything about them needing help to have their children?'

'She did mention it, as a matter of fact, yes. Why?'

'So did they? Did they need fertility treatment to get their children?'

'No. That's just what she said. She said they didn't need it after all, after all the trouble of selling up and moving away like they did. They found they were expecting within three months of arriving. They put it down to the sunshine, she said ...'

I'd known it all along. I'd just known it.

Was this why conversations about the kaleidoscope kept upsetting me? Somewhere in the deep recesses of my mind, did I know something out there was preventing me from having a child? And did I only manage to do so when I was with Rowan, because he wasn't the owner of the clock and so we got away with it?

I rang Peggy.

We met up at Sapphire Silk, to give Indira some business and because it was convenient for Peggy. But it's a nice place, relaxing. Indira served us coffee and the most delicious avocado fudge brownies on the house (although we did leave a large tip), before returning to the kitchen and to her baking.

'So in their case,' said Peggy, 'the curse didn't kill them, it just stopped them having children. Is that what you're saying?'

I nodded. 'They'd obviously been trying a while if they had to move to America for fertility treatment. But then they happen, coincidentally, to fall pregnant as soon as they've left the place – this place.'

'It is possible, I suppose.'

'So what I'm thinking is, and it may be pure speculation. But because Charles Braxton's wife lost both her children, might she have been jealous? Might she have somehow stopped this couple from conceiving?'

Peggy looked at me over her coffee cup. 'Her own baby died, didn't it? And her little girl, bless her. So, yes, it is possible that that's what happened. A mother's love is very strong.'

'So what I'm getting at here is this. Did Mark die because he and Indira were getting together and there was every chance they might have had children? Indira's still very young, isn't she, young enough to start another family? But also, was I hit on the head because I was already pregnant, even though I didn't know it myself at the time?'

'So you're saying because Grace Braxton never got over the loss of her own children, that even in death she was envious of anyone planning on having their own child? You think she planned the attacks?'

'Not just planned them, Peggy. I think she caused them. The CCTV in Peterborough caught pictures of a girl with long hair and wearing a long skirt. Do you remember?'

She looked shocked. 'You're right. It did. And she never really took anything, did she? I mean, we thought it was all about drugs, but it could have been someone else, someone else who found Mark's box and stole them.'

'And I know it sounds surreal and all that, but what if Grace's spirit has hung around her gloves and her daughter's kaleidoscope for all this time, for nearly a century? I mean, if the spirit does exist after death, hers must have been devastated at her children's lives being cut short like that.'

'Not only that, but to then discover that your beloved husband killed your father ...'

'That, too. I'd be surprised if she's ever able to rest in peace.'

'Poor girl,' she said. 'I wonder if she haunted Charles, too, after she died. Imagine it. She wants to hurt him for killing her children, for killing her father, so she taunts him, maybe using the gloves and kaleidoscope in some way.'

My imagination went into overdrive suddenly. 'Maybe she makes the gloves look like they're playing with the kaleidoscope, dangling it in front of him? Or she makes the gloves pick up a rope, shape it into a noose, and threatens him with it? Maybe that's what made him go mad?'

'So he has to hide them. He builds a cupboard at the bottom of the Grandfather clock so she can't get to them.'

'And maybe he places a curse onto the clock to prevent them being moved by anyone,' I said, 'something he learns about from Aleister Crowley's pals. So that if they are moved something awful happens.'

'And even though Grace can't get to them, she continues to taunt him. And his only escape is suicide. Who knows?'

Suddenly, I turned ice-cold.

Because as Peggy spoke I caught sight of something moving behind her. A whisper of light. A rush of air.

But there was nothing there. Just the display dressers and Indira's cushions.

Peggy didn't see it, but she sensed it. I saw it in her face.

'I think you could be right, Sophie,' she said, lowering her voice. 'I also think I agree with Ant's suggestion. We should get this place exorcised. Just in case. Just to be sure. I'll get young Tori onto the job.'

*

So now the deed is done. Saffron Silk is calm and tranquil and Indira is staying. I think we'll become very good friends.

Enid turns to me. 'And how is that little baby doing, Sophie? I hope you're looking after yourself, my dear.'

'It's doing just fine, thank you, Enid. He or she is growing nicely and is due to enter the world on the 28th of September. All being well.'

She beams. 'Oh, how lovely – you have a date. I'm so pleased for you.'

'Funny the way things turn out, isn't it? How one thing shapes another?'

'Some things are meant to be,' she said. 'We just have to believe – in faith and magic and truth. When something's meant to be, it's just that. It's meant to be.'

Soft tears fill my eyes, and I nod. 'I know, Enid. You're right.'

Taking my hand, Rowan turns to me and smiles. 'No tears, my darling. It's a lovely spring day and I want to buy you flowers.'

Wiping my eyes, I grin. 'When we have our own house, *mon chéri*, I'll grow you some of your own flowers. What's your favourite?'

But our attention is drawn suddenly to the taxi pulling up on the road beside us.

The rear door opens and a man steps out. Tall, tanned and good-looking, he stands and waits for the driver to pull his bags from the boot.

It's Anika who sees him first, who goes running up to him.

'Daddy!' she calls.

THE END

Acknowledgements

This book is dedicated to all those who encouraged me to write – especially my mum, who has always believed in me. Also my family and friends, all of whom gave me faith and strength when I needed it.

I wrote this novel during the Covid 19 pandemic, which seemed at one time to be never-ending. I pray we shall reach the end before too long. So once again I am dedicating my book to all the people who helped us out, who lifted our spirits, who kept us strong. The NHS, the shopkeepers, the postal workers, the van drivers. Everyone. Thank you.

Thank you, too, to my amazing proof readers Liz and Michaela, who amended my errors and gave me ideas, with absolutely no comment of 'what an idiot …' Also to Angie, who had to approve my cover design over and over again, whenever I changed my mind – which was far too often!

Forever grateful to you all.

I do hope you've enjoyed ***The Girl at the Edge of Time***.

If you have, the best way to thank an author for writing a book you've enjoyed is to leave an honest review on Amazon.

Thank you so much for taking the time to do this. I really appreciate it.

Alexandra Jordan is the author of The Benjamin Bradstock Tales: *Snowflakes and Apple Blossom, Seasalt and Midnight Brandy,* and *Stardust and Vanilla Spice.*

She has also penned *One Tiny Mistake* and *Murder on Her Doorstep,* both *April Stanislavski Murder Mysteries.*

The Girl at the Edge of Time is a standalone book.

Snowflakes and Apple Blossom was shortlisted for the Writers' Village International Novel Award 2014.
Seasalt and Midnight Brandy was serialised on BBC Radio in 2018.

Alex practises yoga, walks, reads, eats much chocolate, and treads the boards of the amateur stage. She lives in the beautiful Derbyshire Dales. Find her on Facebook, Twitter@Alexjord18, and Instagram.